THE MALADY of ELEGANCE

Jennifer Simmons

www.Holon.co
ISBN#: 978-1-955342-09-4

Published by:

Holon Publishing & Collective Press
A Storytelling Company
www.Holon.co

CONTENTS

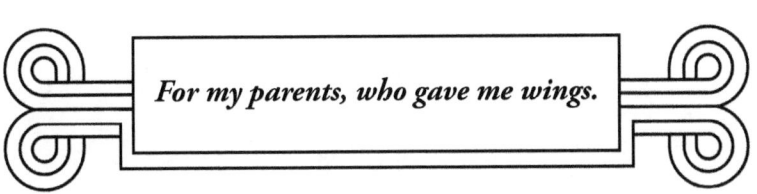

For my parents, who gave me wings.

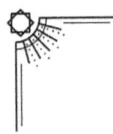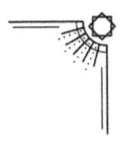

ONE

Arthur frowned.

Sophia Kingsley faced away from him, her dark hair swept into a bun atop her head to reveal the back of her long neck. Her black dress cascaded over her body and fell just short of the floor; the light above bounced off the thousands of sequins causing her to shine in all directions. She was the centerpiece around which the party took place.

He stepped left when a path cleared, but it abruptly closed again and formed a blockade. Arthur awaited a chance to meet his hostess for nearly an hour and not once had even properly seen her face. Each time she turned his direction, the crowd merged to block her from view. Leaving without speaking to her would have been a notable disappointment, for him and for William, who he promised to regale with tales of the Kingsley party.

Arthur had known William Henly since 1918, almost five years before the evening that would catapult Arthur's fate in an unexpected direction. Two years after meeting, they formed a financial advising business together and were tenacious in its growth; Arthur attended a plethora of social events to befriend rich businessmen and further their ventures. It proved to be an effective strategy because in three years, they had achieved unmatched success.

Arthur agreed to attend the Kingsley Summer Ball alone. William, who noticeably decreased his interest in social capital, requested a recap and elucidated his plan to remain home for the evening nursing a glass of whiskey. Arthur's anxiety at attending alone wasn't enough to deter him; he knew the party would be littered with guests of unimaginable wealth, and what's more, Sophia Kingsley would be fixed at its center.

From afar, Sophia appeared to be soft, supple, and welcoming. Her earrings dangled around her jawline, dancing with each turn of her head. He caught himself transfixed by her earlobes, lingering on the slant of her neck. He slowly lifted his glass to take a sip of his diluted whiskey and then set it down on the table behind him, disregarding where he placed it. It was easy to be mesmerized by her, to be pulled in like a magnet to the poles of her body.

She laughed politely as she spoke to an older gentleman, who Arthur noticed often ran his eyes over her when she glanced away for a moment. He chuckled but only to contain his revulsion—the men who never surrendered what they thought they owned, even when time proved they never had, were the ones who became aggressive at the slightest provocation or rejection.

To view Sophia from afar was a certain kind of experience, to get closer to her was another one altogether. Suddenly all of her rounded edges sharpened and stiffened. The closer he drew, the more he feared he might collide into a harsh corner and crash down, taking the walls and the chandelier with him. He swallowed hard, certain that he was being lured into a web, but powerless to stop his feet from advancing.

Then, the scent of vanilla propelled him into nostalgic memories of running around his mother's kitchen at Christmastime as she pulled cookies from the oven. But instantly after Sophia's warmth enveloped him, her hardened exterior once again halted him; his urgency to approach and trepidation to do so battled each other, all the while he struggled to remain composed. He stopped and took a deep breath, in equal parts to calm himself and to pull in her intoxicating scent.

He contorted his face into a forced smile as he approached from behind the older gentleman, who desperately tried to hide that he was balding by piling thin strands of hair on top of his stark-white scalp. He shifted to the side enough to allow Arthur to catch her eyes. Her features were defined and yet somehow soft at the same time. Even her face contradicted itself but fell together in such a way that left one feeling it was exactly as it was supposed to be. He had seen her in photographs, but they had no way to capture the intensity of her eyes, the gleam in her smile, the softness of her cheeks, or the sharpness of her jaw.

Arthur extended his right hand toward her. "I just wanted to thank you for throwing such an elegant party."

She caught his outstretched hand in her left. Silky black gloves covered her skin and Arthur found himself wondering what it might feel like underneath.

Sophia smiled and placed her right hand on top of his as they shook. Her touch was gentle yet firm. "I'm so glad you could make it."

"Arthur." He straightened and with more confidence said, "Arthur Malcom."

She nodded in recognition. "Arthur Malcolm, it is such a pleasure to finally meet you."

Arthur attempted to wipe away the shock of her knowing of his name and quickly recollected that he and William appeared in the newspaper countless times, often with titles like "prodigies" attached. The fact that Sophia Kingsley might have spoken his name, might have discussed him prior to this moment, sent a surge of energy through him.

Arthur Malcolm's exterior exuded confidence; he dressed in a grey three-piece suit, navy tie, and matching pocket square. His shiny, coiffed, chestnut hair had been swept over to one side, and his perfectly shaven face further pronounced his jaw. All of these things, especially when paired with a smile that lit up his face, made him nearly impossible to miss. But Sophia detected a glint of self-doubt in his deep green eyes and felt that whatever lay inside him had a tortured depth about it. In truth, it made him all the more alluring, causing her to feel that she somehow knew him before they even met. She shook it off and decided he was just like most inexperienced men: thrown into success too young, perfectly polished on the outside, but without the bones to support them. With the slightest breeze, they could be knocked over into a pile of formless flesh.

Sophia wasn't a slight breeze. She was a hurricane. Some were blown away before they even made it to her hand, but Arthur managed to sustain the high winds and firmly plant his feet in front of her. Sophia was impressed. The balding man mumbled a few words and then excused himself to refill his drink.

"My late father's accountant," she explained. "Not the most enthralling of conversations, so it was a welcome interruption." She heard the unusually loose comment come out of her mouth and hoped Arthur Malcolm didn't offend easily.

Arthur smiled. "I can't imagine why, accountants are typically so charming."

His wit and confidence relieved and surprised her. "True, like so many men in finance are," she teased and tilted her head.

He laughed. "I promise we become much more so after a few drinks."

"Ah, and how many have you had, Mr. Malcolm? Just so I know what I'm getting myself into."

A sly smile appeared on his face. "I suppose you'll have to tell me your guess."

She smiled and surveyed him. His heart rate quickened but he attempted to disregard it, reminding himself everyone who met Sophia Kingsley felt as he did. Still, he had never met anyone whose eyes penetrated him so deeply.

"I'd venture to say you've had two drinks. Enough to loosen you but not enough to risk embarrassing yourself."

"That's a very astute observation, well done. But the question remains, are two drinks enough to make me charming?'

Sophia, seemingly charmed, averted her eyes and glanced across the room to save her from giving herself away. But then suddenly, her expression changed and she stood straighter.

"Well, Mr. Malcolm, it was lovely to meet you. I must greet some other guests. I insist that you retreat to the terrace; the view of the grounds is lovely from there."

Arthur, confused at the sudden shift, obeyed. He didn't have much interest in the gardens that lay beyond the house, but one motive to attend a Kingsley party was to see the magnificence of the estate. The other was to bask in the opulence of Alfred Kingsley's daughter. He much preferred the latter.

Sophia lived on her late father's estate. Having lost her mother young to a battle with cancer, Sophia was an only child raised by the cold and strict railroad magnate. Her father had no knowledge of how to raise a young girl and left his staff to her upbringing. Several maids and nannies gradually crafted her into a respectable woman capable of holding onto her father's fortune without being conned into marriage by a suitor only looking for her wealth. But Sophia grew into a woman that no man wanted to con, rather, most men saw her as a prize to prove their superiority over all others. If a man won Sophia Kingsley, he reigned supreme.

Arthur made his way out the French doors that had been left open so guests could come and go. He scanned the estate and quickly became bored. He wandered toward the east side of the house and left the other partygoers behind him. He found the side of the house and looked up at its stone face, wondering how one person might ever need so much space.

A door swung open and a staff member exited, shouting

unintelligibly to someone inside. The door abruptly closed and the man rounded the corner to the front of the house. When he was certain the man was gone, Arthur made his way to the door and pulled on it, somewhat surprised to find it unlocked.

Arthur meandered down the dark hallway, careful to ensure he didn't encounter someone who might question him. Though if he had been more confident, he may have known that no one would dare question a man of his stature.

Arthur found a narrow stairway and climbed to the fourth floor; he caught his breath and entered into a long hallway. It was almost eerily quiet, given the noise he knew existed downstairs. A few lamps had been left on in the hall, revealing navy wallpaper flaked with gold accents, not unlike the party invitation. He peeked into the open doors as he walked by; a bathroom, what appeared to be a dressing room, and then he stopped at the third door. Sophia's scent wafted out of it and he knew it must be her room.

Arthur lingered at the open door and peeked in, curious as to what lay inside. Sure no one was watching him, he slipped quietly into the room. Mellifluous fabrics rich in hues of gold and navy covered the bed and the windows, the walls were painted a coordinated cream. A gold chandelier hung high above, placed in the center of the ceiling; imposing dark wood furniture grounded the grandeur of it all. He glanced toward her bed, neatly made, it stood commanding with its four posts. He forced himself away from the thought of getting any closer to it. Instead, he ran his hand over the back of a chair, his fingers tingling upon the silk, and then skulked to one window at the back of the room.

Six large windows opened the rear of the room to the hills behind. From that vantage point, he could see the entire estate, the gardens, the stable, the guests scattered about the lawn clustered in small groups. He spotted a door that led out to a private balcony and pushed it open. The hot and humid August air enveloped his body and he immediately began to sweat under his suit. He reached for his handkerchief and wiped his forehead. The quiet of the balcony struck him, as if everything below had been muted. As he placed the handkerchief back in his pocket, he noticed a small table positioned next to a chaise. An opened book lay atop it, faced down.

He trailed his fingers along the stone railing at the edge and then ran them over the velvet chaise. Everything he touched felt laced with her energy. Compelled to feel her and know her, he couldn't stop himself from his curiosity. He gingerly picked up the book and turned it over to view the cover and then opened it to the first page:

> *Two households, both alike in dignity,*
> *In fair Verona, where we lay our scene,*
> *From ancient grudge break to new mutiny,*
> *Where civil blood makes civil hands unclean.*

He traced his finger under the line and as he was about to move to the next, someone behind him cleared their throat. He jumped and spun around; the book flew out of his hands and landed closed on the floor in front of him with a loud thump. He shot his eyes toward the sound and there Sophia stood with arms crossed tightly over her chest, eyebrows raised.

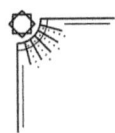

CHAPTER
TWO

Arthur's face flushed with heat and embarrassment and the beads of sweat on his forehead began to run down his temples. He swallowed, bewildered as to how he could ever explain why he was in Sophia's room, on her balcony, touching her things.

Sophia bent over and in one swift movement, retrieved the book from the ground. "Romeo and Juliet," she said without looking at Arthur.

"Excuse me?" he asked, confused, trying in vain to regain his wits.

"The book. It's Romeo and Juliet." She looked at him directly and thrust the book toward him with a force that suggested anger, but her voice came out calm and contained and there wasn't a hint of displeasure in her eyes.

Arthur cleared his throat but his voice cracked anyway. "Oh. Yes. Romeo and Juliet." He took it from her and turned it over in his hand. The edges were tattered and several pages had been earmarked. "Is it your favorite?"

She laughed politely and softly. "It seems so."

He stood holding the book, feeling like a thief caught in the night, still awaiting chastisement. In an attempt to move, he motioned the book back toward her. "I should not have come in here."

She didn't accept the book; instead she drew in a deep breath and walked toward the stone railing at the edge. She placed her hands on top, closed her eyes, and tilted back her head. As he began to move, she interrupted, her eyes still closed. "Sometimes it's necessary to steal a moment away. I come here when I don't want to be disturbed."

Arthur nodded, his hand still frozen in an outstretched gesture to offer her the book. He forced himself to thaw his panic and move beside her, then he nodded again so she could see his agreement. He braced in tense apprehension as they stood in silence for several moments.

She opened her eyes and glanced toward him, a sly smile drawn across her face. "I have told you why I am here. I keep waiting for *you* to explain yourself." Her words were demanding but there was a lightness to her tone, as if she were about to explode into laughter.

"Or perhaps this is one of the many odd characteristics of men who work in finance."

He cleared his throat, too anxious to register her joke, and stammered his way through an incomplete and mostly incoherent explanation. Truth was, he didn't have one; it was if he suddenly found himself standing on the balcony unsure of how he arrived.

She nodded along with him as he stuttered, stopped and started, shook his head and finally landed nowhere with, "I don't know."

She smiled. "And do you regularly find yourself sneaking into women's bedrooms uninvited?"

"No!" he exclaimed, trying to defend his honor. He shook his head again when he saw her smile. "I cannot believe I am about to say this, but this is the first bedroom I have entered uninvited."

Sophia laughed. When she did, her earrings swung around her face and sent reflections over her cheeks.

"I don't know what came over me. It was highly inappropriate and inexcusable. I am trying to gather why you have not yet asked me to leave. Or called security to have me removed."

She tapped her fingers along the railing as if she was considering.

"It was a shock to find you here, I will admit. And there are plenty of men who, if I would've seen them in my room, I would've immediately called for security. Others I would've demanded leave myself." She turned her eyes toward the pasture. "But you... you don't frighten me."

He softened and a strange sensation overtook him; her voice had a hint of flirtatiousness to it. Whether it was toward him or the situation, he did not mind which. Speaking to Sophia alone in such a manner was surely to be a once in a lifetime opportunity.

"I have certainly made a fool of myself at our first meeting. Or perhaps worse and now you will view me as an intruder. I'm certain there will be no recovering."

"Well, this was not our first meeting. Our first meeting, you saved me from my father's tiresome accountant. Have you forgotten already?" She eyed him from the side, enjoying watching his defenses fly.

He shook his head. "No, no, of course not. I could never."

She attempted to withdraw a smile and he studied her face. *She's flirting with me*, he thought. *But then, no, that cannot be true. She is being polite.* But the first thought stuck with him and he held it close, happy to even have the opportunity to consider it.

"I suppose that is a better first impression. I much prefer to be thought of as a white knight than whatever this is."

"You are an interesting man, Mr. Malcolm," she said, scanning his face. He did not appear to be afraid of her. In fact, he did not sound all that remorseful of his actions.

"Please, call me Arthur," he instructed, then caught himself, confused by his misplaced request for informality.

"You are an interesting man, *Arthur.*"

He shook his head at his clumsiness but persevered. "I am not quite certain how to interpret the word interesting."

"Interpret how you like."

"I see you are determined not to give me an answer of your meaning." She stayed steadfast in her refusal.

"Hmm, well then, I shall interpret in the most pleasing light possible. Intriguing, exciting... charming? I never did get an answer on that one. Perhaps attractive?" he dared, surprising even himself with his unabashed insinuation. He seemed unable to hold his body or tongue near her without losing all control of his better senses.

Sophia's stomach leapt with his daring wit. By interesting, she meant stimulating, but she held her tongue, too uncertain to share such a word. Another smile crept over her face, this one charmingly amused, or so he hoped.

"Interesting," she said in a whisper without looking at him, confirming to herself. "Bold, I may say as well," she continued louder, "but I suppose you don't accomplish your noteworthy speed of success with anything less."

He shook his head. "Certainly not. But I assure you, I intend to keep my daringness out of such situations in the future. Better kept to business."

"Well I highly doubt that to be true. But, if I were to be so bold, I might insist that you do not."

"Very interesting," he replied playfully. This Sophia, the one away from prying eyes, stood in stark contrast to the one he saw from across the ballroom, from the one who suddenly stiffened and ended their conversation abruptly, as if she had been caught misbehaving. Here, her charm seemed easy and natural. Even her edge, her willingness to step close to the brink past propriety, had a softness to it.

After a pause, she directed the conversation elsewhere to save her from herself. "Tell me Arthur, what brought you to my party this evening?"

He turned his body toward hers, unwilling to give up the banter. "Well I should think it's quite obvious. How many other men have had the opportunity to steal a moment in your bedroom with you?"

His words caught her so off guard that she opened her mouth in response but could not form words.

With another pleased smile and a look of cool confidence, he turned back to the overlook. Inside, he reeled from his daringness.

"You are telling me that you orchestrated all of this from the start?" she asked doubtingly.

"I suppose you might never know."

"You know, I would venture to guess that you were simply lost and happened on some good fortune that I did not scream and kick you out of my house."

He could not ascertain her intention, whether to tease or to correct him to his place, so he tried her. "I fear you may be correct in that assertion. And yet, I still stand here talking to the most intimidating woman most people, including myself, have ever met. I will reward myself with the word bold for that, at least."

She squinted at him. "Intimidating... is that better than being called interesting?"

"If you want certainty of what others think, then I will say yes. However, if you want the pleasure that uncertainty can bring, of all of the possibilities of meaning, then I will say no."

"Well then I dare say that I came out on top for now I know exactly your thoughts on me."

"And I would argue that I have a much better situation. You merely have my thought of intimidation, which says little more than of first impression. But you have left me with uncertain meaning, so you must have intended it to be on my mind all evening, and in effect, for *you* to be on my mind all evening. If that was the intention, you will have succeeded. And because of that, I can be in no better position than that of Sophia Kingsley intentionally placing herself fixed in my mind."

Her cheeks flushed, or perhaps they turned a deeper shade of red than they already were.

"You are wrong in at least one aspect, though, I did not give you just one thought. I also gave you bold and because I am still standing here with you, it is plain to see how I interpret such a quality."

She looked toward him and he tilted his head, amused in her continued quest for the power.

"But I will remind you that you rescinded your offer of bold and left me with lost." He smiled, somewhat perplexed by the mix of feelings swirling within him. Excitement and intrigue, sure, but there was enough pointedness in some of her words to render him wondering if her full intention was to subtly chasten him.

"You are correct. I have given you *lost* and interesting. One which is simply a lack of knowledge of location, and the other left so wildly open that I might dare to say you could've been correct in your assumptions of my intentions."

He smiled in victory at her last statement. "Well then, I must insist that we agree to disagree on who is the more fortunate one in this situation. There cannot be any harm in that, can there?"

"Not unless you need everyone to agree with you."

"Not in the least." He scrunched his forehead and summarized, "I am interesting, perhaps bold, perhaps lost, most certainly willing to be wrong, and it seems the verdict is still out on charming."

She laughed again. The sound sent swirls of pleasure through his body.

"And I am intimidating. If that is your only thought of me this evening, I suppose I will be satisfied with it."

He shook his head, unsure of how long he could belabor the conversation, but he wanted to keep it afloat anyway, fearing that if he let it drop, her interest in him would die along with it.

"I can assure you that is not my only thought of you this evening." He bit his lip and lifted his eyebrows, like he had a secret. "But, because you are most satisfied with certainty, I'm happy to oblige you and divulge the others."

She stopped in careful consideration. She wasn't sure how much she could bear to hear him say for fear she'd completely lose herself, and she couldn't quite trust what he was flirting with: her or the situation.

Finally, she responded, "Well, I think I would be pleased with one more thought. Any more would be far too demanding."

He nodded and deliberated all he might say. After a few moments, he turned to her, and with genuine spirit offered, "I will not forgo my former claim of being intimidated, that still stands and I would venture to say always will. But, I might dare to say that you are, and the past minutes of conversation have been, incredibly lovely... and, I do not regret one bit that I broke the rules and came here. In fact, if this is the reward for such behavior, the only lesson I have learned is to do it more often so that I might find myself in your company."

His shift into softness touched her; his ability to combine wit and compliment with tender honesty was something unfamiliar to her. The nervous, boyish man who first approached her downstairs transformed into someone unfazed by her name and status. He hadn't bowed to her but he hadn't attempted to overtake her either. She glanced at his lips and her stomach flipped, so she redirected her gaze.

"If I didn't know how much you liked to stay guessing my thoughts, I would tell you the same."

"Ah yes, but best not to, for now I can be left in the pure excitement of wondering how I left Miss Kingsley thinking of this interaction."

"Sophia, please," she teased.

Almost forgetting himself, he moved to touch her arm in playful reproach of her wit. But he caught himself and instead laughed.

"I dare say, Sophia, I had all the anticipation in the world of enjoying myself tonight. I was sure that I would find this party as most described, but I was not anticipating that with you, that I would feel..."
He paused, holding his tongue, wanting to tell her all that he felt, that he wanted nothing more than to stay with her on the balcony forever, that he already wondered how it might feel to kiss her, to release what tension existed between them. But he stopped and inhaled, terror of his feelings freezing him.

She saw his face, felt his words, and knew he was coming dangerously close to speaking aloud what they both felt, but she could not bear it. Too much of her feared being crushed to find it all existed in her head, that he simply would gossip to his friends about speaking to her, and that it wasn't about how he felt for her at all. She interjected before she could not stop herself from engaging with her curiosity.

"Come," she instructed, reaching for his hand, "my guests will be wondering where their hostess disappeared to."

Sophia pulled him off the balcony and through her room. As they exited into the hall, she dropped his hand and pressed hers along her dress to smooth nonexistent wrinkles. She looked at him and smiled.

The sudden shift in manner affronted him; he searched his mind to find what he'd done to cause such a change. Determined to not falter with the shift, he extended his elbow and offered it to her. Arthur had never been so bold in his entire life, but when he was with her, his fearlessness compounded.

To his surprise, she grabbed his arm and allowed him to escort her. Her acceptance appeared to be more than just politeness, perhaps it was a consolation for her abrupt end to their time together, a way to communicate that she was not so much closed off to him as her manner suggested.

To enter a party with Sophia Kingsley on his arm meant that Arthur would be the talk of the town for at least the next week. It didn't matter that they had not arrived together nor would leave together, but it would be clear to everyone in the ballroom they had been alone together for a brief period of time. And for a brief period of time, he had felt like they were the only two people in the universe. Any time spent in the solo company of Sophia was a gift and a great curse. Arthur knew he would have envious eyes burning into the back of his head for some time, but none of that mattered because for a fleeting moment, it calmed the nagging despair that sat too often in the pit of his stomach.

Sophia ran predictions of what was likely turning in Arthur's mind. It wasn't that she minded it, it wasn't so much that she wasn't accustomed to it, it was that against all odds and usual outcomes, she had been drawn into and lost herself in it for a moment. Small adventures were the most she could hope for, and the time she spent with him had certainly been one, but now that she was left with the lingering feeling, she wanted to get away from it as quickly as possible.

When they were about ten feet into the ballroom, back amongst the cacophony of chatter and music, she stopped him and squeezed his arm.

"Arthur," she addressed him again comfortably but her propriety and stiffness of manner had returned. "I must return to my faithful admirers. Thank you for the unexpected encounter."

She pulled her hand from his elbow and left him to watch her walk away and be absorbed into the crowd.

I must return to my faithful admirers. Arthur smiled to himself. If everyone else in the room was just a faithful admirer, a fan adoring from afar, then what was he—*a fool who had been conned into thinking he was something else?*

A deep voice broke into his daydream. Arthur snapped back to reality to see a dark-haired man standing in front of him with his hand outstretched. Arthur reached back and grabbed the man's hand to shake it.

"I'm sorry," Arthur excused himself, "I didn't catch your name."

The man smiled and repeated himself, "James Calwell."

"James. Arthur Malcom."

James nodded. "Yes, yes. I know who you are. I have been following your career for some time now. Was one of the first to predict your success." He beamed as if he had been responsible for it.

The shift from Sophia's elegance to James' garishness disoriented Arthur, like exiting a dark room into blinding daylight. He squinted in an attempt to focus.

"I see. And what business is it that you're in, predicting successes?"

"I'm a reporter. Work in the financial section, been following your career since the beginning, saw you coming from a mile away. You and Mr. Henly, the two of you have certainly been wasting no time. I would venture to guess that your strategy will be taught for centuries to come." He was tripping over one word to get to the next, the way a journalist presses out questions to ensure no one else gets ahead of him.

James continued on, oblivious to Arthur's disinterest, quoting statistics and facts about Arthur's career; he recalled more than Arthur himself. Finally, Arthur tired of listening and interrupted.

"Is there anything I can help you with, James?"

James stopped and looked at Arthur like he had spoken a different language. For a moment, Arthur worried that he offended him.

"No sir." James shook his head. "I just wanted to tell you how much of a fan I am of your work."

Arthur smiled politely and tried to hide his discomfort. James shook his hand again and turned to walk away, but before he did, turned around.

"Unless of course something is happening between you and the beautiful Miss Kingsley, I'd be mighty happy to get that story first."

Arthur later would've bet he saw James lick his lips after he asked the question.

Arthur shook his head. "I'm afraid there is no story there."

James raised his voice as he walked away. "You let me know if you get so lucky!"

Sophia watched as the pesky journalist who arrived uninvited to all of her parties walked away from Arthur. James had been following her around for years, trying to get a story out of her, trying to catch her in a scandal to smear her name in the papers. He was a business reporter but he smelled like a man hungry for gossip. She imagined social scandals sold more papers and propelled more careers. Arthur appeared unshaken. Either he was calm and collected or naive and unaware of the games that were constantly played around her.

Sophia was always one step ahead of those who were looking for something to gain, those wanting to step into a life of luxury and privilege. They believed that Sophia's life was nothing but glamor, but at the end of every night, at the close of every party, Sophia found herself undressing in her room and feeling suffocated.

But that night, after she undressed, she felt something unfamiliar—a sense of longing and an emptiness where she had not noticed it before.

She stepped onto her balcony and lifted her face to the stars shining against one of the darkest nights she'd seen in some time. The moon was just a tiny sliver in the east barely casting any light. For a moment, Sophia thought she saw a figure lurking around her gardens, but as she squinted to focus, saw that her eyes were transforming trees into monsters.

Romeo and Juliet sat perched on the stone ledge and she picked it up so that it wouldn't fall. She looked down at the book and thought of Arthur. What a strange man he had been. What a strange moment it had turned out to be in an otherwise routine night. She smiled and set it down on her table.

Sophia closed the door behind her and drew the curtains closed. She had never considered it appropriate to drink alcohol at one of her own parties, but wished that she had something to quiet the thoughts that raced through her mind.

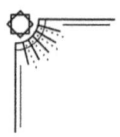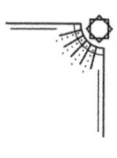

CHAPTER
THREE

"No woman should be living in such a large estate and with such a large fortune without a man of the house to take charge!" William exclaimed, perched on the front edge of Arthur's desk.

Arthur listened while William pontificated about the dangers of women left to their own devices. He tilted back in his desk chair, chewing on a pencil and waiting for William to finish. William often went on diatribes and to keep himself from snapping at his inane comments, Arthur had a habit of chewing the erasers off pencils. He had to learn to work carefully without mistakes because there weren't often erases left to correct them.

William lowered his voice and leaned toward Arthur. "What was she like though? As beautiful as they say?"

Arthur smiled and shook his head. "No, no. You made it abundantly clear that you disapprove of her. It would therefore be insensitive of me to talk about something that upsets you."

William snorted. "Come on! I have to know. I won't ever leave you alone to attend a party again."

Arthur stood up from his chair and shooed William off; William had wrinkled some of Arthur's documents when he sat. Arthur ran his hands over them to try and smooth the creases.

Arthur considered what he might say, how he might describe her and what it felt like to be near her. Electric, enlivening, euphoric. But nothing quite captured her grace and the allure she effortlessly employed.

"Sophia Kingsley is..." Arthur was quickly interrupted by William hitting his arm. Arthur lifted his head and stood.

"Sophia Kingsley is what?" James entered their office and walked toward them.

They had yet to secure a new location, and so their office, a small two room space directly off the street, didn't reflect their success. It bothered Arthur more than William, but because Arthur had been distracted with other things, he hadn't gotten around to finding a new one. Without any gatekeeper, people often wandered in without any warning; sometimes that meant more business, other times, it brought in unwanted visitors. Thankfully, Arthur had already warned William about James.

"A wonderful hostess. Didn't you think it was a wonderful party, James?" Arthur asked, attempting to divert him. He motioned toward William. "This is my business partner, William Henly. William, this is James Calwell."

James and Williams shook hands.

"So, you're responsible for half of this burgeoning empire?" James directed the question to William.

"I suppose you could say that. Though Arthur is the brains behind most of the operation. I just follow along and do as he says."

Arthur laughed because he knew if anything, it was the other way around.

"How can we help you, James?" William asked.

James looked at Arthur. "I just wanted to drop by, that's all. Say that it was nice to meet you again at Miss Kingsley's party." The way he said Miss Kingsley somehow felt like an accusation.

"Of course," Arthur responded. James had gotten the idea that Miss Kingsley was more to him than she was. Or that he was more to her.

"James," William interjected, "how about an interview, since you stopped by and all?"

Arthur was thankful for his friend's social awareness. He knew William had no interest in an interview.

"That's kind of you, but I really only had time to stop in and say hello. It was nice to meet you, William." With that, James turned around and exited.

When the door closed and they were sure he was gone, William turned toward Arthur. "Kind of a weasel, isn't he?"

Arthur nodded. At the party, Arthur had been too distracted by all the thoughts in his head to notice how short and rotund James was. Everything about the man was round—his body, his head, his eyes. If he didn't speak, you could assume that he was a jolly fella, but once he opened his mouth, he became, as William astutely observed, weasel-like.

"He thinks that Sophia and I have some sort of secret relationship, I assume. He appears to be quite relentless about getting information out of me."

"Wouldn't that be something? A secret relationship with a dame like Sophia Kingsley. A man can dream."

"You've never even met her!"

"Yes, but from your lack of willingness to talk about her, I can only assume she is better than I even thought." William smirked at Arthur and walked back toward his desk.

When Arthur met Sophia, he assumed that their interaction would be fleeting, that the evening and her memory would soon drift away and he would return to his daily effort to keep the melancholy away. He had heard about the effect of her, but now he was intimately familiar with the obsession that could arise. Half of him didn't blame James.

***

The sun was setting as Arthur locked up the office that night. William had left and gone home about an hour earlier and Arthur stayed behind to catch up on work he missed due to daydreams. He left his car at home that morning, thinking that the walk might clear his mind. He didn't mind walking; although August days were sweltering, the evenings could be pleasant and cool.

Arthur thought of his mother, who died over three years earlier. Mrs. Malcolm was a spirited woman and when she came to mind, he could feel her loving and commanding presence. She used to scoop him up in her arms when he returned home from school and kiss him all over his face until he begged her to stop. Although he knew his father was in charge of the house, his mother was always his source of security and safety. His father had been cold and distant, like most men were supposed to be with their sons. He worked long hours to provide for Arthur and his mother.

When Arthur's father was around, his mother was different. Instead of the powerful person Arthur knew she was, she became quiet, meek, obedient even. Arthur hated his father for years until he began to understand his mother's complacency in it. Still, because of his mother's love and encouragement and his father's strict expectations for him, Arthur found himself in the position he was—very successful and on the edge of being wildly so. His heart stung whenever he remembered that his parents would never know the man he had become.

Arthur was sixteen years old when his father died and so he took on the duties of man of the house. His father left them some but not enough money for him to stay in school. So, Arthur left school a few years early despite his mother's tears and went to work in a factory. He walked back and forth from that factory for years and saw many sunsets.

It was at the factory that Arthur met William, though William was the son of Arthur's foreman, not a colleague himself. Arthur was insanely jealous of William the first time they met. William's father was light, funny, and affectionate toward William in his own way. Arthur longed for someone to take care of him again, even if it was in the detached way his own father had.

William's father was the one who suggested Arthur and William work together. Despite the fact that the man had never seen Arthur's academic potential, he saw something in him that gave him confidence. Arthur had a way of making himself known without intending. Arthur also had a way of showing his own faults too easily, but he took pleasure in knowing that some could also see his strengths.

After that, Arthur worked the day shift at the factory, then walked to William's house to build a business plan. Before they knew it, with a little money from William's father and some money Arthur stashed away from working over time, they had their business up and running.

The first year was difficult to say the least. Arthur laid in bed at night and questioned his choice to leave certain money for what could have been a colossal failure. His mother never complained; she hugged Arthur every morning before he went to work to tell him how proud she was. She never said a word when all they could eat was potatoes for a week. She didn't flinch when Arthur had to regretfully tell her there was not enough money to buy groceries.

After two years, things at the business began to improve. But Arthur's mother never saw his first big client or the money that resulted. She died two months prior. Arthur cashed the check, deposited some, then stopped on his way home to buy a bouquet of flowers and a bottle of whiskey. He walked to the cemetery, placed the flowers on his mother and father's grave, and drank out of the bottle while sitting on the ground. He regaled their headstones with tales of the business, funny things William had worried about, and how he was terrified when the man in the expensive suit came into his office looking to work with him.

Over the course of three years, Arthur's life changed quickly. After his mother died, he lived with William in a small apartment they could barely afford, constantly annoyed by a loud neighbor and a persistently pesky landlord. After a year there, he and William bought their own brownstones. Arthur hired a small staff of people to run his house, a cook to prepare his meals, and someone to run his errands for him when he worked too much. Attending Sophia's party made his upward shift all the more apparent, especially when people like her already knew his name.

He wondered what his mother would have said about him sneaking into Sophia's bedroom. She would've lectured him, of course, but it was in her nature to smile as she did, amused by whatever trouble he'd found himself in. One thing his mother didn't hide was her worship of the upper class. She never said it explicitly, but he guessed that she had been disappointed to find her life went differently. She smiled when she read articles about the rich and famous, but there was always a sad longing in her eyes.

He thought back to the small apartment he'd lived in as a child: yellowed walls that smelled of stale cigarettes and the little kitchen lined with green floral wallpaper. As his mother prepared dinner, he would perch himself on the countertop and trace his fingers around the petals. His mother would hum to herself and occasionally stop what she was doing, put down her utensil, and plant a big kiss on his forehead. He had since longed for that kind of comfort and resigned that he buried it with his mother.

He hadn't felt comfort in Sophia's presence. What he had felt, in fact, was a feeling he was unacquainted with—and with it came a type of levity, as if whatever it was that held him to the earth released its relentless grip. He wasn't sure if it was the house, if it was her, or if it was being in the company of so many powerful people, but he knew that whatever it was, he wanted to capture it and never let it go. He couldn't seem to learn the lesson that trying to hold onto something for forever is futile.

When he was a child, Arthur would catch fireflies and trap them in a jar to save in his bedroom.

"They can't live under such conditions, sweetie," his mother would say. "They are meant to be in the wild, where they can fly freely and light up the night sky."

Arthur never listened, determined that he could keep them and preserve their beauty. Then he'd cry as they died one by one.

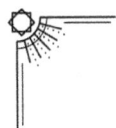

CHAPTER

FOUR

Buried under his suits and firm handshakes, Arthur carried a nagging self-doubt. No matter how many clients he secured or dinners he was invited to attend, the dread that he was about to be discovered as a fraud tagged along like a pesky old friend.

Quite contrary, however, was his belief that he was destined to be someone; and not just a small someone, but a someone of great significance. His belief was so powerful that it kept the self-doubt at bay, at least most of the time. But in the moments when the insecurity arose, it was relentless in its pursuit and he'd find himself in bed unable to lift his head from the pillow.

William always came searching for him to force him out of bed. His empathetic but no nonsense attitude resulted in an odd marriage of soft and stern; demands for Arthur to get up and dress were tucked into a concerned voice. No matter what, without fail, William always came. It had been an unspoken agreement and was understood that neither discussed it after.

Despite Arthur's dread in waiting for the knock, he also welcomed it. He longed for his mother to come into his bedroom and kiss him on the forehead, and he hated himself for feeling so childish. William wasn't his mother, but he was someone who cared, and to Arthur, that was better than nothing at all.

It came on strong and suddenly one morning several months after Sophia's party. When the knock came, Arthur arose and let William inside, and the two exchanged very little words—Arthur knew his role: be obedient, be thankful, and move as quickly as possible. In those moments, when living just the next minute felt unbearably overwhelming, Arthur took his life second by second. *Lift right leg, pull up pant leg. Lift left leg, pull up pant leg. Button, pull on a belt...* If he could break it down into the smallest imaginable chunk of time, it somehow seemed survivable. He'd find himself fully dressed moments later, unsure of how he was able to achieve such a feat.

When they arrived at the office, Arthur removed his hat and laid it down on his desk. A pile of mail lay waiting for him. He stared at it, hoping that he could will it away or somehow open it with his eyes. William cleared his throat, signaling to Arthur that he had been standing there in a daze for a socially inappropriate amount of time, and so Arthur sat.

Arthur shuffled through the mail and disregarded the envelopes that looked like billing statements or official business matters. He wasn't keen to process any significant information in his state. At the bottom of the stack laid a thick envelope made of sturdy paper. Arthur turned it over in his hand and it was only addressed to him instead of the usual "*Offices of Malcolm and Henly.*"

He reached for his letter opener and delicately pulled open the flap, then gently removed the contents, as if they would fall apart if handled too abruptly. A single cardstock dressed in navy and gold letters appeared before him. Arthur's heart began to beat fervently and his breath quickened.

You are invited
Please join us for the Kingsley Annual Halloween Ball
27th of October, 1923

No address. No one needed directions.

Arthur placed the invitation back on the desk and flipped over the envelope. When he did, a small piece of delicate paper slid out and floated to the floor. Arthur bent down to pick it up. Scribbled on the small paper was a handwritten note.

Looking forward to another adventure. —S

Arthur stared at the tiny letters as they drifted in and out of focus. Thoughts raced through his head—*had Sophia really sent a handwritten note along with his invitation? Did she do this with anyone else?* He shook it off and tried to convince himself that she was merely being polite, though he wanted to believe otherwise.

Arthur was still bent over toward the floor behind his desk when William approached and cleared his throat again, thinking Arthur had gotten lost in whatever imaginary place he disappeared to. Arthur snapped up quickly to William's surprise.

"Did we receive anything else with Sophia Kingsley's last invitation?" Arthur asked hurriedly.

William tilted his head and scrunched up his forehead to communicate his confusion. "Uh, something else?"

Arthur turned back toward his desk but shoved the small piece of paper into his pocket, afraid that he might tumble back into mediocrity if he shared it.

"Never mind, I was invited to her Halloween party is all." He hadn't wanted to tell William any of it but he knew that he would have to, so it was as good a time as eventually.

William raised his eyebrows. He noticed how Arthur's demeanor shifted over the course of a moment. Minutes before, Arthur had been off somewhere distant and wherever that was, it brought a tortured expression to his face. Suddenly, he was present and alert, lighter. William treated it cautiously, fearing that he could send Arthur spinning back.

"That's exciting."

Arthur tilted his head and smiled at William. "That's exciting? That's all? I had expected more from you," he teased William, who needed a map to navigate Arthur's sudden transformation in mood.

William shrugged. "I presume that your head will grow five sizes by then and I would hate to make it six."

Arthur laughed. His self-doubt vanished with the simple opening of an envelope. Though his uncertainty of its meaning left him wondering, the invitation itself seemed enough to validate his existence.

He turned the invitation over again in his hand and William walked away, bored by the fixation on a piece of cardstock. William hadn't met Sophia, so he had no way to understand her magnetism. Arthur slid his fingers over the letters and wondered if she had overseen each individual invitation or simply prepared the guest list from the attendees of her summer party. His sense of specialness fell over into mediocrity and then grew, again and again. With each flip, he rose in power and then crashed until it made him dizzy. Finally, he decided he needed to set down the invitation.

***

Sophia stood on her balcony at the moment that Arthur tore

open the invitation. She took a sip of tea while he found the small piece of paper she carefully and secretly tucked into it. By the time she sat her teacup in its place on the saucer, she unknowingly saved Arthur from himself.

Sophia was often the superhero and the villain, but she was unaware of playing the roles. When someone received an invitation, their confidence and importance soared, when she failed to address them directly at a party, it plummeted. She hadn't asked for so much power, but she had been born with it and could wield it without effort or intention. If she had known how capable she was of destroying and saving those who were barely acquaintances, she would've opted out of it altogether. For her sake, it was best she remained unaware, for opting out was never an option. Like every one of her attendees and the non-invited she unknowingly scorned, her birth was unchangeable, her lot in life laid out long before she was a thought in her mother's head.

To some, the Sophia of their mind was charming and gracious, to others, she was exclusive and pretentious. In fact, she could be both over the course of one party. It was no wonder that Sophia didn't know who she was. She measured herself on the basis of other's judgments, and so she had to be thousands of people at once. Sophia did this mostly because that's what she had been taught to do and had never known any different.

"Sophia Kingsley is who others perceive her to be."

Her nannies repeated this sentiment to her as a child; she hadn't understood what they meant, but she obeyed their orders. She dressed in the clothing that was selected for her, she wore her hair how her hairdresser decided to style and cut it, she served the foods the chefs prepared, and she followed the customs her ancestors set and her father taught her. She didn't realize that she was being suffocated because she had never known what it was like to breathe deeply and move freely.

Arthur arrived and expanded something inside her. She felt it as soon as she caught his hand in hers, and even more when she entered into her room and found him on her balcony. The moment she entered, the space felt larger. She couldn't explain the sensation of standing next to him as he fumbled over his words, but she felt as though her feet might lift off the ground, as if she was full of helium and could float away.

When the guest list for her annual Halloween ball was being

drafted, Sophia made sure that the invitation be personally addressed to him so that no one else could intercept the note. She felt giddy when she slid it into the envelope, even though it was her party and she made the rules, she still felt as though she was breaking them. But Sophia was not the type to preoccupy herself with what ifs and regrets; when she made a choice, she left it behind her and waited for its consequences. So once the invitation had been sealed, she left it to fate.

Sophia had no knowledge of Arthur outside of his career successes. She knew he quickly became a well-rehearsed name in her circle, but had not met him until the night of her party. She had almost forgotten she invited him and his business partner until he approached her and saved her from her father's dull and incessantly talkative accountant.

She did not know if he was linked to any woman, though she hadn't heard any gossip that he was, and a man of that success and financial potential didn't stay off tongues if there was any hint of information to share. She thought she might have recalled overhearing someone mention that he was of little circumstance, but that could've been about his partner, Henly. In either case, it didn't concern her where someone came from, nor did it matter to her much where someone was going. Though it may have appeared humble and decent of her, she had hordes of wealth and didn't often think about money because to her, it was largely inconsequential.

In her mid-twenties, Sophia was older than her father would've preferred for her to be unmarried. Sophia promised herself and those involved with the Kingsley estate that not only would she wait for a noble and honest man, she would also wait for someone who could run the house with the grace and dignity her father had. It proved to be an impossible task. Her suitors were unlimited, and it presented a paralyzing amount of options and too much ill-intention to sift through.

Her head staff, Thomas, who had been with her family for decades, often made subtle comments about her loneliness, about her spending all of her time with friends only to find herself alone at night. Sophia knew what he wanted from her, and she knew the person he had selected for the job, but just as subtly as he suggested it, she assured him she was fine.

James, the annoying journalist, did not know of Sophia's skepticism of matrimony and was on post to ensure he could be the first to publish any salacious news. Despite never being on the guest list, he was never turned away.

In fact, no one except James knew, but no arrival was ever turned away from one of her parties. Sophia's father instructed her that it was bad manners to refuse a guest. That was why it was necessary, in terms of beverages and food, to be prepared for more people than accounted for by the list. To others, it seemed that her parties were superfluous but the excess in libations was intentional.

Sophia finished her tea and rang her maid, Violet, to fetch her dishes. With her, Violet brought the newspaper and a daily update on the state of the party planning. Sophia would attend a late morning meeting after she reviewed them.

Sophia watched Violet clear her dishes as she quietly and swiftly worked about the room. If Sophia hadn't called her, she might not have noticed her. The woman worked so routinely and efficiently that her presence was infinitesimal. Sophia was captivated by the lives of others; she tended to live in a fantasy about them—*was Violet happily married, had she been emboldened by numerous lovers who wanted inside information on the Kingsley's? Was she lonely, bored, or content?* To Sophia, anything that existed outside of her was fascinating. She knew that others thought the same of her and found it ironic—everyone, including her, wanted to be someone they weren't, wanted a life that wasn't theirs.

When Sophia reclined on her chaise lounge under the increasingly darkening sky, Arthur was laboriously pouring over work, desperate to keep the invitation off his mind and catch up on the duties he had skirted to favor his fantasies of her. Sophia spread herself on the couch, determined to find the constellations in the sky that might point her in the direction of her fate.

When she was a child, her father, on the rare occasions when he would make time for her, would point to the sky and tell her great myths of the gods and goddesses who lived alongside the moon. He would regale her with sagas of bravery, of love, of spite, and of adventure. Although she knew that they were merely fictions, and perhaps even concocted by her father to intrigue her, she held onto his words and wondered; *if people could dream up such fantastical stories, could they live them too?*

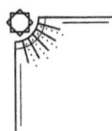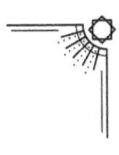

CHAPTER
FIVE

Kingsley parties were always lavish, and the Halloween ball often the most so. Arthur hired his usual chauffeur, Andrew, to eliminate any hassle of driving home. The front entrance of the estate and surrounding fence had been painstakingly decorated in a Halloween theme. Hundreds of pumpkins, gourds, and candles lined the drive to the house; Andrew commented on the amount of resources it must have taken to achieve such a thing. As such, Arthur should've been prepared for what lay inside, but he still found himself in awe—fake cobwebs, cauldrons overflowing with punches made to look like potions, food prepared to no longer resemble food but rather spiders, brains, and all the like. Nothing looked out of place and not one element of the evening was used for any other purpose. Not even a single fork.

Arthur questioned the few people he knew about attire for the party and they responded the same: it was most certainly a costume party. Arthur could hardly imagine what he might do; he hadn't dressed in costume, other than sometimes how he felt in his suits, since he was a child. In the end, Arthur's anxiety led to the ultimate error—being forced to choose from no good options at the last instant. And so, Arthur dressed in one of his father's old suits, put on his father's old spectacles, and went as Herman Malcolm.

As he entered through the front door, Sophia's staff greeted him with a glass of champagne and directed him to the ballroom. The sound of the music increased as he walked down the corridor. The usual paintings and pictures hanging on the wall were draped with black fabric, hanging cobwebs, and some had been made to appear torn.

The ballroom already overflowed with guests and upon entering, Arthur immediately regretted his decision to dress as he had. Guests wore extravagant costumes; it was clear most had been planning since the previous year's ball. Arthur proceeded anyway, attempting to feign confidence as he often had to do.

Arthur greeted the attendees he knew and introduced himself to those he didn't as he made his way about the room. A short man in a goblin mask approached him. Shreds of torn clothing hung off his body. Arthur presumed the look was intended to be haunting, but the man was so short and round that it was instead comical, making him appear like a ball of fabric. The man reached out his hand.

"Good to see you again, Arthur," the masked man said.

Arthur shook his hand. "James, you as well."

James laughed and pulled the mask off his face, his cheeks flushed from alcohol and confinement. "My disguise isn't working as well as I'd hoped."

"You can't get one past me." Arthur scanned the room and didn't listen to James's reply.

Noticing this, James pointed and said, "Miss Kingsley is near the east end, by the red punch."

Arthur followed his hand and regretted giving himself away. James smiled, satisfied.

"Have fun, old boy." James patted him on the back.

Arthur brushed it off and walked in the direction James indicated. If he guessed correctly, Sophia hung about along the edges, no doubt so she might be able to slip away unnoticed. Vexingly for Arthur, almost everyone wore a mask, making it impossible to know anyone's identity.

Arthur glanced up and down the bodies of the costumed people, trying to be discreet but knowing he would recognize Sophia's stature and grace. He looked left and saw a few females he initially thought were her, then decided otherwise. He looked right and saw several men ladling punch into glasses and handing them to women who were too doubled over in laughter to take them. Certainly not Sophia.

"Arthur Malcolm." A soft voice came from behind him and he felt a tug on the back of his suit jacket.

He turned around to find a woman holding a purple and blue glittered mask over her eyes. She donned a long gold, purple, and blue beaded gown with matching iridescent feathers rising from behind her. Sophia Kingsley had approached him at one of her own parties.

"Sophia." He reached out his hand and attempted to stay calm, as if his heart wasn't racing so hard in his chest he thought it might burst out. "What a party. What a costume."

She lowered the mask and offered her hand. "I am happy you made it. And thank you, it was my best attempt at a peacock." Her attempt toward humility was admirable because it was plain that her costume was as elegant and well executed as she. She scanned up and down his body and then lifted her eyebrows at him. "And you are?"

His stomach sank and he unintentionally closed his eyes for a millisecond, indicating his humiliation. Just then another man, tall with broad shoulders, interjected. Because of his size, the man would've been intimidating enough already, but his costume made him even more disturbing. He covered his skin in a thick white make-up and drew dark circles around his eyes to give his face the appearance of being hollow and dead. The places where his clothing had been ripped revealed bloodied wounds.

"You might just have to leave." He wagged his hand over Arthur. "No costume. That's the rule isn't it, Sophia?" The man turned toward him, and Arthur might have sworn he puffed his chest toward him. Sophia appeared to tense but she didn't lose her composure. Still, Arthur saw that this man had an effect on her.

She turned her face toward the intruder and addressed him politely but directly, "It would be quite rude to dismiss someone from a party, don't you think, George? After all, we don't even know that he isn't in costume, isn't that correct?"

The grotesque version of the man called George didn't respond. Instead, he glared at Arthur in silence waiting for an answer.

Arthur looked down over his father's suit, unsure if there was any answer he could give to please George. "Well, I am dressed as my late father, Herman Malcolm. These are his clothes and his spectacles." Arthur tried to sound confident but heard his voice come out as indignant, as it often had with his teachers when he was young.

Sophia clapped her hands together once in front of her face. "Delightful," she said without raising her voice. Then she turned back to George. "You see, darling George, Arthur is dressed as his father. I believe that counts as a costume. And an original one at that."

George snorted in Arthur's direction but upon seeing that Sophia refused to budge, he shoved his way past Arthur and went the direction of the bar.

Sophia looked at Arthur again. "Herman Malcolm? Is that true?"

Arthur nodded his head but allowed some insecurity to break through, hoping his humility would charm her instead of cause pity. "Yes. He was my father and these were his clothes." He gestured over his suit.

She nodded and smiled. It didn't seem that she was taunting him, but he felt silly and exposed anyway. She looked radiant in her dress with her hair curled and pulled on top of her head, secured with a gold jewel-studded headband. Pieces of hair tousled out of it around her face. Arthur caught himself staring at her for a bit too long.

She looked expectantly at him, but he wasn't sure he had anything to give, or what Sophia Kingsley could ever need from a man like him.

Instead he asked, "Who is that George fella?" Not trying to pry, but trying to keep Sophia near him before she fluttered away to another corner of the room to more interesting conversation.

"An old family friend. I suppose that would be the correct label to assign him." Arthur nodded and she added, "George Carlyle."

Arthur choked on nothing. "George Carlyle?!" He spun in the direction the man had walked.

Sophia laughed. "I assume you are familiar with the Carlyle family?"

"Is there anyone who isn't?" He exclaimed and turned to face her again. "Why that name is almost as famous as..."

"Kingsley?"

He hung his head a bit, hoping he hadn't offended her, and lowered his voice, "well yes, that is what I was about to say."

"Almost as famous," she teased and smiled.

Arthur was relieved. He was not accustomed to conversing with people who he had only read about in the newspaper like they were fictional characters, who were discussed like celebrities at his childhood dinner table and gossiped about by his secretary. George Carlyle, the son of Thomas Carlyle, a railroad tycoon, who was to inherit the business from his father. George Carlyle was set to be the richest man east of the Mississippi if he didn't stray from the path his father paved for him.

Arthur concluded that Sophia didn't appear to be charmed by him despite being an obvious choice for marriage—to merge the two most powerful families in the state, perhaps in the country, would have been a move her father would've certainly wanted. And it seemed George wanted as well.

"Arthur, I must know, did you receive my invitation?" she asked, changing the tone.

Arthur blushed at her sudden change in topic and attempted to stammer out words, "Yes. I did." And then later, would berate himself for adding, "thank you."

She smiled anyway, ignoring his awkward delivery, then touched his arm. "As I am the hostess, I'm afraid I must make my way around to my other guests. It was so wonderful to see you again, Arthur."

He watched her walk away and scolded himself for not having a suave answer, for not taking the opportunity to say something alluring or mysterious, to keep her guessing what he was thinking. Instead he thanked her like he thanked the numerous clients he had when they took him out for dinner—detached, polite, formal. He sighed and shook his head. He was a man who was being crushed by the weight of his own insecurities.

Because he had nothing else to do except stand with strangers and make small talk, Arthur opted to wander again. There wouldn't be much new to see save for a few Halloween decorations, but at least it would engage him in something else than his internal madness.

When he again rounded the corner of the fourth-floor hall, Arthur simply peeked inside Sophia's room and wondered if she would be expecting to find him there again. Her note certainly suggested that she found it to be an adventure. Instead, Arthur continued on to the multiple guest rooms where Sophia was often hosting visitors. Arthur wondered who her visitors might be: people like George Carlyle no doubt.

When he reached the end of the hall, he made his way down the back stairs and then out the other side of the house. He walked toward the east through the grass and approached the stable. Arthur had seen it from afar and knew that it was a treasure to Sophia because it was public knowledge how much she adored her horses and loved to ride.

The door on the west end of the stable had been left ajar and so Arthur pushed his way through. Inside it was, Arthur noted, at least the size of his house. Although it smelled like straw and animal flesh, the stables were clean and organized.

Each stall had a sign that introduced the horses by name: Rosie, Lily, Daffodil. The last one, a large brown female with white spots on her flank and nose, caught his eye. Daisy. She looked at him with her big brown eyes as he passed and he felt compelled toward her. He wanted to rub her snout and ask her about the Sophia only she knew.

He petted her gently on her nose and tried to befriend her by speaking in soft tones. He understood why Sophia spent time with them; they were massive animals that could overpower at any given moment, but that made their affection all the more precious.

Daisy nuzzled into his hand as he heard the door creak. A man's raspy voice cracked through the silence. He was speaking to a teenage boy as they pulled open the door that Arthur had closed behind him.

"That one's temperamental, so watch out for her. She'll bite your hand if given the chance. Gotta give her a chance to warm up to ya."

Arthur's heart quickened and without thinking or later understanding why, he carefully lifted the latch on Daisy's stall and slipped in.

CHAPTER
SIX

Arthur heard the clanking of metal buckets as the stable hands dumped feed into the troughs fixed on the outside of the stalls. Arthur ducked behind Daisy and wondered what might happen if he got caught. He wondered if he'd be thrown out and banned from returning, or if they would bring him to the lady of the house and she would decide what to do with him. His heart fluttered at the thought, but he knew he would never be so lucky. He'd be more likely to find himself face to face with a burly security guard.

He listened as the men walked through the stables, stopping at each horse and addressing it by its name.

Arthur whispered to Daisy, "Don't give me away."

She stomped her back foot lightly and shook her mane. Arthur wasn't sure what her answer meant, but he took it as an indication that she'd at least heard his request.

When the stable hands approached her, Arthur deduced that they had been talking about Daisy when they first arrived. A raspy voice again broke through and instructed the boy to reach out his hand and first let her smell it, then to slowly present her with her food.

"Be careful, don't move too quickly, she'll snap at ya."

The boy tentatively reached his hand toward Daisy and she seemed unamused. She slightly sniffed it and then dismissed him as her subordinate. Arthur crunched himself into the front corner of the stall on the same side as the hinge, so that if they opened the door, he could hide behind it. Daisy helped block him from the men's view with her massive body.

He closed his eyes and repeated to himself, "Don't move, Daisy. Don't move, Daisy."

As wild as the man portrayed her to be, Daisy stayed put and gladly accepted the food when offered.

"She's in a good mood tonight," remarked the raspy voice, "unusual for one of these damned party days. Usually the girl hates all the commotion and noise. Consider yourself lucky. Easy first day."

Daisy noisily chewed her food as the stable hands walked back the direction they had come, took care of the buckets and rearranged what needed to be done for the morning. Arthur smiled at Daisy and silently thanked her for her cooperation.

He patted her side and she didn't move or make a sound, just kept eating, pleased to be fed. Daisy's acceptance and immediate befriending made Arthur feel incredibly special. He had hoped it would continue to be a running theme through the Kingsley family.

Alone again, he reached over the gate and tried to undo the latch. He tugged up and out, just the way that it had opened for him to enter, but it didn't move. He tried again. The gate was about four feet tall, but he couldn't get a proper view around Daisy. He felt around it with his hands and noticed something that hadn't been there before- a lock. Arthur pulled on the latch again but it wouldn't budge. Daisy's trough was attached to the outside of her gate and so she chewed away happily with her head hanging over it while Arthur tried to reach around her to pull again.

He stopped and looked at her. "Well, I suppose it's either over or under."

The gate had about a foot clearance under the bottom, so he could edge underneath it and scoot his way out, or he could climb the gate and jump to the other side. Because he wasn't sure how hard he might land, and feared he might twist his ankle and then have to explain himself when he hobbled back toward the house, he decided to go under.

He hiked up his pant legs and thought about what his father might say about him lying face down in straw and dirt to crawl his way under a horse stall. He smiled as he thought about how his father would scold him while his mother stood in the background with her hand covering her mouth, trying to hide her amusement.

Arthur got down on all fours and then laid on the stall floor. It may have been clean, but there was only so much that could be done to get rid of the stench of horse manure. Arthur tried to hold his breath and belly crawled under Daisy; he scooched himself between her legs and then forward under the gate. He tried to ignore the reality that a single decision from Daisy to stomp her hoof could seriously injure him.

He again whispered to her under his breath, "Please don't move, Daisy."

Arthur slid underneath her and emerged from underneath the stall. He propped himself up to his hands and knees and then stood; he looked down and saw that he was covered in straw but wasn't too dirty. He attempted to brush himself off as best he could and when he was satisfied, slightly propped opened the west door and snuck out. He gently closed it behind him and thanked the stars that it hadn't been locked too. He would have no way to explain why he spent the entire night sleeping in the stable when the stable hands found him in the morning.

He rounded the stable toward the house and saw the lights, heard the music blaring and laughter drifting over the hills. He smelled his right arm and then his left, hoping he hadn't carried the stench with him. He detected the faint scent of the stable on him, but he reasoned that no one would get close enough to notice.

He approached the house and entered into the open terrace doors. Not one person noticed he was missing; not having many connections meant he could get away with such things, but also that he had no one happy to see him when he returned. He wished for a moment that William had come with him. At the time, he assumed he'd have to attend to William which would detract from his time to be with Sophia. He chided himself for being presumptuous that he would have such an extended period of alone time with her again.

He politely engaged in small talk with some guests he vaguely knew and excused himself a few times to go to the terrace. He sipped on the most sophisticated drink he could think of- whiskey on the rocks. No water, no mixer. All of that seemed to be the drink of someone beneath who he was supposed to be. He had been trying to drink slowly, careful to remain sober enough as to not embarrass himself.

He swirled the ice cubes in the bottom of his glass and attempted to dilute it. He stood with his back to the house, smoking a cigarette and staring out over the gardens, trying to appear regal and confident, as a man alone at a crowded party would have to be.

Suddenly, he heard screeching coming from the lawn and watched as a thin woman dressed in the remnants of a bat costume darted across it. Trailing behind her was a man in a zombie costume, chasing her with something in his outstretched hand. They ran around in circles a few times before the woman flopped on the ground and kicked her legs up to the man, squealing and laughing for him to stop. The other guests outside watched for a few moments and then bored of it and turned their attention back to their conversations.

Arthur watched as the man helped the woman to stand and then he tossed whatever he'd been chasing her with to the side and wrapped his arm around her. They walked toward the side of the house and disappeared from view. Arthur took the last drag of his cigarette then threw it to the ground and stomped on it.

After five more exhausting minutes of trying to determine how he might again get Sophia's attention, he returned inside and requested a staff member ring Andrew.

Arthur made his way past all of the guests through the ballroom, down the long hall, and stepped out the front entry and into the cool night. The smell of fall lingered but the air already had the chill of winter. He hugged his arms closely around him.

"Arthur!" He heard a man shout from his left.

He turned in the direction of the voice and saw George Carlyle smiling toward him. In any circumstance prior to that evening, Arthur would've been thrilled for a man like George to not only know his name, but also call him over. Arthur sighed and shoved his hands into his pockets, then walked toward him.

George puffed on a cigar and a petite blonde stood on the other side of him. He had wiped some of the make-up off his face and thrown a jacket on, making him look half-refined, half-bloodied and beaten. Two other men dressed much like George excused themselves as Arthur approached. One he recognized as the man from the lawn. The bat woman was nowhere to be seen.

"Arthur Malcolm, leaving so soon?" George asked as he reached for Arthur's hand, giving it a friendly shake. His tone was different than before.

"It's getting late for me, George. Men like me aren't used to parties that go so late into the night," Arthur admitted but wasn't sure why.

Arthur reached to fetch his pocket watch out of his right pant pocket, but it was empty. He fished around and then moved to his left pant pocket, then his jacket pockets, but it was nowhere.

"Looking for something?" George asked as he pulled the cigar out of his mouth and blew the smoke in front of him.

"I was looking for the time, but I must have forgotten my pocket watch," Arthur answered, still patting himself down in pursuit.

"Looking for the time, eh? I heard she's a difficult one to catch." George glanced over at Arthur who was staring blankly back at him.

George stuck his cigar back into his mouth and through his teeth said, "It was a joke." He reached into his pocket and pulled out his watch.

"Eleven forty-two," he said, then snapped it closed and buried it back into his pocket.

Arthur nodded. "I suppose it is a little early."

George was still looking out over the front lawn. "I suppose it is."

The woman beside George had been silent the entire time. Arthur reached out his hand and extended his arm in front of George.

"I'm Arthur Malcolm." She took his hand in her small one with a delicate shake. She dressed as a fairy in a blue leotard with glittery white wings and her face shimmered. Her tiny stature made her even more ethereal.

"Yes, I know," she blushed as she said it, "I'm Elizabeth Barton." Arthur thought that he saw George smile around the cigar between his teeth.

Arthur retracted his hand and shoved it back into his pocket. The woman's hand had been so small that he worried he might have crushed it by accident.

"Elizabeth is the daughter of Thomas Barton. You know who that is don't you Arthur?" He turned toward Arthur, showing his back to Elizabeth and blocking her from Arthur's view.

"I do," Arthur replied, trying to stray away from the conversation.

Thomas Barton was a wealthy investor who moved to the city from out of state. There were rumors, as there were about every new family who had money, that Thomas Barton engaged in some shady business deals to obtain it. But Arthur never knew if that was true or simply a way for the old money to claim their territory.

Elizabeth was short and petite and Arthur thought that she could easily be mistaken for a child if approached from behind. He wondered if she and George had affections for one another, but George's attitude toward her led him to believe otherwise.

George turned forward again and Elizabeth reappeared. She leaned forward and directed her question to Arthur, "You didn't want to wear a costume?"

Arthur opened his mouth to respond, but George cut in, "He's his father. Herbert Malcolm."

"Herman," Arthur corrected.

Elizabeth smiled. "I think that's brilliant... and sweet."

"Thank you," Arthur replied. He appreciated how women defended him but more so how it seemed to perturb George.

George snorted again. "You know, Henry, Benjamin and I put all this effort into being characters from H.P. Lovecraft's *Herman West-Reanimator* and the fella who pulls some old clothes out of the closet gets called brilliant." He shook his head and Elizabeth let out a small laugh.

"Well, I think it's original. No one else here is dressed like Herbert Malcolm," Elizabeth retorted.

"Herman," Arthur corrected her and then immediately regretted it.

"Oh right, Herman," she dropped her voice in contrition.

"I appreciate it though, I really do. I had no idea what to wear to one of these parties."

"It's your first Halloween ball? Why haven't you been before?"

Arthur attempted to blanket his self-doubt with an overdrawn explanation about how he had attended the Summer party, but his insecurity peeked through.

George slapped him on the back. "But here you are now and that's all that matters."

The slap thrust Arthur forward and he took a step with its force. He was thankful that his car arrived at that moment so he kept his momentum toward it.

George threw his cigar on the ground and stomped on it with his foot, and after Arthur had gone, he turned to Elizabeth.

"That fella needs to loosen up a bit, eh?"

Elizabeth shrugged. "A man like you knows what effect he has on people."

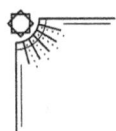

CHAPTER
SEVEN

The next morning, Sophia awoke to the clamor of her staff dismantling the party decor. Muffled bangs and clanks aroused her from dreamless sleep and she rolled over to find the sunlight beaming through her windows. Sophia slept later than usual because she had entertained guests until nearly two a.m. By that time, the remaining partygoers were sloppy and so she knew her staff was diligently working to sweep up broken glass and mop spills from those who lost their manners in inebriation.

Sophia rose and dressed, ran a comb through her hair, and clipped it back with a small gold barrette. A few lingering guests accepted her invitation to stay the night and although the drunkest of them were unlikely to have risen, she still wanted to be presentable.

Sophia sleepily entered the breakfast room to discover George sitting at one end of the table. Immersed in reading a newspaper, he sipped his coffee. Sophia hid her surprise at finding him there; he wasn't one of the people she invited to stay but he often did anyway.

"Good morning, George," she greeted, her voice still raspy.

He looked up from the newspaper and smiled. "Good morning, Sophia." He was already in much higher spirits than her. She forgot how his tendency to be an early riser annoyed her.

"What can I get you for breakfast, miss?" Violet asked politely.

"Tea. And a soft boiled egg." Violet stood at attention and once the orders were given, she turned around and glided away silently. Sophia was mesmerized by her ability to be soundless.

"Not feeling well this morning?" George asked.

"Tired, mostly."

"Yes, Sophia doesn't drink at her own parties," George said aloud as if there was someone else in the room to inform.

"It's inappropriate."

"I hope you don't mind that I stayed the night. I allowed Elizabeth to take my car because she couldn't get a hold of hers."

"That was very kind of you."

Violet returned from the kitchen with Sophia's breakfast and promptly poured her tea. Sophia stirred it, losing herself in watching the liquid turn a shade of brown.

George lowered the paper to the table and pulled his glasses off his face. He was always doing that and Sophia wondered if he truly needed them or just used them for his theatrics.

She caught him staring her way. "What?"

"You're irritable this morning."

She scoffed and noted how irritated she sounded by doing so, so she sat straighter and attempted a civil tone to an irksome comment, "Perhaps it is the company I'm irritated by."

George laughed. "Or perhaps mentioning Elizabeth did it?"

"Why would Elizabeth irritate me?"

"Maybe you're jealous?" He lifted his eyebrows.

"Now why would I ever be jealous?" she asked, feeling the defenses inside her grow. It wasn't that she had anything to be defensive about, but George could provoke her easily, more easily than anyone else. They had known each other all their lives and so he knew exactly which button to press, when to press it, and how hard. She feared it had become his favorite game.

"Oh, I don't know," George drew the words out slowly, "because she seemed to have caught the eye of that fella you introduced me to, Arthur."

Sophia didn't flinch. She learned to contain most of her reactions well. Instead, she shook her head. "Arthur Malcolm?"

"Mhm," George confirmed, unconvinced of her nonchalance.

"That's good, they are both..." she paused and considered what to say, "they should get to know each other. It might be good for them."

George shook his head and picked up the paper as Sophia reached for her tea. Most of the time when George teased her, he fished around until he discovered a fuse that sparked a fire in her. He had seen Arthur with Sophia three times and on all occasions, she had been more contained and rigid than usual, like she was trying hard to hold herself together. The second time, after he saw her enter the room on his arm, her body betrayed her with a blush when George remarked about it.

"Anyway, Sophia, I was hoping that you might accompany me to the stables after breakfast? I have missed Rosie something mad." Rosie was one of the horses that Sophia owned the longest and George took an immediate liking to her. She was beautiful, gentle, and loved George more than anyone. It had been months since George had been able to ride her.

Sophia hoped to go to the stables alone to balance the over-stimulation of the night before, but instead she accepted his offer in proper etiquette.

"Swell. I will meet you there, say, in a half hour?"

"It would be better etiquette to accompany me to the stables." She looked at him, challenging his manners.

"Very well, I will meet you at the back terrace in a half hour."

When they reached the stable, George pulled open the door and immediately ran toward Rosie's stall.

"Rosie, darling! How I've missed you!" He cupped her snout in his hands and nuzzled his face to hers. Rosie let out a whimper and stomped her hooves in excitement. Sophia smiled.

As he was unlatching the gate, he called after Sophia, who was walking further into the stable, "Who are you riding today?"

"Daisy, of course!"

Daisy was Sophia's favorite. She was temperamental, stubborn and difficult to control, but that's why Sophia loved her. Daisy did not give her affections easily; she had to be charmed, and Sophia appreciated when affections were given scrupulously. George led Rosie out of her stall as Sophia unlatched Daisy's gate.

"Hi, girl," she greeted her and rubbed her snout. "Are you cranky after last night? Maybe getting you out of here will do you some good."

Sophia reached for her harness and clicked the lead into it. She would allow George to saddle her. George insisted that the stable hands didn't need to do it for them, he was adamant that the process was therapeutic for both him and the horses. Sophia had to acknowledge that it built trust between them.

Sophia slid behind Daisy and slapped her lightly on her flank, urging her to move. To Sophia's surprise, Daisy appeared unperturbed, but her obstinate character never wavered. With some goading, Daisy stepped forward and Sophia followed. Once, Daisy had taken off galloping before Sophia could grab her lead. She went missing for two days before she returned hungry, tired, and seemingly regretful about her decision.

Sophia was almost out of Daisy's stall when something gold caught her eye. She stopped, bent over, and pulled it out from under some straw.

"That's odd," she said to herself as she looked down at the pocket watch in her hand.

"What is?" George stood in front of her holding onto Daisy's lead. He had already saddled Rosie and tied her up outside the stable.

Surprised, Sophia snapped up her head, then she handed him the pocket watch. "This was on the floor of Daisy's stall."

George turned it over in his hand, looking at the etchings on the front and back. Then he clicked it open to reveal the clock face. There were no engravings on it, but it was an elegant watch and no doubt expensive.

"Certainly doesn't belong to a stable hand," he decided as Sophia shook her head in agreement. "Unless they stole it."

"No," Sophia contested and snatched it from him. "No one on my staff would do such a thing."

"You can't know that, Sophia. Perhaps one of your staff let his greed get the better of him. There were plenty of guests here with expensive pocket watches last night. In fact, I'd dare to say every man who has any sense about him carries a pocket watch and..." George's voice trailed off.

"What?" Sophia asked, wanting George to finish his thought.

He grabbed it from Sophia again and flipped it over thinking he had missed something but there were no markings, no indication of its owner. He was still holding Daisy's lead in the other hand and she shook her head, pulling his hand back and forth, growing in impatience. George ignored Daisy and Sophia and continued to study the watch.

"What?" Sophia asked again, wanting an answer.

"Well I can't be sure, but I believe I know who this belongs to."

Sophia twisted her face in confusion. "Who?"

"Arthur Malcom," George replied, still looking down at it.

"Arthur?" Sophia asked.

"We were standing outside and he was searching for the time to prove it wasn't too early for him to leave. He dug in his pockets, clearly expecting there to be a watch to find, but he found nothing. I made a joke that landed horribly, though I might say that I thought it quite clever. He didn't seem to get it, but I said..."

"George!" Sophia redirected him.

"Oh right, well anyway, after my *delightful* joke, I pulled out mine and gave him the time. He never said he lost it, but it seemed quite clear."

"He could've just forgotten to wear it."

"Sure, but it's quite the coincidence and has to cause you to wonder."

Sophia nodded, admitting that it seemed too strange a coincidence to be one. "I wonder how on earth it ended up in Daisy's stall?"

"He's an odd bird, isn't he? Very difficult to read."

Sophia supposed his behavior had been odd. She discovered him in her room, he attended parties alone and after she sent him a personal note, he did not seek her out once during the party. Finally, his pocket watch was on the floor of her stable.

"I can't imagine what on earth he would've been doing in the stables, but if this is his, there has to be a good reason for him being here."

"Perhaps," George replied, but he didn't seem convinced.

***

About a week later, Arthur arrived at his office to find a small package sitting on his desk. Neither William or Betty had yet come in and so he turned around, as if the empty office might hold the answer of its origins. Too curious to wait, he used his letter opener to cut open the box and then lifted the cardboard flaps to find it stuffed full of navy tissue paper. He rifled through the tissue paper but it seemed to be otherwise empty. Then, he peered back into the box and saw a piece of cream paper at the bottom. He reached in to retrieve it; it was a small envelope with no markings on the outside.

Nervously, he opened the small flap and slid out the card. On it was a short note:

I found your pocket watch. —*Daisy*

Arthur's chest tightened and he felt dizzy. He sat back onto his desk and almost missed on the way down, losing his footing and having to brace himself with his hand. When he stabilized, he closed his eyes and admonished himself for being such a fool.

Later that afternoon, William sat on the edge of Arthur's desk, chewing the last bits of lunch his cook prepared for him. Arthur had told him about the box and William hadn't stopped talking about it since. He was talking between bites, which Arthur found revolting.

"Arthur, you are over thinking as usual. If you ask me"—he took another bite—"she is flirting with you."

"I very much doubt that," Arthur responded, believing himself but hoping William was correct.

"Perhaps we should get a female perspective?" Arthur shook his head no, but William was already waving over their secretary, Betty.

"Betty!" William called, wiping the crumbs off his hands. "We need your opinion on something."

"*We* don't. *William* wants," Arthur corrected and William waved him off.

Betty approached apprehensively. She had worked for them for a year, after their first secretary married. Nineteen years old and always nervous, Betty jumped at the slightest noise. Arthur gathered that her mother strongly disapproved of her getting a job, but Betty's father had been supportive and so Betty applied and was hired because of her work ethic and willingness to put up with William's antics.

William crossed his arms over his chest. "Betty, we need your opinion on something a single woman like yourself might do."

Betty blushed and Arthur cringed for her, but William continued, "If you took time away from your own party to converse with a man you just met, then took the time to write a note to him and slip it into a second party invitation, then approached *him* at that party first, and *then* mailed a note to let him know that he left behind something at that party, what do you suppose your intentions with this man might be?"

Betty looked back and forth between them with uncertainty. She was usually, and rightfully, nervous especially when William wanted something.

"Betty," William pulled her from her anxiety. "We are just asking your opinion."

"If I did those things with a single man?" she asked.

"Yes," William confirmed.

"Well... I have to say I'd never be that bold."

William smiled triumphantly. "Bold about what, Betty?"

"My affections." She stood there stiffly as if she was being interrogated.

William jumped off Arthur's desk. "And how!"

Betty jumped back but smiled, pleased she had given the answer he wanted. Arthur, on the other hand, looked ill.

"Are you all right, Mr. Malcolm?"

"I'm fine, Betty. Thank you. You can return to your desk." Arthur scowled at William. "Why must you be so irritating?"

William slapped him on his shoulder. "She gave you the answer you wanted, didn't she?"

Arthur shook his head. "Nonsense." He waved his hand. "That

means nothing. Sophia is different. Sophia is…"

William tilted his head waiting for Arthur to finish.

"Well she's just different, that's all," Arthur finished indignantly.

"Do you want my advice, old friend?"

"Not in the least, William."

"Well, you're going to get it anyway. Arthur, listen," he said, attempting to get Arthur to focus but Arthur was intent on staring at the pencil in his hand, wanting to stick it in his mouth and chew on the eraser. "If you have any interest in Sophia, it is time for you to reciprocate. Think about it, if she does have affections for you, she is not getting anything in return. And what can she conclude from that? Don't be a sap."

"How in the world am I supposed to impress a woman like Sophia Kingsley?"

"I didn't say impress, I said show your interest." William rolled his eyes. "It's Sophia Kingsley; even pondering the idea that she might be interested seems reaching. You're lucky to even be talking about the Jane in such a way."

Arthur couldn't argue, but that didn't solve his problem.

"So what do I do?"

William stood up again and then leaned toward Arthur. "Shall we ask Betty again?"

"No!" Arthur screamed barely above a whisper and grabbed at William's shirt sleeve to pull him down. They were both unaccustomed to women being interested in them, but since they had money and people were learning their names, it happened more frequently. Still, both men were lost with how to manage such situations.

"Fine, but the two of us are hopeless."

"We can come up with something, we built this!" Arthur waved his hand around their office.

"That's a little different than a woman, Arthur."

Arthur thought about the activities he might ask Sophia to do with him, but he couldn't imagine her at the soda shop or cinema with him and he certainly couldn't imagine her at a speakeasy.

"I got it!" William shouted and Betty jumped twenty feet away.

"She didn't return your watch, right?"

"Right."

"And she signed the note from Daisy, right?" He held the note up to Arthur as if he hadn't seen it.

Arthur squinted, wanting him to get to the point. "Right?"

"So she's playing coy," he concluded. "Set a date with Daisy!" He slammed the note back down on the desk in triumph. Betty jumped again.

"You really need to stop doing that to Betty."

William swung his head around toward Betty and then back at Arthur, ignoring him.

"It's brilliant, don't you agree?" He sat wide eyed.

"Maybe not brilliant but good." He tapped his fingers on his desk, trying to decide his next move.

Suddenly, from the far corner of the office, they heard a small voice. "You should call her."

Both of their heads spun and Betty was blinking toward them, then she looked nervous again and more softly said, "At least that's what I'd want."

"Thank you!" William exclaimed and threw his hands into the air.

She smiled and the light returned to her eyes. "I could do it." She stood up and walked toward them, excited. "I could ring and say that it was you calling for her. That makes it very official. Even more mysterious."

"Why Betty, you are marvelous!" William praised her as she blushed. "Don't you think that's a marvelous idea, Arthur?"

Arthur looked to Betty. "You think that would work?"

She nodded quickly, still smiling.

"Ok," he agreed. Although he was terribly embarrassed, Arthur needed the assistance and appreciated the support.

"Attaboy!" William would've rooted for Arthur any time, but he was hopeful that finding Arthur a wife might make him happy again and a wife like Sophia Kingsley would surely do the trick.

Betty was already back at her desk dialing.

"What are you going to say?" He whispered, but she stuck up her hand, already speaking to the telephone operator.

"Yes, Sophia Kingsley, please."

She covered the mouthpiece and whispered to them both, "I am being patched through."

Arthur and William had been leaning over her desk but Arthur had to stand up and walk away. He paced back and forth in front of her desk until she spoke again, then he stopped and resumed his position.

"Yes, hello. This is Betty Farris from the offices of Malcolm and Henly, I have Arthur Malcolm for Sophia Kingsley."

Arthur felt like might vomit but he was impressed at Betty's handling of the situation.

"Of course, thank you." She covered the mouthpiece again and whispered toward them, "He's going to get her." She giggled then composed herself.

Arthur felt childish but every inch of his body felt alive. His toes tingled, his heart raced, his hands shook. He wasn't sure he'd ever felt so terrified and elated. He didn't even know the two could exist together, but it was awfully exhilarating.

"Am I supposed to talk to her?" Arthur leaned in further and whispered at her, but she waved him away.

"Sophia Kingsley, this is Betty Farris calling from the offices of Malcolm and Henly." Betty was nodding. "Yes, Miss."

Arthur twisted his hands. He started to walk away but couldn't, feeling as though he might faint.

"Mr. Malcolm received Daisy's letter. He would like to set up a time that they might meet." Her brilliance aged her past her nineteen years.

She nodded. "Mhmm," and again, "Yes, Miss. Thank you. He will look forward to seeing Daisy again." And with that, she said goodbye and set the receiver down. Then she looked up and covered her mouth, her eyes wide. Talking to Sophia could do that to a person.

"What?!" Arthur screamed, desperate to know.

"She said Daisy would be delighted to host you this afternoon, around four o'clock!" Betty screeched.

Arthur's stomach dropped. It hadn't occurred to him that he would actually have to see her.

"This afternoon?" His voice was lower, fraught with fear.

"I couldn't very well say no, could I?"

CHAPTER
EIGHT

Arthur paced his office until William, knowing Arthur would never get there on his own, finally called Andrew. Arthur felt too paralyzed with excitement. As he got into the car, William and Betty both waved after him, as if he was going to accomplish a brave and magnificent feat. But wasn't he?

He swallowed many times trying to get rid of the excess of saliva. And then, halfway there, his mouth went dry and he wished he could bring it all back. His heart raced and he wasn't sure how long it was healthy for a man's heart to be beating so fast. At one point, he lost the feeling in his fingertips and had to shake them to get the blood back.

This is ludicrous, he thought, *Sophia is not interested in a man like me.* And then her name hit him and he felt it all rush back in.

As they pulled up to the estate, Arthur noticed how different it looked in the daylight. He had not seen it except at night, when it was packed with people and decorated in a theme. During the day, it looked even more refined—well-groomed lawns, trees perfectly lining the drive, all trimmed and shaped. He stared out the window as they passed, as if he'd never seen anything so splendid before.

Arthur had dreamt of such things as a child. His mother regaled him with tales of the rich and famous, and as she did, her eyes lit up with fierce desire. Arthur would stare up at her and silently promise that he would give her everything she wanted one day. He often felt resentful that his father didn't seem to want more. His heart stung as he thought of her. He wished she would be in his home when he returned, that he could tell her all about his day. Or maybe she would accompany him to parties. He imagined himself walking into Sophia's with Ida Malcolm on his arm; women would pine for him.

The car came to a halt and Arthur snapped back to where he was and back into his nervous state. He exited as Andrew pulled open his door and the massive house appeared, standing over him with its prominence. He took a deep breath and stepped toward the house. As he climbed the stairs, the front door opened and one of Sophia's staff members was behind it.

"Mr. Malcolm, welcome. I'm Thomas," the man greeted. He was tall, thin, and at least sixty years old.

Thomas instructed him to wait in the foyer until he returned. Arthur looked up, he hadn't noticed the majesty of the entry before. He had been focused on the party inside; now he could see that that ceiling was storeys tall and a large gold chandelier hung at its apex. Arthur had his head tilted back when Thomas returned.

"I shall show you to the stables," he informed Arthur.

"The stables?" Arthur asked, surprised.

"You are here to see Daisy, am I correct?"

Thomas's question was dry and left Arthur wondering if Sophia had taken him seriously or gotten her staff involved in the joke.

Thomas led him out to the back terrace and then toward the east. They walked through the lawn in silence. Thomas seemed disinterested in Arthur and so he stayed quiet.

When they approached the stable, Thomas motioned toward the open door. "She's waiting for you inside."

"Who?" Arthur asked.

Thomas turned and simply lifted his eyebrows at Arthur.

Arthur pushed open the west door, which was ajar, but only slightly so. He wondered if Sophia had been making a joke of him and he'd really only find Daisy and the other horses inside. Before his eyes adjusted to the darkness inside, he blinked, trying to see if Sophia was waiting for him at the other end.

He continued making his way toward Daisy's stall and let out a small "hello" in case she was there and hadn't heard him enter. No response.

He reached Daisy's stall and she was there waiting for him, alone. He petted her on her snout.

"Hi, Daisy." She nuzzled into his hand. He didn't see what those men had been talking about when they called her temperamental.

She made a few noises indicating that she was happy to see him as he rubbed her head. She lifted her head back and he saw something fastened around her neck; a ribbon with something dangling from it. He reached for it and laughed. His pocket watch had been strung around her. He gently tugged on it and pulled it off.

"You've got to be joking," he muttered to Daisy, but mostly to himself, and shook his head.

"I thought it was you who was doing the joking." A voice carried down the corridor and he snapped his head in the direction of it.

Sophia was dressed in riding attire, a helmet in her hand. She walked toward him stunning him with how she managed to look so elegant. She smiled as she neared him and it was all he could do to smile back instead of taking off running in the other direction.

When she reached him, she held out her hand for the pocket watch. He placed it in her glove.

"I must know, how did this end up on the floor of Daisy's stall?"

If she was offended or suspicious, he couldn't hear it in her voice.

"How did you know it was mine?"

She tilted her head and handed him the watch, then looked him up and down, ignoring his question. He was still dressed for work in his suit and tie. "It's such an unusually warm day, I thought it could be fun to ride. You might want to change clothes first but what do you think?"

"But, I…"

"We have plenty you can borrow."

They walked back toward the house in silence. Sophia wondered if he really was so casual about her that he had nothing to say. He continued to intrigue her with his strange turns in personality and behavior. One minute he could be coy, the next serious, only to be nervous the moment after that. She glanced over him while they walked but he simply stared ahead. If she could've read his mind, she would've found it cluttered with worry, but he had practiced looking confident even when he felt the opposite.

Sophia instructed her staff to show him to a room and bring him appropriate attire. As, she waited for him on the back terrace, she stared out over the hills and wondered what he was doing with her. Sophia was used to men being either very direct with her or so nervous they couldn't speak. Arthur didn't seem to be either. She heard George's voice tell her that Arthur was odd with a hint of concern in his voice, but she never knew how much she could trust George's initial impressions of someone.

When Arthur remerged, he felt more insecure than ever. His clothes were ill fitting, given that they were not tailored to his build, and it made him feel even more displaced and awkward. He lifted his chin as he walked back toward where Sophia had been waiting, trying to act as if it didn't weaken his composure.

When Sophia saw him, she noted how funny he looked in her father's riding clothes; her father had been a tall man and slightly bulkier than Arthur. However, just as he had worn his silly Halloween costume with poise, he seemed completely at home. Instead of becoming larger and more boisterous to cover up insecurities, he seemed genuinely assured of himself for no good reason.

His assurance deeply impressed her, no other man had ever seemed so happy when he was thrown off balance by her. His stability felt grounding, like she could be attached to the earth and her surroundings, when so often she felt tethered to nothing yet contained by everything.

When they reached the stable, the west entrance was still open. They entered so Sophia could ask the stable hands to saddle the horses. They would be taking Rosie, a gentler horse for Arthur, and Daisy for Sophia, who chose to ride her whenever she could.

But to both their surprises, George was standing at Rosie's stall, unlatching her gate.

He jumped a bit and called out "Sophia!" and then "Arthur!" with an even more stunned tone in his voice.

Sophia didn't falter, she simply approached him. "George, I trust that you remember Arthur Malcolm?"

"Of course." He reached out his hand to shake Arthur's. "Good to see you again, Arthur."

Arthur reciprocated the sentiment though he didn't trust that George had been surprised by his presence.

"I hadn't expected to see you here," she directed at George.

"It's so unseasonably warm today, I thought I might get a chance to take out lovely Rosie. I apologize if I caused an inconvenience." His eyes shot back and forth between them.

Sophia shook her head. "Not at all..."

The three of them stood in awkward silence for a few moments, George still holding onto the gate latch, frozen in space.

Sophia cleared her throat. "It would be wonderful to have you join us, if you'd like."

George smiled and then looked at Arthur from head to toe, noticing his ill-fitting outfit. He smiled. "Were you planning on riding?"

Sophia nodded. "Arthur's never been riding before, I thought I'd give him a lesson."

Arthur had never disclosed that information, but she was correct.

"And I suppose he wanted to see Daisy again?" He pointed the question at Sophia but then turned to Arthur. "Did you get your pocket watch?"

"Yes, I did."

For some reason he pulled it out of his pocket to show George, as if he needed to prove that it was real. At the same moment, he became aware it hadn't been a secret between just him and Sophia. His mistaken sense of exclusivity crushed a piece of him and he had to swallow down his embarrassment.

"Well, I can take Lily if you would like Arthur to ride Rosie."

Arthur shook his head. "Of course not, you should ride Rosie if that's what you came here to do. I can ride Lily."

Sophia nodded her head, amazed by how collected he stayed during the past few minutes; she knew how George's presence was naturally intimidating.

"Lily is a good horse. Easy, like Rosie. You shouldn't have a problem," she assured him.

George offered to prepare all the horses and so he and Sophia removed them from their stalls and led them outside. Then George carried the saddles out and laid them next to each horse. He called over Arthur to teach him the maneuvers.

Sophia leaned against the stable wall and watched as George instructed Arthur. "Loop this through this way and then... whoa girl." He held Daisy as she started to back away. "Tie this here."

Arthur's genuine interest softened any trace of George's typical condescension. It was a scene she was not accustomed to; George's interaction with unfamiliar men were typically fraught with inferiority complexes. When they finished, Arthur looked proud. She smiled at him in silent praise.

Arthur found that riding Lily, while destabilizing at first, was actually quite enjoyable. But unfamiliar with the sport, he had to pay extra attention to his movements so he trailed behind Sophia and George most of the way. They occasionally turned around to check in, making him feel like their child.

Despite Arthur's internal struggle, Sophia believed that he was as confident as ever. Sometimes maybe even aloof toward her. He seemed to be more interactive and affectionate with George, in fact.

She refrained from engaging with the growing disappointment of George's interruption. Manners dictated she extend an invite, so she did, even though she knew George well enough to know he'd feel obliged to accept. When she scanned Arthur's face for disappointment, she saw none, and therefore assumed he was perfectly content with spending the afternoon as a threesome.

On top of a hill that overlooked the entire estate, George and Sophia both dismounted their horses. Arthur caught up and followed suit, thankful that they had their backs turned so they didn't witness as he awkwardly climbed off Lily.

Sophia turned around and approached Arthur. "I had my staff pack some refreshments and a blanket so that we might take a break."

George laid out a few blankets while she unpacked the satchel attached to Daisy. She pulled out some fruit, crackers, and cheese. Then she retrieved a bottle of wine and two glasses. She motioned for Arthur to sit and he obeyed, leaving space between him and George for her to sit.

She handed the food to George and a glass to Arthur.

"I only packed two glasses. I didn't realize we'd have you with us, but I'm happy to share mine with you."

George nodded and he pulled the cork from the bottle of wine she brought. Arthur had never seen her drink before. George first filled Sophia's glass and then handed the bottle to Arthur.

Sophia took a sip and studied the glass for a moment. She smiled and offered it to George, who accepted.

After he had a drink, he smiled back at her. "Good choice. Your father was a big fan of this wine."

"I know. It always reminds me of him. Just the smell reminds me of those days we'd run around the estate while they all talked and laughed and drank."

"You two have known each other for a long time?" Arthur asked, feeling like an intruder.

"Our entire lives," Sophia answered. "George is two years and one month older than me, to the day. Our parents were very good friends. So I have never known life without him. Sometimes unfortunately for me."

"Sometimes unfortunately for me," George teased back. He beamed when he looked at her, but then he seemed to remember Arthur's presence and it quickly faded.

"Most of the time, people show up in the middle of each other's lives, you know? Friends, lovers, they all have a history you will never fully be privy to because you weren't there to live it with them. There is a before and an after to almost every single relationship you'll ever have, and only a rare few who have been there since the beginning. For most people that's only parents and maybe an older sibling. And it's earth shattering to lose those people, because when someone is there right from the start, it is impossible to imagine they will ever be gone. It's devastating to lose others, sure, but possible to imagine a future without them because you know a version of yourself without them. But Sophia and I are a rare constant. We are, fortunately or unfortunately, depending on when you ask, forever interconnected. We cannot imagine a future without the other because we know no version of ourselves separate. It is a blessing and a curse to be so intertwined, as she will well admit." He took Sophia's glass from her hand with a wide grin as she rolled her eyes. Then he took a sip as he stared out over the hills.

Perhaps George intended to convey a warning or a threat. That, Arthur couldn't discern. But he knew George felt it at least necessary to send the message: *I'm here to stay, Arthur.*

***

Twilight began to settle into the hills, casting soft pink and orange hues over the horizon. Arthur wondered what it might be like to run to it, to become wrapped in its effulgence and let it fill him with its tranquility. But like Sophia, the object of his longing, the light would continue to be just beyond, seemingly forever out of reach.

Arthur felt the wine calm his nerves and allowed himself to relax on the ride back to the stables. He swayed with Lily's steps; side to side, back and forth. It lulled him into a meditative daze and he understood why Sophia loved to disappear into her horses. But as he dismounted Lily and handed the rein to George, with a smirk, George quipped,

"Make sure you've secured your watch."

Each time George brought attention to it, Arthur became more aware of his status as the outsider. Earlier, George boasted about being correct that it belonged to Arthur, implying either he discovered it himself, he was there when Sophia found it, or she consulted him on it. In any case, the afternoon solidified George as a larger player in her life than he had thought.

It surprised him then, when Sophia invited them both to stay for dinner, that George declined the offer. While George explained why he couldn't stay, Arthur stood wondering if proper etiquette dictated that she ask but they both refuse because dinner on such short notice would be an imposition. He still hadn't worked it out for himself when George slapped him on the back and pulled him out of his worry.

"But Arthur, you should stay! The Kingsley cooks are some of the best!"

George's encouragement further confused him. He noticed Sophia shoot George a glance, which undoubtedly had meaning to them, but he couldn't read it.

Sophia turned to Arthur, waiting for his response. Arthur misread everything and filtered it through his self-deprecating lens which convinced him it would be rude to accept the invitation. In truth, nervousness to be alone with her overruled his desire.

"I'm afraid I cannot either. I have a business dinner with a client. Thank you for the invitation, though," he lied.

Sophia's heart dropped. "Of course. I understand."

George glanced between them and again sent Sophia a look, this one different than before. Arthur didn't know if it was an attempt to extend her pity or relief.

"Why Arthur, why don't I give you a ride then? My car is already here and I'm staying at my place in the city tonight, so it won't be an inconvenience to me at all."

George had just purchased a Rolls Royce Silver Ghost, the car Arthur lusted after since childhood. Arthur almost talked himself into buying the Dusenberg model A, which would've cost about half of what George spent, but William brought him back to his senses. He settled on the Packard 'twin six.' By all means a luxury car, but still nearly a fifth of the cost of the coveted Rolls Royce.

"This is my baby, bought it only a few months ago." George rubbed the leather covered steering wheel. "Probably more precious to me than any child ever could be. All set?"

Arthur hated how much he envied him. He feared he would never stop feeling small near George.

They pulled down Sophia's long drive and through the front gate. George waved at the gate attendant and called out his name as they did. If George knew even the name of her gate attendant, Arthur imagined he knew everything.

As soon as her house was out of sight, George turned to Arthur. "I ruined your plans for a date, huh?"

Anxiety shot through Arthur's chest and into his stomach and he stammered, "No, I, no I went to get my pocket watch."

George briefly looked over to him and then back to the road. "Well in case that isn't true, I did not know you were going to be there and had no intention of getting in the way."

"So is that why you stayed to ride?"

George tilted his head back and laughed as Arthur realized he just admitted his lie.

"That's why I lied about my dinner plans, you sap. The tension between the two of you in the stable was palpable and I was behind the eight ball. How could I refuse an invitation at that moment? I thought you would at least seize the chance to be alone after."

Arthur turned toward the passenger window and watched the trees fly by. "I have a business dinner." Admitting his affections for Sophia to a man like George would surely make him look even more foolish.

"Sure you do."

The two men sat in silence for a while with Arthur staring out the window feeling exposed and vulnerable, two things he did not care to feel.

George's voice broke Arthur from his thoughts. "All I am trying to tell you is that if you do have affections for her, you'd better make it clearer."

"You think I'm some sort of patsy? I'm not."

George tilted his head back again and laughed, irritating Arthur. He didn't find any of it amusing.

"Now why would I ever think that?" George asked, innocently.

Arthur shook his head, frustrated. He didn't want to have the conversation; he knew he couldn't compete with George Carlyle.

George lifted his eyebrows and noted that it was the first time he'd seen Arthur's face show expression. They rode the rest of the drive in silence.

When George finally pulled up in front of Arthur's brownstone, Arthur exited the car and thanked him for the ride. He wanted nothing more than to be away from him and from thoughts of Sophia. Leaving the car would at least accomplish one of the two.

"Enjoy your phony business dinner!" George called out the window as he drove away.

Arthur's shame yearned to go inside and hide, but his fury had to resist the urge to throw a rock and dent George's car; he reveled in the idea of something about the man having a flaw.

Arthur's house was dark and silent; his staff had finished their tasks long before. He smelled the faint scents of garlic and onion and his stomach rumbled. The silence opened space for the day's events to hit Arthur, the embarrassment, the foolishness of presumptuous thinking, the shame of feeling lesser than George.

In an attempt to console himself, he thought of how fortunate his younger self would've considered a day with George and Sophia. Inevitably though, it crumbled and he recoiled at the memory. William and Betty's confidence cost him his dignity.

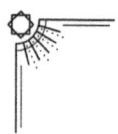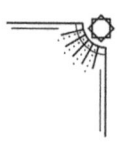

CHAPTER
NINE

Arthur chewed on the end of a pencil; he stared over a business contract, trying to determine if the client had erred in his substantial generosity or had cleverly hidden something that would end with William scolding Arthur for entering into the agreement.

The door opened and the bell that hung at the top, the one he installed after James had silently slithered in, rang loudly. Arthur, assuming it was William returning from a meeting, didn't look up; instead he leaned closer toward the paper on his desk, as if getting nearer would somehow make it more comprehensible.

"Ahem," a man cleared his throat in demand of attention.

Arthur snapped his attention toward the man, annoyed that it hadn't been William and that he'd have to shift his focus away from the contract and start again later.

A tall gentleman stood in front of him; he was sturdily built with a demanding presence. Arthur guessed he was about fifty-five years old. His age distinguished him but he had a youth in his eyes, a man still vibrant despite the creases that had formed. He was impeccably dressed and although some clients dressed well when they came to visit to portray having more wealth than they did, there was a certain kind of class that couldn't be faked. It was often easily differentiated by a man's clothing and manner. No one other than a very rich man could afford his attire or stand in it so confidently.

"Excuse me, sir. How can I help you?" At seeing the potential of the man, Arthur reprimanded himself for being inattentive. He'd become habituated with Betty being the one to receive guests. But even in his regret, Arthur made a habit of not apologizing because he'd learned somewhere that it signified weakness; he wasn't sure where he heard it or even if he believed it, but he'd noticed that once he stopped using the word sorry, he felt less of it.

The man gestured toward the chair in front of Arthur's desk in a request to sit.

"Of course, please." Arthur obliged.

"Arthur Malcolm?" The man asked.

"Yes, how can I help you?"

"Well, I am looking for a new financial manager." His eyes drifted away for a moment as he continued, "as my current, well now former, manager had other best interests than mine. And I hear that you are going to be the best. You and your partner, but you came personally recommended."

Arthur nodded; since vigorously climbing the ladder of the social elite, he'd gained numerous referrals. In fact, his were nearly doubling William's.

"Well I appreciate the referral, I am happy to see what I might be able to do for you. Typically, we would schedule a meeting to go over all of your finances together. Then I can determine a plan for you and you can decide if you would like to move forward."

"I can have my secretary compile those easily. I have some other business associates who need to be present, but I imagine that we can arrange a meeting soon."

"Of course, whatever makes you most comfortable."

"Oh it's not about comfort, Mr. Malcolm. I imagine that my business partners would also like to meet you to know where their money is going."

The way the man responded felt familiar—confident in a way that was adjacent to condescending.

Arthur shook his head. "Forgive me for perhaps forgetting, but have we met before?"

The man stared blankly back at him and then the smugness intensified. "When I walked in here, I asked if you were Arthur Malcolm. Don't you suppose that if we had met, I would've already known who you were?"

Arthur resisted the urge to snap back at him; each patronizing comment flung toward him was another reminder that he did not yet belong in the upper echelon. He swallowed his pride, reminding himself that creating powerful enemies was a sure way to go the opposite direction. "I suppose you would have. You just seem very familiar."

"Ahh, you know my son. In fact, he was the person who highly recommended you. He told me I'd be a fool to go anywhere else and that I would be in the best hands here. He was quite adamant about it." He paused for a moment and then added, "I imagine that the first few minutes of this encounter are not representative of the rest of your work."

Arthur again ignored the jab. "Your son referred you to me?"

"Yes. My son, George," the man replied, accustomed to being recognized without introduction.

The men shared an unmistakable resemblance. Thomas Carlyle was George thirty years later: the same broad shoulders, the same dark hair, the same confident swagger. Even the way they spoke, with a cool arrogance that made people want to impress them, was the same.

"Ah George!" Arthur exclaimed, surprised at the recommendation. George confounded him.

Mortified, Arthur continued, "You must be Thomas. Please excuse my manners. I had been wrapped up in a complicated case when you walked in the door and I'm accustomed to our secretary handling guests, not that that is an excuse for my negligence of course."

Thomas nodded. "I can appreciate a man who pours himself into his work. That is why people like you and I are successful at what we do."

Arthur noted the inclusion and it momentarily swept away the inferiority; an account from Thomas Carlyle would mean more than just copious amounts of money, it would also be social prestige. George would know that, making it all the more perplexing why he'd assist Arthur in ascending the social ranks. But perhaps men like George didn't feel the need to compete because they knew they'd never be beaten.

Thomas continued, "I have to be honest that I was more than skeptical at George's insistence. I am a man accustomed to a certain style of doing things; young men don't often understand the importance of tradition in the same way that my generation does."

Arthur nodded genuinely, not bothered by what Thomas insinuated; he'd heard all of it before and was keen to make it known how he aspired to be different from his peers.

"I believe that there are time honored techniques and manners of doing things that should be respected. I know that is why my partner and I have gained the success we have. Why change something that has been effective for decades?"

Arthur watched the great men before him carry out tasks and comport themselves in a style that seemed so classic it was baffling why anyone would ever want to change it. When he heard and watched his peers behave in ways that rebelled against it, he merely shook his head at their insolence.

Thomas almost smiled; his lips parted and the corners turned up ever so slightly. It was the most emotional expression he'd dare to give in public.

"George has yet to steer me in the wrong direction. He will be happy to hear he was correct. When are you available to arrange a meeting?"

Arthur paused; he had not taken care of his own schedule in months. Most of what he did was based on Betty's scribbles on his desk calendar. He looked down at the scratches on it then back toward Thomas.

He scrambled for an answer. "I would prefer to work around you, sir. I can arrange my day to meet your busy schedule."

Thomas seemed pleased. "Very well then. I will have my secretary ring yours?"

"Of course. I will inform Betty to expect the call."

"How nice that you learn their names," Thomas muttered as he rose from his chair. Arthur followed him to stand.

"Well we only have the one right now. I imagine it's a bit different when you are running such a large business like yours." The words felt dirty leaving his lips; he had just dismissed Betty's importance as if she was expendable, which was proving to be untrue.

Thomas raised his eyebrows as if he hadn't understood the explanation; Arthur thought of how George made a point to know all of Sophia's staff by name. Surely Thomas did no such thing for his own.

Arthur accompanied Thomas to the door and shook his hand. "I am looking forward to doing business together, sir."

Thomas nodded but didn't reciprocate.

It wasn't more than five minutes before William and Betty came bursting through the door, ringing the bell violently. Arthur had tried to settle back into his earlier task but was again interrupted.

"Arthur, you brilliant man!"

Arthur looked up and found William breathing excitedly with his hands perched on the back of the chair where Thomas sat. His eyes were wide with disbelief.

"Thomas Carlyle!" William shouted and threw his hands in the air. William saw Thomas leave the office and waited with Betty across the street until they were sure he was far enough away where they could convey their excitement at the proper volume.

Arthur smiled. "Ah yes."

William laughed loudly. "Look at you, you smug fool! Calm and collected as if you planned on Thomas Carlyle himself sauntering into our office."

"It was a surprise, huh? I think I'm still in shock."

"A handsome man, isn't he?" Betty asked in an excited voice from across the room.

Arthur deduced that Betty was on the prowl for a husband despite her assertions that she wanted to wait. She was constantly noting the handsome men who came in and walked by the office.

William waved his hand to dismiss her thought. "How about powerful? Rich?! That man is lousy with dough. Why he will single handedly pay our salaries with just his business."

Arthur remained seated and didn't match William's enthusiasm. "Now don't get too excited. This is all preliminary. Nothing has been signed or decided yet."

"Ah, I have no doubts in you." William hushed him. He sat down and the phone on Betty's desk began to ring. She answered as William leaned toward Arthur and whispered,

"Is he as terrifying in person as they say?"

Arthur admitted that he was intimidating, but in a way that had been earned. Before he could continue, Betty called to him from across the room, which Arthur asked her several times to cease doing.

"I have George Carlyle for you."

William's face twisted in curiosity.

Arthur waved William away but William didn't budge. Finally, William realized that Arthur wasn't going to answer until he was gone and so he pouted his way back toward his own desk.

"This is Arthur Malcolm," Arthur answered, pinning the receiver between his cheek and shoulder and reaching for a pencil to jot down notes.

"Yes, Arthur, hello. This is George Carlyle."

Before he could swallow it, Arthur heard it come out of his mouth, "Calling to ensure I didn't embarrass you in front of your father already?"

"Ah, the old man came to see you?" George laughed and Arthur could picture him throwing back his head in the way that caused Arthur to feel like a joke had just been made out of him.

"He left only minutes ago in fact."

"I'm impressed by his promptness, why I just mentioned your name yesterday. But my father takes his business dealings very seriously."

"I suppose he needs someone fast. Wait, if you aren't calling in regard to your father's meeting, then why are you ringing?"

George laughed again, this time quieter and seemingly out of discomfort.

"I am having a few friends over for dinner this evening. I am ringing to ask you if you'd like to join?" He sounded confident but slightly insincere. "Unless of course you have another *business dinner.*"

Arthur frowned. "No, George. I am free. I would love to join you."

"Swell. I will inform my staff to set another place."

Arthur couldn't reason why George would ever invite him or group him into the people he referred to as friends. He resisted the urge to ask about Sophia's attendance.

"Dinner is at 7 o'clock and of course drinks to follow." George informed him. Arthur had attended a few dinners in the last several months where the night progressed into early morning and after dinner drinks progressed into normally dignified men falling over drunk.

"And Arthur?"

"Yes?"

"You are welcome to bring someone if you'd like. No need to let me know; we will be prepared to set another place if you do."

Arthur stammered, "No, no. Just me. Thank you."

"All right then. See you at seven!"

Arthur held the telephone in his hand for several moments after George hung up. He caught Williams eyes on him, twisted in an expression as if to say *what was that about?*

Arthur shrugged and set down the phone.

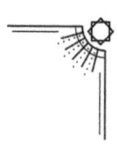

CHAPTER
TEN

The gates to George's estate were just as grand as the Kingsley's. The Carlyle's decorated their property in a distinct way; Arthur heard that George's mother adored flowers from Asia and so trimmed the grounds with plants that Arthur had never seen. Giant yellow petals and bright red spiky ones lined the drive; Arthur turned to examine them out the window and hoped a dinner party at George's house didn't involve a property tour like some of the others he attended. He was tired of feigning interest in the expense paid for foliage.

George's head staff, Robert, greeted Arthur at the door and took his top coat, then led him toward the sitting room. The sound of chatter intensified as they got closer. Arthur looked at the paintings on the walls, members of the Carlyle family stared blankly back at him. Most of the men in the paintings looked like George; all large and commanding.

"Arthur!" George rose from his chair as Arthur entered the room and walked toward him, his hand outstretched. "So glad you could make it this evening. I know how busy you always are."

Arthur took a deep breath at the second prod George made about the same incident in one day.

Arthur took his hand and shook it. "Never too busy to decline your invitation, George."

George laughed. "Please, please come in. We are just sitting here until dinner is ready then we will move to the dining room." George motioned around the room. "You remember Elizabeth Barton."

Arthur nodded; although it hadn't been long since he'd seen her, he'd forgotten how tiny she was. Arthur towered over her as he greeted her.

"And this is Henry Westin." George gestured to a thin light-haired man whose pale skin against his grey suit made him look monochromatic. Henry was in the business of trade and made his fortunes working off the docks. He was infamous for his demure style.

"Trixie Westin." George continued, and Trixie rose from her chair as she clutched Arthur's hand.

"My name is Tara but my friends call me Trixie," she explained. Arthur couldn't imagine why someone would ever let a nickname like that stick. Trixie wore her brown hair cropped short around her chin and straightened it so there was little volume left. Her black dress hung from her slender body; it was difficult to tell where she was underneath it.

"And this is Benjamin Avery." George motioned toward the final person in the room. Benjamin, dressed in a black suit and painted with an unimpressed look, didn't rise to meet Arthur's hand. Instead Arthur found himself shaking the hand of the sitting man and having to lean forward in an awkward position.

Arthur let go of Benjamin's hand and stood with his back toward the doorway.

"And you know Sophia—late as always!" George announced.

Arthur turned around to see her enter the room accompanied by Robert. She wore a loose-fitting navy dress that hit just below her knees to reveal stocking legs that ended in matching heels. She tied her hair up around her head, curls falling out of the gold headband that matched her earrings.

She smiled toward George and rolled her eyes. "I am most certainly not late."

George pulled out his pocket watch. "Seven o'clock on the dot! Of course!" George laughed and she reached out and brushed his arm, playfully conveying her annoyance.

Arthur scanned the room—Henry and Trixie shared the same last name, and so he paired them as married. If it had been intended as a couple's dinner party, that left Elizabeth and Benjamin as the other couple, though they didn't appear particularly fond of one another.

Sophia made her way around the room hugging the women and kissing the cheeks of the men. Benjamin did not stay seated to greet Sophia. Lastly, she walked toward Arthur who had yet to take a seat. She reached out her hand and Arthur caught it, again feeling the electricity of her skin.

"Arthur," she said softly, "it is wonderful to see you."

Arthur lifted her hand and kissed the back of it. He'd never done such a thing before, but taking the action in front of George satisfied a competitive part of him.

"It's always lovely to see you, Sophia," he said as he lifted his face. She averted her eyes briefly and Arthur thought he saw her cheeks flush.

Arthur didn't get a chance to see George's reaction, because immediately after, Robert announced that dinner was ready, breaking Sophia and Arthur's attention away from one another.

Sophia turned away from Arthur and again approached George, who was in the middle of standing from his chair. Reflexively, he offered her his arm and she took it. Arthur walked behind them to the dining room.

"I know my seating arrangements are a bit untraditional," George shot Sophia a glance as he said it, "but I think it is fun to break tradition with friends."

"Arthur?" A butler with a gentle voice approached him. "You will be seated here." He motioned toward a chair and pulled out for him. There were only seven of them at a table that was built for at least twenty guests so they all clustered around one end. George sat at the head of the table. To George's left were Henry, Trixie, and Benjamin. To his right sat Sophia, Arthur and Elizabeth.

As soon as they all sat, the meal service began—salad with sheep's cheese and walnuts, followed by rolls with soft and salty butter, then the main course of lamb chops and boiled potatoes. They all chatted with each other, sipping on wine and becoming increasingly loose as the drinks went down. Arthur made small talk with Elizabeth while Sophia spent most of it talking to George. Every once in a while, he would turn to her in an attempt to say something and catch George's eyes on him, as if he was waiting for something.

When they finished their meal, George motioned to one of his staff. Without pause, the table was cleared and each guest offered a glass of champagne. Trixie immediately gulped it down. George clinked his fork against his glass as he stood and Trixie clasped her hand over her mouth, realizing her error. George raised his glass into the air to make a toast.

"As you are all aware, we are here to celebrate a most wondrous occasion this evening." He looked toward Sophia who tilted her head to convey her annoyance at his show but was smiling and blushing just the same.

"Please," George instructed, "let's all raise our glasses in a toast."

Arthur reached for his glass and felt the warmth of the alcohol creep into his cheeks. Sophia reached for hers as well; it was the second time Arthur had seen her drink.

When she raised her glass, Arthur caught a glimmer of gold reflect off a finger on her left hand. Before he could investigate further, she wrapped her hand around her glass and he lost sight of it. He tried to turn his attention toward George and away from his curiosity.

"My darling, Sophia. It has been an absolute pleasure being the one to annoy you for all these years." George's ostentatiousness seemed to have little effect on the others, all of whom appeared perfectly aware of the occasion. Arthur held his glass in the air wishing he would've gotten more information from George over the phone.

"And I cannot wait to continue to do the same for the rest of time." Sophia smiled and rolled her eyes.

"You know she's going to end up unhappily engaged to George before you ever do anything about it." William had said to him after he told him about the afternoon horseback riding. *"Might be already with how long it's taken you."*

Arthur felt his throat tighten. His mind, increasingly fuzzy from the alcohol, tried to prepare. He hated William for putting the idea in his mind, but even more, he hated himself for wanting it to be untrue.

Arthur flashed his gaze around the room as George went on about the qualities of Sophia; charming, elegant, and alluded to a few inside jokes everyone but Arthur seemed privy to. All of them turned their faces into big smiles, laughed with the jokes, and made eyes toward Sophia when George teased her.

Arthur turned his attention back to George, who lifted his glass further into the air, ready to conclude the toast.

Arthur swallowed and braced himself and then George bellowed, "Happy Birthday, to our lovely Sophia!"

"Happy Birthday!" The rest joined in unison, and then clinked their glasses together.

Arthur's heartbeat slowed and he joined the others in their well wishes. He took a few sips of his champagne simply to calm his nerves. His stomach settled and his energy plummeted. It had taken all his resources to prepare himself for the news he thought was coming. And finally, when he recovered enough to think more of it, though it hadn't been the worst that he'd expected, he still wished he'd known it was her birthday.

"Thank you, all." She beamed. "Thank you for coming. And thank you George for hosting such an excellent meal."

She placed her hand on top of his in sincere thanks. He covered hers with his other and reassured her that he wouldn't have had it any other way.

Arthur was certain he could eat no more, but then they were presented with a decadent chocolate cake. A treat from George for Sophia's birthday. The light gleamed off the icing as the butler cut into it, and everyone sat silently, waiting for an acceptable time to express their interest.

After the cake had been eaten and chocolate crumbs were strewn atop the white tablecloth, George asked everyone, "Shall we move to the den for drinks?"

Elizabeth giggled in her increasing intoxication and rose from the table without explicitly answering. The rest followed suit, but Benjamin announced his intention to leave before anyone had left the room. Arthur noticed that the man hadn't been drinking and appeared irritated with Elizabeth and Trixie who were starting to giggle and whisper to each other. Benjamin and Elizabeth still seemed no more interested in each other than he was in Trixie.

"My cousin isn't always the most sociable person," Sophia leaned in and whispered to Arthur. It was becoming clearer that Arthur knew little of the world he now inhabited.

"Well let the rest of us have some fun. I have some very fine hooch just waiting to be drank." George winked toward Sophia after Benjamin said his goodbyes and excused himself. She again reached for his arm to walk together toward the den.

The den was at the other end of the house; there were two large doors on the back of the room that would've opened to a terrace during warmer weather. Instead a fire blazed in the fireplace and as soon as they entered the room, George reached for the poker to push at the logs that were burning. It was as if he was always trying to prove his manhood; hardiness clothed in the finest garments. He was everything Arthur dreamt of being—tough and masculine but refined and intelligent.

Arthur pulled his attention away from George and toward the rest who huddled around the bar, making drinks. Henry poured drinks for the ladies first and then himself. When the women took their places on the couches, Henry offered one to Arthur who happily obliged.

"It is nice to finally meet you," Henry said as he dropped an ice cube into Arthur's fresh glass. "I recognize you from the Halloween party but I was just going inside as you came out." Henry poured a generous amount of whiskey over the ice cube. "I have heard of the great things you and your partner are doing."

"Likewise," Arthur reciprocated as he took the glass from Henry. "I am interested in the work you're doing in trade. Seems to be a business not going anywhere soon."

"I hope not."

Just then, George approached and slapped Arthur on the back, almost spilling his drink. "Henry, care to make me a drink?"

Henry nodded and went through the steps he had gone through five times before.

"I can only assume you're discussing business," he said and then toward Henry, "you always are."

Henry didn't look up but instead kept his eyes fixed on the glass in front of him. "That's what happens when your father didn't build one for you."

Arthur choked on his sip and snapped his head up to see George's reaction but George just threw his head back and laughed in his classic way.

"Attaboy, Henry. You slay me." George took his drink from Henry and seemed delighted with the jab.

Henry smiled. His bright blue eyes shone against his pale skin and light hair. He appeared the opposite of George—thin, delicate, with a kindness to his face. His lips were pink and revealed pearly teeth when he smiled.

"Please tell me that you aren't over there chinning about business," Trixie interjected from across the room.

"Politics!" George raised his glass toward her. She rolled her eyes and turned her attention toward Henry.

"Now I know that isn't true." She gestured toward Henry. "Henry wouldn't dare do that until he's good and zozzled."

Henry held his drink in the air. "I'm working on it, Trix!"

Arthur turned toward Henry. "Henry, excuse me for asking, but are you here with Trixie?"

Henry let out a loud laugh. George smiled into his glass then shouted toward Trixie.

"Trixie, Arthur wants to know if you're here with Henry!" Arthur felt his cheeks flush and wondered why George always had to make a fool of him.

Trixie squealed and jumped up from the couch. Sophia didn't react and Elizabeth looked amused but pained for Arthur.

"I never!" Trixie exclaimed and then clutched her chest. Arthur looked back and forth between them, confused.

George again slapped Arthur on the back but Arthur preemptively repositioned his drink in anticipation of it. "Trixie is Henry's cousin," George explained.

"Oh," Arthur replied, not understanding what all the drama had been about.

Trixie wandered over and looped her arm through Arthur's. "Oh, don't worry, Arthur, everything's jake. My dear cousin is the cat's pajamas and he has been awfully kind in letting me tag along with his friends." Trixie leaned into Arthur which felt more necessary than flirtatious.

"You've certainly made yourself right at home," Henry flung back.

"Oh shush!" Then she leaned her face closer to Arthur and in a softer voice said, "don't listen to anything anyone says about anyone around here. None of it is true. All caught up in the gossip of it all."

She spun around toward Sophia who sat quietly on the couch next to Elizabeth. Still clinging onto Arthur, she continued, "Except for Sophia. Our birthday girl doesn't stoop to our level."

Arthur looked toward Sophia who shifted slightly with discomfort and sat straighter. "I don't see any reason to contribute to all the nonsense."

"But where do you get all your fun?" George teased her as he took a seat in the large leather armchair perpendicular to their couch.

She scoffed at him. "Not everyone thinks that it's fun to destroy the lives of others by spreading rumors."

He laughed. "I don't have enough power to destroy anyone." They all knew it wasn't true. George could take down every single person in the room apart from Sophia.

Trixie rejoined them and sat on the couch across from the other women. "You are not great at faking modesty, George."

Henry sat next to her. "No one can be as good at it as you are, Trixie."

Arthur sat in the armchair across from George, who was half listening, half nursing his drink. They all loved to tease each other and didn't know or perhaps care that it was pompous to make light of their power and money; Arthur thought of the people he used to spend his evenings with and how revolting the current conversation would be to them.

"So tell us about you, Arthur." Trixie took a sip of her drink and looked at him.

"What about me?" Arthur asked, frowning.

"Well, for starters, any dames you're dizzy with?"

Elizabeth coughed at the brashness of it. Henry shook his head, amused how Trixie always jumped to the topic when there was a new man around. Arthur's cheeks reddened, he took a sip, then lowered his glass to find them all staring back at him, waiting.

"A man like me has no business dating," Arthur replied, trying to join in the self-deprecating humor they all seemed so amused by.

Trixie retorted, "Applesauce! A man like you? What's that?"

"Successful?" George asked.

"Rich?" Henry chimed in.

"Handsome?" Trixie finished.

Arthur was uncomfortable at the way they were portraying him. He feared they were all joined in some sort of joke, making fun of him.

"A man like you can have any woman he wants," Elizabeth stated, plainly. "You shouldn't be so unsure of that."

"Not any woman," he mumbled into his glass.

Trixie snorted. "Name one!"

Arthur tried not to glance toward Sophia; he wanted to see her reaction. Instead he kept his gaze down toward his glass then looked up to Trixie and shrugged. "I don't know, but I'm not so arrogant to think I can have any woman I might want."

Elizabeth nodded. "I like that." She smiled toward him, giving him a reason to look in her direction and therefore in Sophia's. Sophia appeared to be actively listening but her face gave him no indication of opinion.

Then George butted his way in. "Sophia, you've been awfully quiet. What do you think?"

"Think of what?" she asked, feigning ignorance.

"Of Arthur. Do you agree that he is selling himself short?" George was persistent and when she didn't answer he continued, "You know this city better than anyone. If anyone knows, it's you." He sipped his drink in victory.

Sophia had no way around it; everyone, including Arthur, was looking in her direction waiting for an answer. Any instance they could draw Sophia Kingsley into social drama was satisfying.

"I suppose Arthur has his pick of women, yes."

George didn't let up. "But can he have *any* woman he wants, as Trixie insisted?"

Trixie tilted her head. "I still think I'm right."

"Of course not!" Sophia exclaimed and Arthur's heart dropped. "There are plenty of married women who he surely can't have." She smiled toward George, proud of herself for evading the interrogation.

Trixie whooped with laughter, Henry shook his head and took a drink. George sat back in his chair, his eyes locked with Sophia's. He squinted at her with a look of disappointment, or at least that was Arthur's best guess. Elizabeth smiled tightly and took another drink.

"Let's lay off poor Arthur, please!' Elizabeth pleaded. "The man will never come back to one of our gatherings."

"Oh all right," Trixie conceded, "but you will have to get used to us."

"I'll do my best." Arthur nodded his head and was just drunk enough to be nosy. "And what about all of you?"

They all glanced around at each other, then Elizabeth took up the question, "It doesn't quite work that way around here."

Henry explained, "What she means is that It's tough when you're..." he hesitated, the reluctance of a man who had not always been wealthy, "when you're us."

Trixie giggled. "He means rich."

"Gosh, Trix, thanks." Henry replied.

"Well you do! But it's just because people are always after the money. You'll see, Arthur, if you haven't already. It makes it tough to know who likes you and who doesn't. Why do you think we stick to our dysfunctional little group? It's certainly not because we like each other all that much."

They all laughed and Trixie continued, "It doesn't matter anyway, all these men think they're fat cats now and just want the chippies."

"Trixie!" Elizabeth scolded her.

"Well it's true," Trixie continued into her drink. She spoke nonchalantly but it was obvious she had been hurt.

George, who hadn't spoken in longer than was characteristic, joined in. "You'll see, Arthur, unless you find someone amongst the few up here." He lifted his hands to convey some sort of hierarchy. "You will always wonder if they're on the up and up."

Arthur attempted to blink away the intoxication he felt. "This is all very depressing."

Trixie spoke up again, "Oh no! We're sorry, dear! It is all sorts of fun—all we're saying is be careful unless you find a dame with just as much or more money than you."

The way they all talked about money so casually was new to Arthur. And the way they all knew he had money was even more so.

Elizabeth smiled. "There are plenty of single women 'up here,' for you." She motioned as George had, making fun of him.

"You know what I mean, Lizzy." George drew out the nickname.

"I told you not to call me that!" She yelled toward George.

He shook his head. "I like it."

To that, Elizabeth rolled her eyes and turned her attention toward Sophia. "Sophia, let's refresh ourselves, shall we?" Then she turned toward Trixie. "Trixie?"

Trixie and Sophia answered by standing up and following Elizabeth out of the room. Apparently, the expected answer was yes.

"They're going to bump gums. Well Trixie and Elizabeth, at least. Maybe Sophia does in private. I don't know," Henry said.

George snorted. "Sophia gossiping is a rare occasion."

George then turned toward Arthur. "How does it feel, Arthur?"

"What?" asked Arthur.

"To have it all—money, success, dames clamoring for you." He seemed to be bating him, but for what Arthur was unsure.

Arthur shook his head. "I don't think I have all of that..." But George and Henry were both shaking their heads at him.

"You'll see." George raised his glass toward him. "You have much more than you realize."

CHAPTER
ELEVEN

Henry crafted Arthur another drink but he let the ice melt a bit before he began to drink it. He felt himself getting looser which led to sloppy honesty. He reminded himself he barely knew them, despite their inclusion of him in their world. The last thing he needed was to make a drunken fool of himself at the very first dinner party to which he'd managed an invitation.

George stayed in his chair most of the evening, sipping his drink and staring into the fire, lost in a world where no one else was permitted. He hadn't interacted with Sophia much since he goaded her about Arthur.

Henry, Trixie, and Elizabeth got increasingly drunk as the night progressed. Soon, they all squealed in excited voices and Henry's usual cool demeanor gave way to that of a giddy boy.

Arthur wondered what he would've thought of it all just a short time before. Then, it seemed like a wishful aspiration to be entertained at the Carlyle house. Life's pace quickened exponentially and landed him in a position where the social elite were referring to him as a friend. William had been his best friend for years and it felt strange not to have him there, but it seemed the harder Arthur tried, the less William wanted to join. The more Arthur immersed himself into their world, the more distant he felt from William and the life they'd materialized from a dream.

Sophia sat next to Elizabeth until Elizabeth tipped over her drink and spilled it over the couch. Sophia jumped up to Elizabeth's apologies and reassured her that she had not spilled on her. Even so, she made the intelligent decision to move away from the couch. She walked toward George and leaned over toward him. He nodded and then motioned toward the wall. Sophia walked to it and pressed a small button until a staff member magically appeared.

She turned toward the rest of the group. "I'm getting my coat to go outside and look at the stars. The sky is supposed to be particularly clear tonight and there might be a chance at seeing a meteor. Would anyone like to join me?"

Henry, Trixie, and Elizabeth ignored her and George shook his head. Then he turned his gaze toward Arthur and lifted his eyebrows. Arthur took it as a dare.

"I'd like to, if that's alright," Arthur replied.

"Wonderful," Sophia replied, then instructed the staff to fetch both their coats along with some hats and scarves to keep them warm.

When the staff returned, Arthur rose from his chair and took his coat. He then placed the borrowed scarf around his neck as Sophia wrapped one made of fur around her and pulled a matching hat onto her head. Some of her hair fell out of her headband as she did, framing her face and making her look more casual than she normally appeared.

Arthur followed her to the terrace door, then walked around her and held it open. He closed the door behind them, muting the drunken guests who were laughing in the den.

Arthur exhaled and watched his breath swirl in front of him. He wished he'd worn his warmer coat but resisted the urge to pull his arms around himself, wanting to appear collected in front of Sophia. Not that it would have mattered because at that moment, Sophia was already staring up at the sky, searching for the illuminated tail of a meteor.

Arthur joined her and turned his attention up toward the black sky dotted with thousands of stars. It was clearer than Arthur had ever seen it, or perhaps the thrill of being near Sophia made everything feel heightened. They stood aside each other for minutes in awe of the magnitude of the universe.

"It makes you feel small, doesn't it?" Sophia broke the silence but kept her gaze up.

"Mhmm, like you're so tiny. Almost like what we do doesn't really matter."

She considered this for a moment. "It's funny how both things can be true at the same time—that what we do matters a lot and then hardly at all."

Arthur laughed lightly under his breath. "The enigma of being a human."

Sophia smiled up to the sky. "Some of us are more mysterious than others," she replied, then lowered her face and looked at Arthur.

He looked back at her, her nose starting to turn pink in the cold. "Are you categorizing yourself as a mystery?"

"I wasn't, no. And how am I to know if I am anyway? I don't know if people are confused by me or not. To me, I'm pretty straightforward... boring."

"You are hardly those things," Arthur replied, dumbfounded.

"I live with myself every day. Trust me, it gets awfully boring to be inside my head."

Arthur nodded. "I suppose I know what you mean. I get tired of the same thoughts that seem to run through my mind at a relentless pace."

She tilted her head in curiosity. "You don't strike me as the kind of man who worries about much."

Arthur laughed. "I'm doing a good job then."

"Of?"

"Of seeming like I have it all together."

"And you don't?"

"Do you?"

Sophia sighed and then looked out over the grounds. "No."

They stood in silence for a moment until she spoke again, "My mother used to sing a song to me at night—about the stars. I always think of her when I look up at them."

Arthur was touched by her sentimentality. "She sounds wonderful."

She nodded. "She was an amazing woman, an amazing mother. Sometimes I wonder how things might have been if she didn't die. I think maybe my father would've fought harder against his own death. He loved her immensely."

Arthur's thoughts drifted to his own mother and his longing for her but he decided against sharing.

"How did he die?"

"The influenza. End of 1918."

Arthur nodded. The world opened up again in the last few years and in ways it felt like the influenza was lifetimes ago, but for those who lost someone, it was forever present.

Sophia could feel Arthur holding back, clammed up and fighting against the alcohol's push to relax. In contrast, she softened. The hard edges she felt earlier sitting on the couch diminished as soon as they walked out onto the terrace together. She'd been pleasantly surprised when Arthur accepted the invitation.

"Tell me, Arthur, what do you think of all of this?"

Arthur, unsure of what she was looking for, guessed at an answer. "I appreciate George including me."

"You think that George was the one who wanted you included in my birthday?" She asked, raising her eyebrows toward him.

"Well, I guess, he was the one who called, so I—"

She laughed. "He called at my request."

"Oh." The word dropped dead, unwittingly halting the conversation and hindering Sophia's attempt to disentangle Arthur's reticence.

She forced her gaze back to the sky, confused by his refusal to unwind.

Arthur fretted over his blank mind and empty lips; something about being in George's house clammed him up, as if he feared the man might pounce on him at any second. He could sense Sophia disappearing back into herself.

But then, as if to take pity on him, the universe interceded. Sophia gasped and pointed toward the sky. "Look!"

Arthur spotted a streak of light whiz across the black sky and as fast as it appeared, it vanished, absorbed into its celestial resting place. He looked toward her, her hand still extended in the air, her mouth wide and eyes awestricken. Her gold ring shimmered in the moonlight and he again caught sight of it.

Curious, he reached for her finger and almost grazed it. "What is this?"

"It was my mother's." On her left middle finger, she wore a simple gold ring. She touched it gingerly with her right index finger and then traced it, engrossed in memory.

"She came from very modest means; my father seemed so traditional but then he did such a controversial thing and went against my grandparents' wishes and married for love instead of status. My father gave her the ring when he was courting her. She was skeptical of a man of such status and was insistent that she did not have any interest in his fortunes. He tried to give her more expensive gifts and she continued to refuse him. Finally, he realized that what she wanted was an indication that he knew her. And that's when he gave her this ring. It was a lot for a man like my father to give his love interest something of such little value. But to my mother, it was everything."

Sophia stopped and pulled herself away from the memory of her parents. She looked diffidently at Arthur to find him listening intently, captivated by every word.

"It's funny, the things that we'd be most devastated to lose sometimes have no value to anyone else."

Arthur thought of his father's suit, his mother's broken grandfather clock, and the few pictures he had of them both. There were only a few cherished things that remained of them.

He nodded. "I think those are the best things. They're full of memories…"

Sophia waited for him to continue but when he didn't she rescued him from what seemed to be pain.

"Exactly," she agreed and again ran her finger over the ring. "I never take it off."

"Never?"

She shook her head. "No. I'm terrified to lose it. I always want to make sure it's safe. It's strange, but I know that as long as this ring is with me, I'm somehow safe too."

Arthur nodded, understanding. When Sophia's mother died, she exposed her vulnerable young daughter to a precarious world; one whose ambiguity brought terror instead of excitement. Arthur resonated deeply with that experience. A strange sensation engulfed his body and he wanted to hug her close in an attempt to quell an overwhelming and insatiable wistfulness.

Sophia broke her concentration away from her mother and her ring. Her calm countenance faltered when she drank and she no longer retained the ability to keep her thoughts from escaping her mouth.

"Arthur?" In her voice was a hint of vulnerability which immediately pulled Arthur's attention away from the sky.

"Yes?"

"You didn't know it was my birthday, did you?"

A lump formed in Arthur's throat the way it had when a schoolteacher was about to reprimand him for his careless impropriety.

"I'm afraid that I didn't."

She nodded, already knowing as much. "I thought George may have failed to mention it. May I ask why you accepted his invitation?"

Arthur frowned and considered; he knew the honest answer was that he didn't want to shrink away from George, but he feared Sophia would judge him if he confessed his insecurity.

"I suppose I enjoy being in… everyone's company. It promised to be an enjoyable evening." In truth, he hadn't known what was in store when he accepted. The most he hoped for was a chance to prove to George he wasn't afraid of him.

Sophia softly laughed. "Sometimes I'm not so sure that's true."

"Why is that?" he asked calmly, astonished that his anxiety didn't spill out of him. His desire for her coupled with the whiskey made his internal longing for her near unbearable. He held himself even tighter to keep it from spilling.

She laughed again. "I've seen you with George. Half the time you seem to enjoy him and the other half you seem to want to punch him in the face."

"Hmm, well I suppose we both know I'd be lying if I refuted it."

"It's not an uncommon feeling, we all feel the same sometimes... but I'm glad that you're giving him a chance; he's a good man."

Arthur wanted to contradict her, to tell her that George wasn't worth her time, but he knew he had no evidence to prove it. It was a simple case of envy.

"I suppose you know him better than anyone," Arthur gritted through his teeth. As obnoxious as George was, he had been good to Arthur—inviting him, making him feel welcome, sending him business.

"George is just... conflicted."

Arthur frowned. "Conflicted? About what? About you?"

Sophia jumped in quickly. "Oh no, no. Not about me. About life I suppose. He feels so small against the universe and yet so big in it too. Like a lot of us do."

"You seem worried about him."

"I am. I always am. George is the only person left who has known me my entire life."

Arthur felt the pettiness of his competition with George.

"That's important, I wish I still had that," he admitted.

"You don't?" Sophia asked, intrigued. Arthur had a habit of being a good listener without sharing in return.

Arthur shook his head. "No. My father died when I was sixteen, my mother when I was twenty-two. I was an only child. Now William, my business partner, is the person who has known me longest I suppose."

"I'd like to meet him."

"Why?"

"You're a difficult man to know. Perhaps he could offer some insights into what is happening in that mind of yours."

"Trust me when I say it is not that interesting."

"Maybe to some people it is." She swallowed hard and waited for him to reply.

"Not to me," he said, ignorant to what she just admitted. For a man obsessively interested in what Sophia thought of him, he failed to read obvious cues.

"Well let's start with something simple," she said.

He looked at her with amused suspicion. "Ok?"

"Do you still find me intimidating?"

He smiled. "I told you I always would."

She nodded slowly, satisfied and feeling perhaps she had finally bated him. "Remember when you said you had a lot of thoughts of me that first evening and I asked for only one more? I'm thinking I erred and missed my chance to get it out of you."

"Should've taken up the opportunity then," he replied.

Why he wouldn't pick up the banter, she didn't understand. In her excitement, her heart beat hadn't slowed since she came outside with him. She wondered if he could hear it pounding out of her throat when she spoke. She closed her mouth tighter as if there was a sound to be muffled.

"Are you hurt that I didn't know it was your birthday?" he asked.

"No. Of course not. I was just curious. You seemed a bit... shocked when George announced it."

"I was, I just never know what that man is going to say. The vicissitudes in his behavior are perplexing."

Sophia drew in a deep breath. "May I ask you a very personal question?"

Arthur swallowed and continued hesitantly. "Yes."

She chose her words carefully. "You are awfully curious about George, so what, well do you..." She paused and tried again, "what exactly are your feelings about him?"

"Does it matter that much to you what I think of him?"

"It might."

"I don't know him well enough to know, I guess," Arthur answered honestly. Outside of his jealousy, which often colored everything, Arthur didn't know what he truly thought of the man.

Sophia nodded. "I see. Well, George is... well he's not... I guess what I'm saying is that if you are so inclined, I think you could be friends."

Arthur frowned and pursed his lips, not wanting to comply.

"Perhaps. I suppose if you are asking me if I approve of George, I hate to say that I probably do." He heard the words fall loosely out of his mouth and hated their sound.

"Approve?" Her voice rose with the word.

"Yes. As you said, he is a good man, as much as sometimes I'd hate to admit it."

She frowned. "What do you think that—"

Before she could finish, the door behind them flung open and Trixie and Elizabeth fell through it, laughing.

They hadn't put on coats over their sleeveless dresses and their breath fogged in front of their faces. Trixie's cheeks were red with cold and intoxication.

They both stumbled toward Arthur and Sophia. Trixie wrapped her arm around Sophia.

"We wanted to see what was so enthralling out here. Something has to be the bee's knees. You two have been out here for so long," Trixie mumbled out her words, having gotten considerably drunker.

Elizabeth straightened and pulled herself back. "It is a beautiful night, isn't it?" she asked, trying not to slur her words but she failed to enunciate as much as usual.

Sophia wrapped her arm around Trixie to help keep her upright. "Trixie, are you going home tonight or are you sleeping in one of the guest bedrooms?"

"Henry had Jasper drive!" she replied, half answering the question.

Sophia nodded and then looked at Arthur. "I am going to take her inside and get her some water."

Sophia aided Trixie in leaving the terrace, trying to hold her up as she tripped over her own feet.

When they made it inside and shut the door, Arthur watched through the window as George rose from his chair. He and Henry had been seated perpendicular to each other and appeared startled at the interruption in their conversation. George wrapped his arm around Trixie and practically lifted her feet from the ground. Arthur saw George and Sophia exchange a few words, then say something to Henry before they carried her out of the room. Henry sat alone and looked down at the empty glass clutched between both hands.

Elizabeth pulled Arthur's attention back. "Are you enjoying the evening?"

Arthur nodded, not wanting to be cruel and tell her that he had been enjoying it much more moments ago.

"It's strange isn't it, to join a new group like this, people who have been in the same circle for years?"

Arthur nodded again wishing he could follow the others inside. He remembered how George positioned himself with Elizabeth the night they spoke outside of Sophia's party and wondered if he had been just as annoyed by her.

Elizabeth continued on, oblivious to Arthur's disinterest.

"You know we were just teasing you earlier, don't you?"

"About what?"

"About women, wanting you and such." She was trying hard not to slur and to remain composed.

"Yes, Elizabeth. I know."

She didn't pause in her response. "Except it is true, you know," she said, looking down at her hands. Her skin had become paler in the cold.

"Look at you, you're freezing." She wrapped her arms around herself and giggled. "I hadn't realized how cold it was."

He placed his hand softly at the small of her back. "Let's get you back inside."

"It's too beautiful out here to go back in."

He sighed, realizing he might have to pick her up and throw her over his shoulder to get her back inside. It wouldn't be difficult to lift her with one arm.

Arthur pulled his hand from her back and she turned to face him. "Well alright, I suppose I will let you escort me inside."

Arthur turned to the door and the moment he faced her, Elizabeth grabbed his forearms, lifted herself up to her tiptoes and attempted a kiss, except, given that she was about a foot shorter than him, she missed and planted it on his chin instead.

Thinking she was falling, he instinctively grabbed her shoulders in an attempt to steady her. At that exact moment, the door popped open and George leaned out, catching them in that position—both grasping at each other, Elizabeth descending down from her toes and Arthur gazing down at her as if they had just kissed. Arthur was unsure if George witnessed the error or assumed that it was mutual. Arthur pushed Elizabeth away, making him look even guiltier.

George cleared his throat and tried to continue but his voice faltered, "Uh, Elizabeth?"

Elizabeth turned toward Arthur but kept her hands grasped around Arthur's forearms.

"Henry is going to ring Jasper to bring Trixie home. He wanted to know if you would like a ride," George said.

Elizabeth looked up at Arthur as if he might have some input and Arthur wanted to shake her grip from his arms. She finally released him and walked toward George.

"Of course, that would be kind of him." George ushered her inside and then turned to Arthur who was still half frozen in shock. He shoved his hands into his pockets as if he was trying to hide something he had stolen.

"Arthur would you like to ring Andrew?" George's voice was harsh and clipped.

Arthur nodded. "I think that is a good idea."

George held the door open for him, so he could return inside. As he passed George, he could feel his eyes burning into him. Arthur swallowed and wondered why George felt that all the women around him belonged to him.

George closed the door behind them as Henry was standing to leave. He assumed that the three women were gathered in the foyer waiting for Henry and the car, Sophia likely still struggling to keep Trixie upright.

Henry said goodbye to them both and then glanced briefly at George. Both of them seemed annoyed.

After he left, George turned to Arthur. "Robert called on Andrew. He should be here soon."

Arthur again felt like he was in trouble. He didn't care for the feeling that George was the self-appointed authority over him.

Arthur cleared his throat. "Is Sophia already gone or is she staying here for the evening?"

George stared blankly back at him, unaffected by the daringness of the question. George didn't break his gaze, but he didn't answer either.

Arthur pondered whether he had spoken the question aloud.

Just then, Sophia broke the tension. "They left," she informed them as she reentered the den.

George spun around; he loosened and dropped the harsh tone from his voice, "Thank you, Sophia."

She approached and looked back and forth between them. The tension in the space was thick and it hit her as she took her place next to George.

"Is everything alright?" Sophia asked, concerned.

George nodded. "Everything's jake."

But Sophia knew otherwise; George's tone meant *we'll talk about it later.* She nodded and dropped it but scanned Arthur's face for clues. He looked like a deer caught in the scope of a gun. She wondered what Arthur could have done to cause such anger.

She knew better than to resurrect it. "I believe my car is here." She gently touched George's elbow to break his attention away from Arthur.

George nodded and offered his arm. "I'll walk you." As they turned he called back to Arthur, trying to contain himself. "Arthur, Andrew is no doubt almost here. Why don't you come as well?"

Arthur followed them, again walking behind as Sophia clung to George's elbow. Arthur's habit of finding himself behind them grated at him.

Sophia kissed George on the cheek and thanked him for the dinner. "And it was lovely talking to you." She looked Arthur in the eyes and her genuineness softened him; it made him want to blurt out that he wished it had been her who tried to kiss him on the terrace. But he held his tongue. Instead he just nodded and smiled, fearing that if he opened his mouth, it might come pouring out.

George walked her to her car and helped her get into the back seat. He then closed it behind her and waited until her car was halfway down the drive before returning to join Arthur.

George shoved his hand into his pocket and pulled out his pocket watch to check the time.

Arthur's chest filled with anger at the passive implication that it was he who was keeping George so late.

"He should be here soon," Arthur replied. George nodded and then Arthur added, "You don't have to wait here with me."

"That would be bad manners, old boy."

They stood in tense silence for a moment until George couldn't contain it any longer. Though he was still drunk, he held his intoxication in and feigned sobriety well. "Just like other behaviors are bad manners."

"I don't understand how any of it concerns you," Arthur retorted. His defensiveness came off as petulant, but he felt no need to provide an explanation to George. Elizabeth and his interactions with her did not belong to him.

"The audacity." George shook his head.

Arthur frowned and shoved his hands into his pockets. He didn't feel drunk any longer but his words were driven by alcohol. "I don't see why you should care so much what I choose to do or not to do."

George scoffed then shook his head. Then in an act uncharacteristic of him, he walked toward Arthur and stood about a foot in front of him. Arthur started to step back but stopped, holding his ground.

George lowered his voice. "Let me be very clear. What you do in my house is very much my business."

Arthur's heart pounded and he willed the beads of sweat forming on his forehead to subside. He had never before been in a fight and he didn't want George Carlyle to be the first.

Arthur held his breath and tried to contain the shakiness in his voice. "I have done nothing to you." He knew he didn't sound as tough as he'd hoped.

Just then, George surprised him. He stepped back, shoved his hands into his pockets, and hung his head for a brief moment. If it had been a face off for dominance, Arthur would've won.

George swallowed and his voice shifted. "I just care about her."

"Elizabeth?" Arthur asked, surprised.

George shook his head. "No, Sophia."

Arthur's heart sent pangs through his body. "I know."

Then Arthur softened his voice and his intoxication allowed him to be more honest. "I don't want to compete with you."

George tilted his head up and lifted his eyes. "You're competing with yourself, Arthur."

The answer infuriated Arthur. "Why must you always speak in platitudes? Can't you be transparent with me for once?"

George looked squarely at Arthur and laughed. "You seem to believe that you yourself are transparent. You want to have an honest conversation with me?" he asked, though it sounded more like another accusation.

"Yes. For once," Arthur replied, exasperated at the riddle he was always trying to solve to no avail.

"Swell. Let's meet for lunch soon, say next Tuesday?"

Arthur was taken aback, he hadn't expected George to take him so seriously. His shifts in mood were impossible to follow.

Arthur nodded in silent agreement and then George said, "Andrew is here."

With that, George left the foyer. Manners only dictated so much.

CHAPTER

TWELVE

George called Arthur's office to confirm lunch. Betty gave him the note that Monday and Arthur sat staring at it, surprised that George not only remembered, but followed through on his offer. It occurred to him that George may have intended on lecturing him again. Arthur resisted the urge to cancel out of anxiety.

Betty had drawn multiple exclamation points next to the location. George made reservations at the *1913 Room*, a restaurant usually for conducting important business. A lot of money had been made and lost over deals made within those walls.

***

On Tuesday, as Arthur left to attend the lunch, William stopped him on the way out. "Sure are spending a lot of time with this George fella."

"I imagine it will be a lot more once we're business associates," he lied, pretending the lunch had anything to do with business.

When Arthur arrived at the *1913 Room*, George already waited for him at their table. He sipped on a drink and had taken the liberty of ordering one for Arthur.

As Arthur sat he motioned toward it. "I don't drink at lunch."

George replied, "I think you will change your mind."

Arthur took his seat and as he did, George sat his drink on the table. He didn't offer his hand or stand to greet him. George was still upset for reasons Arthur couldn't quite discern. If George was trying to intervene in his liking for Sophia, then his anger over him kissing Elizabeth didn't stand to reason.

George clasped his hands in his lap and looked across the table. It was set formally, as if they were meeting for an elaborate meal. Arthur had never been to the *1913 Room* but the men surrounding him were all wealthy and powerful. He wondered if George had made the reservation to have territory on his side.

"Well?" George prodded, forcing Arthur to go first.

Arthur took a deep breath to calm his nerves and annoyance that George acted as if he was doing him a favor. "I was surprised you followed through."

"You don't know me very well," George replied, non-defensively.

Arthur wished he could rattle the man, but he seemed unflappable, that is, until Sophia became involved.

"I suppose I don't." Arthur took a sip of his whiskey. It was smooth and balanced and he tried not to show he was impressed. George had been correct again, he did feel the need to drink. "I have to be honest, I don't understand what happened last Friday night."

"Happened with what?" George asked.

"You." Arthur replied directly. With a simple nod of his head to the right person, Arthur knew George could likely ruin his entire career. But thus far, George proved not to mix business with his personal life and so Arthur saw no reason to be indirect.

George picked up his glass and swirled the ice cube in the bottom, then looked at Arthur. "You don't understand what I was upset about?"

"No," Arthur replied. He had no interest in drawing out the conversation. Either they were going to discuss it or they weren't. And either they were going to be friends after or they weren't. It felt clear to Arthur there were only two directions to choose and they were opposite ones.

"You have to be careful in this world, Arthur. With what you say, who you say it to, what you do, who you do it in front of."

"I'm aware of that," Arthur replied sharply. He hadn't wanted a lesson, he wanted an explanation.

"I don't think that you do, but you will learn. Probably pretty painfully, unfortunately."

"Are you implying that your anger was an attempt to protect me from myself?"

"Not at all," George replied plainly. "Maybe someday we will be friends and that will be the case, but if you were to disappear tomorrow there is only one reason that would impact my life."

George didn't want to disappoint his father. Arthur was well aware of his expendability in all other matters.

Almost as if he was reading Arthur's mind, George leaned forward and added, "And don't make so many assumptions about things for which you have no idea."

Arthur shook his head. "You're doing it again. Giving me all this baloney instead of real answers."

George sat back in his chair and swirled his drink again, but this time he didn't look away from Arthur.

"You recall what I said on the hill that afternoon when we went riding?"

"You said a lot of things."

George didn't flinch. "About Sophia and I being intertwined in our lives."

"Yes, I recall. Vividly, in fact."

"Good. Then you understand that Sophia is a permanent fixture in my life, and I in hers."

Arthur swallowed his anger. "And that you own her? Is that what you came here to tell me?"

George didn't laugh as he usually might have. Instead, he narrowed his eyes and shook his head. "No. We do not own each other. But I do have interest in what she does with herself. Who she spends her time with, you see. But—" he sat forward and his voice lifted, becoming more casual in tone. "—I don't always have a say in that nor do I always get what I want."

"And what is it that you want?" Arthur finally asked.

George didn't hesitate. "Her happiness, of course."

Although Arthur wanted to grant him selflessness, he knew George had motives that were more self-motivated than he'd publicly let on.

"And we both know what you want," George said, his eyes locked on Arthur.

Arthur's stomach flipped and he searched his mind for a rebuttal.

"There's no use refuting it, Arthur. I thought we were here to level with each other."

Arthur sat straighter and took a deep breath. "Fine."

"Good." George smiled. "To that end, I need to ask you a question and I need you to answer me honestly. If the answer is yes, I need you to leave immediately. If the answer is no, I need you to stay."

"Why?"

George shook his head. "There are things that are not mine to share. I do not spread gossip, as much as others might claim I do."

"Ok." Arthur agreed, though he hesitated in believing him.

George leaned forward again. "Did you make a move on Elizabeth?"

Though he wasn't sure what he expected, George's question surely was not it. He shook his head. "I don't understand. You just said that you knew I was interested in Sophia. Why ask me about Elizabeth?"

"I just need to know if you did or you didn't."

"What makes you think you have the right to pry into my personal life?"

"Is the answer yes then?"

Arthur shook his head. "No. The answer is no."

George sat back. "Ok then. Thank you for answering."

"I would still like to know why it's necessary for me to reveal these personal things to you."

"It isn't, Arthur, until you get yourself involved in a mess that suddenly I am being forced to sort through." George now sounded fatherly, and it irritated Arthur that once again he felt like he was being lectured.

"My life is not yours to clean up."

"I didn't say your life."

"So what? You're acting as Sophia's keeper?"

George shook his head. "No. I wouldn't ever act as that, not unless she elected me to. But I will always be protective of her. And I will always give her what she wants."

Before Arthur could reply, George stood and his demeanor completely changed. In confusion, Arthur started to stand too, thinking that the lunch was over before they'd eaten, but then George smiled and reached his hands forward to someone else.

Arthur looked behind him to find Sophia approaching. Sophia appeared just as surprised to see him but greeted George with a kiss on the cheek. George pulled out the chair he'd been sitting in and offered it to Sophia.

She looked back and forth between them as she sat. "I'm sorry, Arthur, I didn't know you were joining us..." She looked to George for an explanation.

George swallowed the last of his drink and then leaned forward over the table to address them both.

"Arthur didn't know you would be here either, but I needed to get you both here without argument. I am afraid it is also out of my own selfish desire."

Sophia frowned. "George, I am confused, what..."

But George interrupted again. "I have to admit that I am getting quite exhausted from this."

Arthur swallowed hard and braced himself for what, he didn't know.

George took their silence as an invitation to continue. "I am going to excuse myself from this lunch. I must be getting back to the office. I hope that this will give you both the chance to discuss some much needed things without interruption. I have ordered the wait staff to bring you a set meal and they will not interrupt with any questions unless of course you instruct them to."

"George—" Sophia attempted to stop him, but he shook his head.

"I am excusing myself from this. It is your turn to be honest, about everything." He emphasized the last two words toward Sophia, leaving Arthur immensely curious.

Sophia grinned as he walked away. "George is always doing things like this."

"Like what?" Arthur asked, confused.

"Just... this."

Arthur shook his head. "Well it's all new to me."

"George is just being protective." Arthur looked at her, a question in his eyes, and she finished before he could ask, "of me."

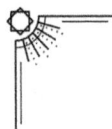

CHAPTER
THIRTEEN

When Arthur told William about the argument and the upcoming lunch, William of course had his theories. "He was clearly upset with you because he knows Sophia is interested. Is he being protective or possessive? That's the question."

"Well I think the assertion that she's interested is a bit too presumptuous," Arthur argued.

William shook his head and Betty joined. Arthur allowed himself to believe it for half a second until William added,

"I think it's obvious she is interested. Just be careful, you know? I know that we have more freedom to marry who we like, but these old money types often don't. I've heard cautionary tales about them having their fun while they can before they have to succumb to expectations."

"I can't imagine Sophia being someone who would do such a thing. And why would George ever allow it?"

"Perhaps he knows he'll ultimately win, so he's letting her have her fun."

"I can't believe the two of you!" Betty scolded. "You're speaking of her like property."

William and Arthur both closed their mouths, ashamed of themselves. But William's words left a nagging doubt inside Arthur.

***

Arthur played with the condensation running down his glass as he replayed the conversation with William in his mind.

Sophia sat straighter in her chair to feign confidence, but truthfully, she was confused. She understood George's motivations and trusted him to not set her up for hurt, but as far as she knew, he'd never had a direct conversation with Arthur about his feelings.

Finally, Arthur cleared his throat. "I, um, I'm, I should apologize to you for what happened on your birthday."

Sophia studied Arthur's face and frowned.

"Listen, I am aware that a woman like you and a man like George are just naturally destined to... well, you know. But in some small chance that isn't true, I want you to know that it was Elizabeth and I wanted nothing to do with it."

"Arthur." She leaned forward. "I have no idea what you're talking about."

"Really? I thought George would've immediately told you..."

She shook her head. "No. What happened with Elizabeth?"

Arthur closed his eyes and admonished himself for not letting her lead, but then explained himself.

"Oh, and?" She asked sharply, trying to sound unbiased when he'd finished.

"No," Arthur replied definitively. "You saw her, she was half seas over and probably not thinking. She tried to kiss me but missed, so nothing even happened."

Sophia laughed lightly and the knot in her stomach untwisted. Then she tilted her head and asked, "And a man like George and a woman like me are naturally destined to what?"

Arthur straightened and put on his business exterior—formal, stiff, and yet cool. "End up together." The words came out indifferently and he congratulated himself for containing the jealousy.

Sophia leaned back in her chair but remained expressionless. Then she swallowed, unsure of how to respond. She twisted her mother's ring around her finger.

"Naturally destined, huh?"

"I don't know, Sophia. I'm just trying to understand what is happening, trying to ascertain George's motives."

"Perhaps we don't have to base our actions on George." She smiled.

Arthur's embarrassment grew. *Why was he being compliant in treating George as his authority?*

Before he could reply, a waiter approached with soup and placed the cups on the table without a word. Sophia touched the man on the arm as he set hers down in front of her.

"Excuse me, sir?"

"Yes, Miss Kingsley? How can I help?"

"Is there perhaps a telephone I may use?"

"Of course, Miss. Shall I ring someone for you?"

She shook her head. "Thank you, no. I'd like to call myself if that's possible."

The man ushered Sophia away from the table leaving Arthur alone with his confusion. First, he decided that her answer to his question about George was a clear no. Then he decided it was too dangerous to assume anything. He finally settled on it meaning that George wanted to marry her, but she hadn't yet made up her mind. Arthur felt the pressure and excitement of having the chance to prove to Sophia that he was the better option.

The smell of the soup wafted to his nose and his stomach rumbled. He had not eaten that morning because his anxiety prevented him from doing so. In the end, he decided it was poor etiquette to eat while Sophia's sat there untouched.

Several minutes later, Sophia returned but her expression had not changed. As she sat she explained,

"Forgive me for the rude interruption, I needed to take care of something very important."

"Not at all." Arthur motioned with his hand to signal nonchalance. "When business arises, it is of utmost importance to handle it immediately."

Sophia looked at Arthur with some disappointment; when he was in business mode, he became stiff and sounded like her father, or every other man who sat in the *1913 Room* trying to be someone. She took in a deep breath and held it for a moment, hoping that maybe it would bring back the man she'd met on the balcony the first night.

"Arthur?"

"Yes?" He had just picked up his spoon to dip into his soup.

"Would you like to take a walk with me?" He glanced down at his soup and she added, "if you'd like to eat first, that's okay too."

He shook his head. "No. I would love to take a walk."

He rose and then positioned himself behind her chair to aid her in standing. Then, in a move he often saw George do that was successful, he offered his elbow to her. She smiled and accepted gladly.

As they were leaving the restaurant, Arthur noted feeling the effects of whiskey on an empty stomach. Sophia leaned over to him and whispered, "This place can be very stuffy. The food is wonderful but the conversation often gets stilted."

"Of course," he replied, as if he had many encounters there defined as such.

When they opened the door, Arthur was grateful that he'd worn more layers than three nights before when they stood together on the terrace. The air was cold and he was thankful that the morning wind had subsided. Still, he could see his breath when he opened his mouth. The warmth of Sophia's body next to him captured his attention and caused him to forget his hunger and chill.

"I know that you've lived in this city your entire life," she said, "but I wanted to show you something."

The city used to be tough, cruel and unforgiving, but it had changed for Arthur in the last few years. It had shown itself to be friendly, easy, and sometimes even beautiful. She led him down the sidewalk as cars whizzed by and honked at one another; important people on their way to important places.

Men lined the sidewalks signaling for taxicabs, women pushed children in strollers. The sounds of chatter, laughter, and street vendors filled the air but all that filled Arthur's mind was that he was strolling down the most prominent street in the city with the most eligible woman in it.

After they had walked a few blocks in a more comfortable silence, she pulled at his arm to follow her down a side alley. He knew that alley ways were usually no place for a woman, but she was insistent.

The hiss of the heat flowing out of the grates filled the air and the stench of the sewer, the one that reminded him of the city he once knew, filled his nose.

The alley led into another street and across from them, a square. In the middle of it was a giant Christmas tree. Though it was day and the lights unlit, ornaments of green, red, and silver gleamed in the sun, causing it to shine. Tinsel twinkled as it danced in the wind. People gathered around it in groups, smiling and pointing to the massive silver star on top. Shrieks of children's laughter and calls of men selling candied nuts from their carts filled the air. Although Arthur passed the square many times, he had never seen it from the perspective Sophia was showing him—it was as if the city—cold, grey and noisy—opened up to reveal itself as a joyous carnival.

"Isn't it lovely?" She hugged Arthur's arm closer to her and he squeezed her back.

"Yes, but I'm confused. It's only November. Don't the trees usually go up in December?"

She smiled. "Well, I will be away for the month of December and because Christmas is my favorite holiday, I would've missed seeing the trees here. So, it was a birthday gift to have it erected early. This has always been one of my favorites."

"Oh," he replied, wanting equally to ask about her being away and who gifted it to her.

She turned to him. "Have you seen this one before?"

"Yes. But never in the company of someone like you." He gave her arm another squeeze. "My mother used to bring me here as a child, but I don't think I've been back since then." The breath formed in front of his face and he could almost smell the peppermint candies she bought for them. He used to pop one in his mouth and then suck in hard to create a freezing sensation. It was invigorating. Suddenly, he got an idea.

"Come on. I want to see something."

She obliged and clung to his arm as he pulled her down the street. He stopped in front of a store and she almost bumped into him when he did. Women with small children opened the door to enter and exit, and each time they did, they could hear the cacophony of voices and children's screeches behind it.

"I knew it had to still be here!" He beamed as he looked over to Sophia, who was staring directly ahead, her eyes glistening.

"Come on." He nudged her and pulled her again. He grabbed the door as another person exited and held it open for Sophia.

Masses of children crowded the counters and the smell of sweets, chocolates, peppermint, and peanuts filled the air; it scooped Arthur up into the comforting arms of his childhood. He could see his mother standing at the counter pointing at all the candies and dreaming with Arthur about what it would be like to buy them all. In the end, they always each picked one piece of peppermint to accompany them to the tree. It was all she could afford but it was all he had ever needed anyway.

Sophia smiled and spun toward the counter in excitement. The crowds made it difficult to keep any space between them, and so he stood close behind her and whispered over her shoulder.

"Have you ever been in here before?"

She shook her head no and her hair brushed up against his cheek as she did.

"Oh it's so wonderful!" she exclaimed as she reached back to grab his arm again, attempting to pull him closer to the counter. After a space cleared by a few patrons who finished their purchase, she nudged her way up to it and leaned over, almost pressing her face against the glass and the confections behind it.

Arthur took the spot next to her but instead kept his focus on her in her childlike wonder.

"I have had candies and treats prepared by my bakers but they are always so nicely plated and presented at dinner or a party," she said, almost talking to herself. "But this is an entirely different experience altogether. The smells, all of the colors at once. It's marvelous."

"What do you want?"

"We're buying some?"

"Of course!" He laughed at the absurdity of her amazement.

"Oh..." She drew out her breath considering. "What should I get?"

He pointed out a few things to her and then the shop owner approached them.

"Good afternoon sir, miss. How might I help you?"

Sophia looked up with delight. Arthur spoke first, "I'll take a peppermint please."

"Just one?" The man asked as he reached for a small bag.

"I'll have one too," Sophia agreed.

Arthur turned to her. "You can have anything you want."

"I trust you," she said, smiling.

"No, no, we have to get more." He thought of all the times he had come in with this mother and wished for this moment. It felt wrong to not seize it. Arthur wondered if it was the same man who asked him the same questions years ago.

"Yes!" She clasped her hands together. "What else?"

Arthur got an idea and his smile widened. "I'd like two boxes of chocolates."

"Two?"

Each box contained at least fifty pieces. For Arthur, it had been the crown jewel of the shop, always out of his reach.

But Arthur nodded convincingly. "Yes. Two please."

Sophia shifted her attention to the fudge at the other end of the counter while the man delicately packaged the boxes of chocolates and two peppermints into a bag. Arthur pulled out his billfold and handed the man the exact change. The fact that it hardly made a dent in his wallet was not lost on him.

Arthur gathered the bag and reached for Sophia to usher her back out into the cold. When the door closed behind them, she reached for his arm and hugged him closer to her.

"That was magnificent! And here I thought I was going to show you something special."

"You did," he answered, looking at her and then the bag in his hand. "Let's cross the street and get closer." He motioned with his head toward the Christmas tree.

She allowed him to lead her across the street and then they took their places on a bench near the tree, so they could smell the pine when a gentle breeze swept through.

Arthur unrolled the top of the paper bag and peered inside. It was more chocolate than he'd ever had in his possession at once.

"How are we ever going to eat all of that?" She looked at Arthur and laughed.

He looked at her and smiled. "We're not." And then he turned his attention toward the hordes of children and families gathered near the tree. He reached in and pulled out a peppermint and handed it to her.

"Here," he said, offering the peppermint. She accepted it in her glove.

She pulled at the two twisted ends to unroll the paper from around the hard candy. He reached in and fished out his and then did the same. She looked at him and they popped them into their mouths in unison.

He showed her how to suck in the air to experience the cooling sensation. She laughed and shivered and then leaned her head onto his shoulder. He stiffened for a moment, fearing he might disintegrate into happiness if he didn't hold onto something.

Without lifting her head, she tucked the hard candy in her gums so she could speak. "So what shall we do with the boxes of chocolates?"

He reached down and fetched one box and opened the lid. Under it were chocolates of all sizes and shapes, each individually wrapped in white waxed paper; each a surprise only to be revealed once it had been bitten into. He glanced around at all the children playing and running around the tree.

"Would you like one?" he asked Sophia, but she shook her head.

"No, I couldn't possibly. I have a feeling I know your plan for them."

He exaggerated playing with the opened box until a child near him took notice. Once the child's gaze hit the box, he could not distract himself from it. Arthur smiled at the boy and handed a piece to Sophia, encouraging her.

She looked over to him and accepted it, and then held it out to the boy and lifted her eyebrows, offering an invitation. The boy tugged on his mother's arm who was trying to wrangle a smaller girl with her other arm. The woman pulled back on him in annoyance until she followed his gaze toward Sophia.

Immediately, the woman's face lit with recognition. There were people who didn't know who she was, mostly because they didn't care to, but for those who paid attention, Sophia was royalty. The boy tugged on his mother's arm and she obliged, taking the girl with them too.

They approached Sophia and Arthur cautiously. "I'm sorry, my son seems to think..."

Sophia interrupted her. "No need to apologize. I offered," she said as she held up the chocolate until the boy reached out his hand. She gently placed it into his bare hand.

The girl turned her attention from her tantrum and fixated on watching her brother. She reached out her hand to Sophia, hoping for a similar response. Arthur handed another to Sophia and then she placed it in the girl's hand.

"What do you say?" the woman reminded her children and in tiny excited voices they responded, "Thank you," without taking their eyes off the candies.

"Would you like one too?" Sophia asked, but the woman shook her head.

"No, thank you. And thank you." She smiled and then encouraged her children away from the couple on the bench, peeking back a few times as if to confirm who she had just spoken to.

Soon, other children caught on and Sophia felt like Santa with a long line of children waiting to see her. Arthur allowed her to hand out each piece, even when she suggested he get in on the fun. He found it more pleasing to watch her joy with every child she delighted.

"Arthur, we're starting to run low," she informed him as she peered into the near empty box. He peeked inside and then jumped up from the bench.

"I'll be right back!" He jogged across the park then the street to the store. Sophia watched him briefly and then turned her attention toward the girl in front of her, a blonde with curly hair who appeared to be about five years old. Her mother stood over her, seemingly skeptical of the well-dressed couple who were delighted in handing chocolates to children. Even still, no one forgot their manners and she directed her daughter to thank the nice woman and then promptly pulled her away. Some were more thankful than others of their generosity.

Arthur returned with two more boxes and set them down next to Sophia as he sat.

"This was all he had left," he informed her breathlessly.

"I had no idea how many children there were!" She laughed as she handed out yet another.

"When there's chocolate, there are hundreds of attentive ones." He crossed his legs and leaned back on the bench, spreading his arms across the back, one extended behind Sophia.

After all the chocolate boxes were empty, Sophia joined Arthur in leaning back on the bench. She brought her hands over her face then blew into them, hoping to bring some warmth back.

"Are you cold?" Arthur asked as he leaned forward to look at her.

She shook her head no but then stopped. "Ok. Yes I am."

He stood and offered her his hand. "I have eaten exactly one peppermint today; I'm hungry. Are you interested in joining me for a proper lunch now?"

She smiled, accepted his hand, and nodded in agreement.

They walked toward a small soup restaurant that Arthur frequented often. People often ate from their bowls while standing, slurping it in a hurry to return to work.

"Here it is," he said, pointing to the small sign about fifty feet in front of them. "Are you ok with standing to eat?"

A moment of hesitation crossed over her. "I suppose."

***

Later, between bites of soup, hers split pea and his potato, she looked up at him. She worked to balance her bowl in one hand and use the spoon with the other. It wasn't proper etiquette but to keep it from dribbling down her chin, she brought her face closer to the bowl.

"Arthur," she said, interrupting him mid bite.

"Hmm?" he asked, his mouth full of potato and cream. He wiped at his chin with the back of his hand to catch any that may have dripped.

"What are you doing for Christmas?"

He swallowed and then used a napkin to wipe his mouth, just in case. "Well, for the last few years I have had Christmas dinner with William and his family."

"What about the morning?" She tilted her head in concern.

He shrugged. "Sometimes I work."

"No!" she said, causing the few who were left lingering late at lunch to turn their heads. "I won't hear of it! You must come to Europe."

He lowered his bowl so that it was in line with his stomach. "Europe?"

"Yes. It has always been a dream. That's why I will be away most of December. You must come."

"I'll consider it," he replied, unsure if it was true.

"Oh you should. Everyone would be so happy if you did."

"Everyone?"

"Mhmm," she replied. "Well me, for one. But Henry, George, Trixie, possibly Elizabeth if her father will allow it."

Arthur knew she hadn't been asking only him to join her, but the thought briefly crossed his mind and so when it was revoked, unwarranted disappointment washed over him.

"Please think about it," she pleaded with him again. He wasn't sure how he could ever say no to her.

***

By the time Arthur returned to his office, it was almost time for Betty to leave early for an appointment. She was walking away from his desk as she saw him come in.

"I just left a message for you on your desk." She turned and pointed to the small note.

"Thank you, Betty."

William sat behind his desk reading intently over something. Arthur sat down and scanned the note.

Scribbled in Betty's handwriting, he read, "*3:45 p.m. George Carlyle. Return call.*"

"Betty," he called after her breaking his own rule not to shout across the office, "did he leave any other information?"

"No, sir. He just asked that you return his call." She waited for Arthur to add more and when he didn't, she turned to the cabinet to finish filing the last few documents before she left.

Betty was organized, efficient and concise. Most of the time, Arthur enjoyed those things about her, but he wished in that moment that she'd asked George more.

William looked up from his desk. "Strange that he's calling right after you met..." William waited for Arthur to add an explanation and when he didn't, William remarked, "and after such a long lunch at that." He looked directly at Arthur as if Arthur had just been discovered.

"Sophia was there," Arthur said coolly and shuffled some papers on his desk to make it seem as though he was disinterested in the information.

"Ah, I see."

Betty smiled at William from across the room and Arthur thought he saw them share a look.

Arthur stopped messing with the papers and looked back and forth between them. "What?"

Betty spun around and returned her attention to the filing cabinet. William shrugged and looked back down at his desk. "Nothing. I was just saying I see."

"No lecture this time?" Arthur asked, wishing that William hadn't just dampened the mood Sophia elevated.

"Lecture for what? It's perfectly acceptable for you to have a long lunch with Sophia Kingsley and George Carlyle." The way he said both of their full names stood out in stark contrast to the way Arthur knew them. He recalled a short time ago referring to them in the same way.

"Then what are you getting so sore about?"

"I'm not."

"I know you, William. I can hear something in your voice."

"I just don't want you to take any wooden nickels, that's all. Those types can treat us like we're easy marks."

"Those types? You realize we are becoming those types?" Arthur's voice rose in annoyance.

William abruptly stood from his desk making Betty jump. "We are not becoming anything."

Arthur frowned and scoffed. "Bushwa!"

"Arthur, I just don't want you to be a chump! You can throw on your glad rags and toss your dough around all you want, but just be careful."

"You were the one who wanted me to ask her out, now what? Jealousy, is that what it is?"

William laughed mockingly. "You think you're sitting pretty but I've seen what happens to new money when things go sour."

"Are you talking about your father? That won't happen to me, William. I'm no sap."

"Are you calling my father a sap?!" William's face turned red and he clenched his jaw, ready to return the attack. Arthur's defensiveness had grown exponentially since he met Sophia but William wasn't about to let him dump it on his family.

"Fellas!" Betty shouted over them, surprising them both. "Break it up! I'm sick of listening to this nonsense!"

Arthur and William both stood frozen; neither had ever heard Betty raise her voice in anger.

"Everything copacetic?" she asked.

"Everything's jake, Betty. And I wasn't calling your father a sap," Arthur replied, dryly.

William shook his head as Arthur stood, put his coat back on, and walked out of the office, forgetting the note's insistence on calling George.

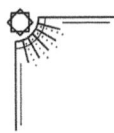

CHAPTER

FOURTEEN

Arthur didn't return to the office until the following morning when he had calmed down and the night allowed him to relive the memories of the afternoon with Sophia. When he arrived that morning, William greeted him as usual and handed him a mug of peppermint tea.

"Here," he said, shoving a few files toward Arthur. "I need you to review these."

"Are they new?"

William shook his head. "No actually. But they are coming up on the end of their contracts and I would like to head them off before they can consider cancelling with us." William was good at the parts of business that involved forethought and strategy. The only way Arthur contributed to those things was through his social networking, which had become much more personal than business.

As Arthur sat, the doorbell chimed and ushered in George. He looked down at the note that was still there waiting for him.

"George, I saw that you called. I..."

George waved him off. "Don't worry about it, Arthur." His usual tone had returned and the disdain in his voice was nowhere to be found.

George took the seat in front of Arthur's desk.

"Is there something I can help you with?"

"My father asked that I meet with you to review some of the financials." He set down the newspaper he had folded in his left hand, then reached in his briefcase and pulled out a thick file and set it in front of Arthur, laying it on top of the newspaper.

"I know it's not much time, but my father had hoped you would compile something by Friday and we could meet again for lunch? Say around noon at the *1913 Room*?"

Arthur wanted to be upset about the entitlement, but he had no business dismissing the biggest account he might ever hope to land.

"We can certainly take care of that for you." William's voice came from behind George as he approached. He extended his hand to

George who stood to take it.

"I'm William Henly, I don't believe we've met."

George shook his hand. "We have not. George Carlyle. It is nice to see you." He motioned toward Arthur with his head. "You have one hell of a business partner here."

William laughed and released his hand. "I sure do."

"We're excited to do business with you and your father," William said.

"We're happy to have found the two of you. William, you should come out with us sometime. You're always invited."

"I'll have to take you up on that," William said, nodding.

"Well I shall leave you to it. I appreciate this. Don't make me look like a sap."

William laughed again to keep the lighthearted tone. "We will do our best to never make you look foolish."

"All I can ask for, I suppose," George replied. "Have a good day, Arthur, William." He nodded to them both and then on the way out the door he turned to Betty, saying, "and Betty." Betty blushed as he said it and tried to drop her head to conceal her face, but her red cheeks were obvious.

After the door shut behind him, Betty smirked. "What a nice man, no one ever even acknowledges me!"

"I have to admit he was less arrogant than I anticipated," William agreed.

Arthur added nothing. Once again George was maddeningly inconsistent.

Arthur lifted the file from his desk. It was heavy, stuffed full of papers. Arthur knew neither he nor William would be getting to much else over the next two days.

"Not common for someone to leave something like this here with us, is it?" William asked.

"Sure, but then again, we have never done business with anyone like them."

"True," William replied as Arthur leafed through the file.

"He also left his newspaper," William noticed.

Arthur peeked around the file to see the folded newspaper still sitting in front of him.

"Looks like he already read it," he remarked, noting its rumpled state. He handed the file to William to view. "Take a look at this and let me know what you think the next steps should be. I'm happy to review the numbers once you're finished." William nodded and accepted the file.

William liked to look over a file in totality before Arthur began to break it down into details. He said that the details distracted him from his process. Arthur wasn't sure what that meant, but it had worked thus far, so he thought better than to change it.

William walked back to his desk, his eyes fixated on the file. Arthur returned his attention to his own desk and opened one of the files William gave him. He would use the time before William was finished with the Carlyle account to get as much else accomplished as he could. Other clients weren't so expectant, but they were still paying them for their services.

Arthur flipped another page in the file and caught sight of the newspaper still at the front edge of his desk. Though his desk was often littered with remnants of eraser, for the most part, he preferred a tidy workspace. He reached for the newspaper and then turned to his left to toss it into the wastebasket. As it landed, the part that had been folded together opened, revealing the front page of the section.

In a millisecond, Arthur's brain registered the title story and it snapped his attention back to it:

SOCIALITE SOPHIA KINGSLEY CAUGHT
COZYING UP TO NEW MAN IN TOWN.

Below the headline was a black and white picture of them, Sophia's arm wrapped around his, walking down the street toward the candy store. Sophia was smiling wide and Arthur had a pleased expression on his face. It certainly looked as though they were more than friendly.

He reached down and fished the paper out of the wastebasket, then fully unfolded it and placed it open on his desk.

He reread the headline and then again scanned the image. He hadn't been able to see Sophia from the picture's view and noted how elated she looked next to him. Underneath the picture the caption read:

Sophia Kingsley, right, with businessman Arthur Malcolm, left.

Under that was a brief article:

Sophia Kingsley, socialite and heiress was seen on an outing with Arthur Malcolm on Tuesday, the 13th of November. According to witnesses, they attended lunch at the 1913 Room and then enjoyed sitting near the Christmas tree, where they handed out candies to children. One mother we spoke to noted that Sophia looked "very happy with the man" and offered her well wishes on their relationship.

This is the first time Miss Kingsley has been spotted with a male suitor outside of her estate in some time. It is reasonable to assume that "their relationship has gotten quite serious," according to our expert who has followed Miss Kingsley's life closely.

Arthur Malcolm is a partner in the successful financial advisement business—Malcolm and Henly. Mr. Malcolm is newer to the area, notes our staff, so he has been widely unknown to the public until now. "We shall certainly see a lot more of Mr. Malcolm as his relationship with Sophia continues to blossom," says our expert.

Arthur shifted his attention to the author of the article but it was one he didn't recognize—Earl Metters. However, when he looked closer he noticed that the photo had been credited to James Calwell.

He scoffed. He hadn't even noticed anyone taking a picture but remembered how silently James could move around, especially for someone as round and uncoordinated as he appeared. He laid the paper down on his desk, feeling violated. His life hardly interested anyone until recently when everyone had a budding captivation of it.

Betty watched Arthur's horror and confusion with intrigue and quietly walked to his desk.

"Sir? Is everything alright?" She asked quietly.

He snapped his head up at the question. He slid the paper across the desk toward her and she sat, pulling it off the edge and in front of her face. Her eyes widened as she guided them down the page, over the headline and picture, then scanned the article.

"Oh dear."

William caught onto the commotion and joined Betty in reading the article. He was peering over her shoulder, though less interested than Betty.

"Strange. Is this true?" William asked.

Arthur shook his head. "No, I've lived in this city my entire life."

"Well I know that, ya goof. I meant the rest of it."

"Oh... well yes and no. She wanted to look at the tree and then I took her to the candy shop that my mother and I used to go to. I wanted to see if it was still there." It was half-truth but truth nonetheless.

"And you handed out candies to children?" Betty asked, a mixture of disbelief and affection in her voice.

Arthur nodded, embarrassed. He wanted that to be something only he and Sophia shared.

"That's funny," said Betty as she flipped over the pages.

"What?" Arthur and William asked together.

"George left this, didn't he?"

Arthur nodded. "Yes"

"Well he only left this one section. See." She held it up for them both. "This isn't the front page. This is only the social section. The rest is missing." She turned it over again as if the rest would suddenly appear.

Arthur frowned and reached for the paper. "You're right. That is odd."

"I wonder if he did that on purpose," William added, which gained both Betty and Arthur's attention.

"Why on earth would you say that?" Betty asked.

William continued cautiously. "It's George Carlyle. I don't think he does anything carelessly, does he? It seems odd he would only have that section of the paper and then leave it behind. And on Arthur's desk too."

"Wow," Betty chimed in, as if Arthur's life had just become a mystery novel, "I would bet that you're onto something."

"That's preposterous. You're both reading too much into simple absent mindedness."

William knew that Arthur was trying to convince himself. "Is George absent minded?"

"Well... no, at least not that I've ever noticed. But that doesn't mean anything."

"If we say, for argument's sake, that he did leave it here on purpose, what would be the motive?" Betty asked, amused.

William contorted his expression into deep thought and Arthur considered, despite his assertion that there was no truth to their allegations.

"He wanted you to know that he saw the article," William concluded.

"And that he knows about you and Sophia!" Betty triumphed.

"Applesauce! There is nothing to know!" Arthur insisted.

"Not according to this." Betty held up the paper in Arthur's face, reflecting the photograph back to him. He grabbed it out of her hand and slammed it on his desk.

"This is all baloney! None of this"– he waved his hand toward them and then down to the paper– "is true!"

"Wouldn't it be marvelous if it was, though?" Betty asked, her eyes shining with excitement. Those who were outside of the gossip dreamt of being in it. But once they made it there, as Arthur now comprehended, it was not as glamorous as it seemed. In fact, it was far more violating than he'd presumed.

***

Arthur clutched the phone to his ear; he instructed the operator to connect him to George's office and waited to find someone on the other end. At six p.m., it was unlikely anyone would still be there, but Arthur found it too risky to ring his home for such a matter. If he could pretend that he was calling for business, perhaps he could determine George's state of mind and intention.

The phone continued to ring and just as Arthur was about to hang up, he heard the receiver on the other end pick up.

"Hello?" asked an exasperated voice that Arthur didn't recognize.

"Yes, um," Arthur stuttered, having given up hope that someone would answer, "this is Arthur Malcom calling for George Carlyle. I know that it is after business hours..."

"Arthur! Hello!" the voice exclaimed in recognition, "this is Henry. Henry Westin."

Caught off guard, Arthur replied, "Oh Henry... Hello. Is, uh, is George with you?"

Arthur heard a voice in the background he recognized as George, and then heard Henry explain to him it was he on the line.

"Yes. Arthur," he was saying to George before he heard George take the receiver.

"Arthur?"

"Hi George, I was just calling to check in. I know our meeting isn't until Friday but..." He hadn't thought through his pretense for calling well enough and then Henry answered the phone, muddling what little he'd prepared.

"Henry was just here to meet me before we make our way out for the night," he cut Arthur off, offering an explanation Arthur hadn't asked for.

Arthur stammered again at the interruption, "Oh. Ok. Well as I was saying–"

"Why don't you just join us?"

"Well, I – "

"We are going to *Seventh*, the juice joint. You know the one?"

Arthur forgot his original statement and frowned; he frequented several speakeasies and thought he knew all the *it* ones.

"You mean Connie's?" Arthur asked.

"No, no, it's not located on seventh street, it's named *Seventh*."

"Oh, then no. I am not familiar with that one."

"Good, that means we're doing a good job at keeping it exclusive." George laughed. "Why don't we swing by and pick you up?"

"Well... I suppose that would be alright."

"Swell! We'll be there soon, say fifteen minutes?" George hung up before Arthur could protest otherwise.

As soon as he set down the phone it rang. Thinking it was George again, he picked up.

"Offices of Malcolm and Henly."

"Arthur, where are you?" William asked, concerned.

Arthur glanced at the clock on the office wall. 6:05 p.m. He frowned, trying to recall if he was meant to be somewhere. In his silence, William realized he'd forgotten.

"Dinner at my parent's house tonight, remember? My mother is making meatloaf for us?"

Arthur's heart dropped. Backing out with George was not an option. He hated to disappoint William's parents. They had become like surrogates since his mother died.

"Oh, I did forget."

William waited and then said, "So are you leaving now? I tried ringing you at home but when I didn't find you there I realized you must have lost track of time at work."

Arthur was nodding even though William couldn't see him. "Right. The thing is, William, I'm a bit behind the eight ball here. I just got a call from George asking me to meet. He and Henry are on their way here now."

William was quiet; Arthur held his breath in waiting.

"I see," he said slowly. "Well my parents will be disappointed, but business is business."

Arthur knew William had no misconceptions about what the night truly was—not a business endeavor but another social gathering in which Arthur and the others would congratulate themselves on being masters of the universe while they drank too much.

"Please give them my regrets."

"Of course." William replied and Arthur knew him well enough to hear the faint disapproval in his voice.

William said goodbye quickly and then hung up before Arthur could reply. William always had opinions of Arthur's actions and how he chose to spend his time but Arthur noted that he'd been particularly irritated recently.

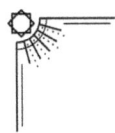

FIFTEEN

Seventh was housed under a laundromat. They entered through the front door, as if three men in expensive suits without laundry bags looked at all like they belonged. When they reached the back of the room, George pushed open a door that led to a smaller room which sat empty save for a lopsided laundry cart in the corner that was missing a wheel. It smelled musty; the paint on the walls had yellowed and no one had bothered to retouch it. Based on what he saw so far, Arthur didn't find it very promising.

At the other side of the room was another door; George knocked on it three times before it opened and a man appeared behind it. The man was large, even bulkier than George, but he didn't speak a word. Without a smile, he reached out and shook George's hand and then let him descend down the staircase behind him. Henry approached second and the same thing happened.

Arthur then approached, and following their lead, reached out his hand. But instead, the man crossed his arms over his chest. Arthur peered around him down the stairs to see George and Henry almost at the bottom. He considered calling out to them but didn't want to appear insecure. The man looked Arthur up and down.

"And who are you?" the man asked in a gruff voice.

"Arthur Malcolm," he replied, trying to feign confidence.

The man plainly replied, "Sophia Kingsley's candy man." Then he lifted his eyebrows while waiting. The words were playful but everything else about the man was not. His face still wore a grimace and his arms were hugged tightly across his chest.

"Yes. That was me in the paper."

The man nodded slowly and then moved out of his way to let him to the stairs behind him.

Arthur had to squeeze by because the man didn't bother to fully move over to let him through. He brushed across the man's arms as he did and the man pulled the door shut behind them. The man stayed at the landing at the top while Arthur made his way down, grateful that the burly mad hadn't followed him.

Sounds from below grew louder as he approached: a piano, perhaps a saxophone, laughter, screeches of delight, and a dissonance of chatter. As if it had been planned, it all reached a crescendo as Arthur landed his feet at the bottom of the stairs and pushed his way through the curtain into the bar. As they swung closed behind him, the music stopped and the chatter erupted into applause. If Arthur hadn't known better, he would've thought that everyone was cheering his entry.

He spotted George and Henry who had already taken seats at a small booth across the room. In the center of a room was a raised platform that contained the piano and a man sitting behind it on a bench. A light dangled over it cascading a spectrum of colors on the floor below. Surrounding the platform were small tables, each seated about two or three people, most of whom had their chairs turned in the direction of the stage. On the back edge of one side were the booths, lined with deep red leather that shone against the lights. They looked as though they were polished every night. On the other side of the platform, there was an empty area where people could dance and to the left of it all was the bar.

Besides the light that hung over the piano and the few that hung dimly lit over the booths, the lighting was sparse. The bottles of liquor lined up behind the bar were backlit and drew attention simply because they were brighter than anything else in the room. There were two male barkeeps behind the bar, both dressed in tuxedos, flitting their way back and forth, pouring drinks, sliding glasses across it, not stopping to hear anything more than a simple order.

"You want something, honey?" A woman, clad in a short sequin dress that hung off her body so that when she spun it twisted around her, approached him immediately as he sat. Her heels were higher than any he'd ever seen but she managed to maneuver around in them well. Whiskey already sat on the table in front of George and Henry; it was clear they were regulars and not only was it their booth, but it might've also been their bar.

"Whiskey on the rocks," Arthur replied. The music picked up again and he saw he'd been correct about the saxophone, but there were also trombones, rounding out a makeshift jazz band.

The waitress leaned over Arthur so he could hear her and touched his shoulder as she spoke into his ear. He could smell her perfume, strong and floral and he tried not to breathe in too deep. "You let me know if you need... anything else. Ok, honey?" Her voice was sweet with a slight southern drawl.

Arthur nodded. He caught both George and Henry smiling at him out of his periphery.

"They certainly employ some beautiful dames, eh?" George commented, watching her as she walked away. She had a swagger in her step, dominating the heels as if they were the most natural thing in the world.

"She's always our waitress when we come here. Name's Virginia." He smiled and then added, "She likes us." Arthur's stomach turned at the way he said the last part. Henry remained silent and stared ahead at the band while sipping his drink.

George and Henry sat on one side of the booth and let Arthur have his own. George leaned over so that Arthur could hear better over the noise.

"Isn't this place swell? Sure, there are other joints that are great places to be seen, but this is where you come when you *don't want* to be seen. We have a lot more freedom here."

Seventh existed solely for the most elite men in the city. Sure, they went to others like *Chumley's* with the rest of the socialites, wealthy, and famous, but *Seventh* was so exclusive that even its name was only known by men like George Carlyle. It was nearly impossible to be admitted without someone like him.

Virginia returned, carrying his drink on a black tray, and set it down on top of a napkin in front of him.

"Thank you, Virginia," Arthur tried.

She flashed her bright white smile, her lips were painted bright red. "You can call me Ginny." And she winked at him before walking away.

George laughed. "I told you, she's a doll."

Arthur's discomfort grew as George leaned back in the booth and then scanned the floor, casting his gaze up and down as he did. The tables were occupied by men and the only women to be found were the ones serving the drinks and flirting with the patrons who may have been too stupid to realize they were working on tips.

The piano stopped again and people clapped. Arthur took a sip of his whiskey; it wasn't nearly as smooth as the ones he'd had at George's or Sophia's. The chatter ceased and Arthur turned his attention to the center of the room where all the men fixed their gaze. A spotlight turned on and Arthur noticed there was a single microphone held by a stand in the center.

People began to clap and holler. One man shouted out a name Arthur couldn't decipher. Then, the music began and from the back of the room, the side where there were no booths, a woman appeared. She too wore a sequin dress, but instead of silver like the rest of the women, hers was red. She wore black stockings, with seams running up the back, and black heels that elongated her legs. Her blonde hair fell loosely out of a headband, not unlike the one Sophia wore to her party. Arthur noted how much more sophisticated Sophia looked in hers but this woman's entire outfit and demeanor exuded sex.

She stepped toward the stage and then up the two stairs to the cheers of the men. She took her place behind the microphone, faced in the direction of Arthur, and pulled it to her lips. Then she closed her eyes. For a moment, the music ceased and it seemed as though every person in the room held their breath.

Then, the music started up again and she opened her mouth. Out came a smooth, bluesy voice that felt like velvet on Arthur's skin. Her red lips traced over the microphone and then she pulled it from the stand so that she could move around the stage. Her backside jiggled as she did and Arthur found himself captivated by her; her long legs, her red lips, her golden hair, the way she worked her heels and held her body.

"That's Margaret." George pulled Arthur away from his thoughts. He smiled toward Arthur, understanding. Every man in the room shared the same understanding. Arthur saw why there was so much fuss.

Arthur swallowed and attempted to turn his attention back to the men across from him but Margaret's voice continued to pull him away, into a world Arthur hadn't even known he wanted to be a part of.

George smiled again and Arthur realized that he and Henry had been carrying on a conversation while Arthur lusted after the woman in the red dress.

"It's difficult to keep your wits about you with them around isn't it? Probably why so many bad business deals are made here. I've made it a rule to never conduct them here," George stated.

Arthur was disgusted by George's belief that all women were for his pleasure but had to admit that he saw the allure of being so powerful.

Henry rolled his eyes and George caught it.

"What's the matter, Henry? Don't share the same sentiments?"

Henry shot him a glance that Arthur couldn't read and then nudged George, indicating he wanted to get out of the booth.

"I need to go to the john," he explained.

George stood to let him slide out and then he slid his way back in, taking his place right across from Arthur.

"You have to excuse Henry. Once he's splifficated, he'll be less of a bluenose." George grabbed his drink and realized it was empty. Arthur had hardly even started on his.

"Splifficated?" Arthur frowned.

"Zozzled, smoked... drunk... and a bluenose is—"

"I know what a bluenose is," Arthur retorted.

"You've been spending too much time schmoozing our parents' generation. You need to be around more people your own age, Arthur. Good thing you've got us now."

George waved his empty glass in the air and in what seemed like too short a time, Ginny appeared.

"Yes, darling?" she asked in her smooth drawl.

"Ginny, my love, I need another whiskey please. And can you bring one for my friend Henry as well? He could use a few more," George said as he smiled.

"Sure thing." Ginny smiled then turned to Arthur. "How about you, sweetie?"

Arthur shook his head and then motioned toward his glass. She nodded in recognition and then turned on her heels in the direction of the bar.

The drinks came and Henry hadn't returned by the time that George had finished his, so he took the liberty of drinking Henry's as well.

"Where'd he go?" Arthur asked, looking around the room. He guessed it was about eight o'clock and some men had already given into their intoxication. They pulled the female staff onto the dance floor, who happily obliged and pressed their bodies into them.

George shrugged. "The back room, maybe."

"Back room?"

"You know..." he looked at Arthur and then enunciated, "the back room."

"Oh." Arthur replied, embarrassed.

"You interested?" George asked. Arthur couldn't tell if he was teasing. Arthur shook his head vigorously. "No."

George laughed. "Alright, but all you have to do is ask. Not me... one of them." He pointed out toward the women.

"Have you ever?" Arthur asked cautiously.

George laughed. "A gentleman never tells."

Arthur caught sight of Henry standing at the bar. For whatever reason, it relieved him to see that Henry was not in the back room but was instead speaking to another man dressed in a nice suit.

"He's over there." Arthur pointed, as if he had a point to prove to George.

George spun around. "Must be all finished." He smirked at Arthur. "Come on, let's dance. What good is a joint and all this free flowing hooch if we aren't going to put it to good use?"

Arthur wanted to say no but he often went along with George so he didn't even attempt to fight. Instead, he downed the rest of his whiskey, his second, and stood up to join George who was already making his way across the room.

Arthur had never so much as slow danced in public, let alone danced with a strange woman to upbeat music. His throat tightened as women approached them, hoping to be invited onto the dance floor. Other men's faces twisted in annoyance as the women turned their attention away from them and toward George; in those moments it became obvious the benefits of being a Carlyle.

Ginny grabbed Arthur's arm. "Come on, sweetie, I'll show you how." Arthur had no interest in dancing with her, but if forced to pick from the ones available, at least he knew her name.

George picked a small brunette who was about half his size. When they sauntered out to the dance floor, it was easy for him to pick her up and throw her around as if she weighed nothing.

Ginny was gentle with Arthur and although he stepped on her toes a few times, she simply laughed and forgave him. He was grateful he'd downed two glasses of whiskey to calm his nerves.

The music stopped and they parted to clap. Margaret took the microphone again as the band turned out a ballad.

"Shall we?" Ginny extended her hand but Arthur shook his head, "I think I'll sit this one out."

"Well that's fine, I'll just find me someone else." She winked and made her way to the other side of the floor.

George and his partner had chosen the opposite and held each other as they swayed to the silky voice in the red dress.

Arthur joined Henry who was still standing at the bar, alone.

"Not bad." He congratulated Arthur.

"Yea, I'm a regular Oliver Twist," Arthur laughed, knowing he was not talented in the least.

"I don't even try," Henry conceded. "Would you like another drink?"

Arthur replied in the affirmative which led to quick work by the bartender in pouring him another.

George, who was at least six drinks in, walked his way to the bar, his arm wrapped around his dance partner's shoulder. She threw her head back in laughter and unlike many of the women who half volunteered to accompany the patrons on demand, she appeared to be having a genuinely good time.

"Mary, would you like some giggle water?" George asked, knowing well that she wasn't supposed to be drinking while at work.

"Mr. Carlyle," she teased flirtatiously, "you know that would be breaking the rules."

"Oh alright, I suppose I have to let you get back to work then."

She beamed up at him. "Thanks for the dance, as always."

He released his arm from around her and allowed her to walk away. He turned his front toward the bar to get the barkeep's attention, positioning himself between Arthur and Henry, interrupting their conversation. From Arthur's other side, he heard the velvet voice, this time without the song behind it.

"Lawrence," she said, getting the attention of the bartender and pulling him to her instead of George. "I need a water, please." She kept her front side pressed up against the edge of the bar.

George, upon seeing that Lawrence was first going to attend to her, turned his body toward her and spoke past Arthur.

"Always stealing the attention," he accused.

She turned her head but kept her body forward. "If memory serves me correctly, I'd say you could stand to put some space between you and your next whiskey."

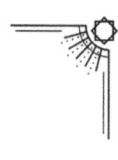

CHAPTER
SIXTEEN

Arthur spun his eyes to George, awaiting a reaction. In classic fashion, he laughed, but it wasn't as jovial as usual. Arthur stood in tense space between them, feeling their history push at him from both sides. He wanted to move but feared that it might incite more drama if he did.

Instead, George turned back to the bar and waited for Lawrence to finish fetching Margaret her water before attending to him. Arthur had never seen someone wait on anyone before George. Margaret took a sip and then turned to face Arthur, her right side leaned against the bar no doubt to take some of the pressure off of her feet that had been shoved into heels.

"Hi, I'm Margaret," she introduced herself. She smiled, the tension of interacting with George draining from her face.

"Arthur," Arthur replied and then added, "Malcolm."

"It's nice to meet you, Arthur Malcolm." She leaned over further to glance around him. George had his back turned and was facing Henry. "I gather you're here with..." She nodded to the men behind Arthur.

Arthur affirmed with a nod. She sighed and lifted her eyebrows; clearly it meant something to her that he answered yes.

Usually, getting up close to someone meant that you could see the flaws that were nonexistent from far away. With Margaret, however, she looked even better up close, if that was possible. Red lips and dark eyes, long lashes, and rosy cheeks. Arthur imagined what it might be like to run his fingers over her smooth skin. She smelled sweet and fresh, like springtime. Arthur again found himself lost too long on her, blaming it on the alcohol but also her intoxicating presence.

Margaret smiled, she was accustomed to men being lost in her. "First time?"

"It is," Arthur replied. "It's a bit... overwhelming."

She laughed. "I've been here three nights a week for over a year and it's still overwhelming to me too."

"Where were you before that?" Arthur asked, unsure if he really cared.

"I wasn't anywhere I guess. Home with my parents. Working around their house to help. My father had a friend in the entertainment business. He came for dinner every so often. I happened to be singing a little as I was helping my mother cook dinner one night and my father... well he agreed I'd come here."

Arthur's face contorted just a bit and she recognized the disgust.

She waved it off. "At first I was upset, felt like I had been sold. But truly this is the best thing that could've ever happened to me. Has given me much more power over my own life than I could've imagined." She paused and then glanced around, her eyes lingering over George's back for a bit longer. "As soon as I learned how to weed out the bad eggs, at least." She sipped her water and Arthur noticed that she left no lipstick behind.

George turned and wrapped his arm around Arthur's back so that he was standing partly behind, partly beside him. "She's referencing me," he said, looking at Margaret. And then his voice changed into something Arthur had never heard—the tone was dripping with sarcasm and taunting. "Come on, doll, what's the matter, haven't found your daddy yet?"

She rolled her eyes and Arthur wanted to shake George off of him. Margaret incited something in George that caused Arthur to feel dirty.

She shook her head and kept her eyes focused on Arthur. "It was nice to meet you, Arthur. I have to be getting backstage," she explained and then she set her glass down and walked away.

"It was nice to meet you too," Arthur called to her back.

He shook George off and then stood to face him. Henry, who still looked irritated, took his place next to George.

"Maggie. Nothing but gams with a voice." George shook his head in exasperation. "Would you like to go to the backroom with her, Arthur? I imagine we could arrange that."

To Arthur's gratitude, Henry stepped in.

"Must you always be like that?" he asked, sending a chill down Arthur's spine with his tone. People teased George, people became irritated and short with him, but none of them challenged him like he sometimes saw Henry do.

"Like what?" George snapped back; there was no trace of playfulness left in his voice. The only other time Arthur had heard that tone was the night of Sophia's birthday party when George confronted him.

"Such a bimbo. What does George Carlyle have to prove to anyone, huh? Why don't you lay off?" Henry replied, the harshness of it landing over the three of them.

George didn't laugh like Arthur expected. Instead he slammed his drink down on the bar and took a step away from them, putting a few feet between him and Arthur.

"It's not my fault that these broads are gold diggers, skating around, treating men as pocketbooks. And I'm not supposed to say anything when they treat me like a chump?" Arthur had never heard George even begin to reference anyone in such a way. He could be condescending and pestering, but never cruel.

"I'm going to go iron my shoelaces," George said and then walked away in a huff.

"He and Margaret have beef?" Arthur asked Henry whose eyes were filled with something akin to disgust.

Henry shrugged. "Sort of, I guess. Margaret isn't used to being refused. She thought that she had more of a chance with him than she did. She tried to get George into the back room several times but he always gave her the icy mitt, not wanting to give her the wrong impression about him. She didn't take it well. She's not as sweet as she'd like you to think. But I don't know why George has to razz her. It's like he loves to remind her that he rejected her."

Arthur frowned; with the way she reacted, he assumed George used her and then spit her out. He was surprised to hear that George had turned down the possibility.

"He's not a bad guy." Henry suddenly came to the defense of the man he'd just criticized. "Just a little..." he paused, searching for a word.

"Conflicted?" Arthur jumped in with Sophia's word.

Henry considered and seemed impressed at Arthur's accuracy. "Sure. You could say that."

"People do." Arthur replied.

Henry frowned. "You're awfully interested in George, you know that?"

If it was an accusation, it didn't sound like it. Arthur's defenses lit up anyway, wanting to refute it but acknowledging that he did spend more time worrying about George and wondering about his motives than even about Sophia.

He shrugged. "Not really, at least not on purpose. I'm just trying to understand, I suppose."

Henry laughed. "I doubt you ever will, if anyone is an enigma, it's George. Can't ever tell what that fella really thinks."

"You're good friends."

"He's a good man, a good friend. Truly, one of the best you could ask for. But you have to get past the... well, like I said, he can act like a bimbo."

Arthur pictured George poking at the fire during Sophia's party or teaching him how to saddle a horse. He did often position himself in ways that proved his masculinity.

Henry reached out and slapped Arthur on the arm. "I heard you might be joining us in Europe."

"You did?" Arthur replied, it had been less than two days since he'd been asked. Information passed quickly.

"Sophia mentioned she invited you. You should come," he encouraged, sincerely. "Ever since Elizabeth moved, it's been off balance. Sometimes Benjamin comes but as you saw, he can be a bit of a wet blanket."

"I'm thinking about it," Arthur said, wondering if he was lying.

"You should. Truly. George and Sophia—"

"Are they... do they have a... history?" Arthur interrupted. The whiskey finally allowed the question to escape his lips.

Henry laughed. "George has a history with everyone, in one way or another. Or at least everyone thinks they have one with him, as you can see with Margaret. And as you can see, George tends to dislike easy marks. Maybe because his whole life has been that way. Sophia on the other hand has never been something easy for anyone to get. They've known each other for so long, sometimes it's hard to tell. I can say that there are a lot of people who would like for them to marry."

"Like who?" Arthur asked.

"George's parents, mostly. I think Sophia's parents wanted it too."

Arthur frowned and realized that maybe even George and Sophia didn't know if there was something between them.

"You're actually stuck on her, aren't you?" Henry asked.

Arthur didn't react. He wasn't sure if he should bring himself to answer. Henry and George spent a lot of time together and information given to one often made its way through them all, including Sophia.

"You don't have to spill," Henry offered. "I wouldn't blame you for not trusting me. In fact, I wouldn't blame you for not trusting anyone. You shouldn't really."

"You all keep saying that," Arthur replied.

"That's because money and power do odd and often awful things to people. Holding onto decency is like trying to grasp onto sand while you jump into the ocean. Most people come up with nothing left."

"You're a killjoy, you know that?"

Henry laughed. "I'd like to say that I've been the exception, but I've done things I'm not proud of. When you've had no power and suddenly you're some big shot who can have anything and do anything you want, it's almost impossible not to get swept away into it." He lifted his glass toward Arthur and used it to point in the direction of Margaret who was making her way back up on stage. "I mean, are you really going to tell me that you would easily be able to refuse her?"

Arthur spun his head around to watch her red dress sparkle as she moved.

"I can't have her."

"Sure you can. You can have any Jane in this room if you want. It just depends on what you're looking for."

Arthur froze; he wondered if what Henry said was true.

"It gives you more respect for people like Sophia and George doesn't it? That they don't just take whatever they want all the time? It's easier for them sometimes, though, because they've lived with it their whole lives. They don't know what it's like to have nothing, how it feels to fear that things might be ripped away from you at any moment. We're constantly teetering on the edge of uncertainty, wondering if maybe we're going to be thrust back down to where we belong. It gives them a sort of power over us because it almost feels like they're the ones who determine where we belong. Why do you think so many people are afraid of George? He wouldn't ever do it—maybe he doesn't even have that power, but it certainly feels that way."

The words stung because they were true. Arthur often felt like one of the children in the candy store, nose pressed up against the glass pining for the sweets behind it and then gobbling them down as soon as he could, worried that someone might swipe them away before he had the chance to taste them.

"I'm not trying to scare you, Arthur. I'm just trying to level with you. No one really warned me. Maybe they didn't know, I don't know. It's why I'm always trying to reign in Trixie, which is proving to be quite impossible."

Arthur glanced down into his glass at the melting ice cubes. He related to their fate unnervingly.

"I feel lost." It may have been the most honest thing Arthur ever uttered.

Henry smiled empathetically. "Places like this don't help."

"Not at all. So overstimulating. I don't understand why all these men seem so enthralled."

"We have lower thresholds than them," he said, gesturing around the room. "The regular world in itself is overwhelming for me, but for them, they are so bored with it that they have to seek out adventures anywhere they can find them. Problem is, they have to get more and more extreme to have the same effect."

Arthur had never heard Henry say so much. He'd always taken him for the quiet, analytical type, not the deep thinker he was proving to be.

"Eventually, we all realize that what we're searching for, what makes us feel alive, doesn't exist anywhere out there." Henry set his empty glass on the bar.

Arthur let his words sink deeper and felt dangerously close to baring his soul to Henry, so he pulled himself away from it and steered the conversation in a different direction.

"Do you get tired of trying to wrangle George?" Arthur asked.

Henry laughed, lightening the mood. "I've never understood why no one puts him in his place. It's actually quite easy. And he's pretty receptive to it. He gets mad but he moves on fairly quickly. He's intolerable otherwise. You have to learn to not be scared of them." He looked Arthur in the eye. "Trust me. They're just as insecure and flawed as us. Maybe more so."

Arthur didn't believe it but couldn't shake the feeling that Henry was trying to give him a very important lesson.

"Anyway, let's blouse? I'll find George."

Arthur took the last sip of his drink and then set it down. "I can pay while you find him?"

"You don't have to do that, it's already taken care of." He walked away and left Arthur there alone anyway while he went in search of George.

Arthur played with his empty glass until Lawrence took it and asked him if he wanted another. When he declined, Lawrence lost interest and moved on, again leaving Arthur alone, having nothing to do with himself.

"Lonely?" He heard the voice come from his right. Margaret

returned to the bar for another glass of water. She twisted her right foot behind her, putting most of her weight on the left. Even the normal movements she made felt different, more alluring.

"We're about to leave," Arthur informed her.

"Pity, I've just finished my last song. I'm free for the rest of the night now. Spending it with—" she spun her gaze around the room, scanning all the men left. "—anyone else doesn't seem appealing."

Arthur swallowed, her lips were still bright red, plump, and wet from the sip of water she had just taken. "Well I..." he said and began to believe what Henry had suggested.

She twisted a curl that fell from her headband around her finger. "You what?" she asked and slightly parted her lips into a smile. He was entranced by her. The part of him that longed to feel powerful and desired overtook his body.

"You want to..." She motioned her head toward the back, where Arthur had seen plenty of women lead stumbling men.

He blinked quickly, shocked that Henry's prediction had come true and come true so quickly.

"Well?" she asked, waiting.

Arthur's mind was clouded with whiskey and lust. Her dress grew brighter and the radiance was almost blinding; he felt like he might have to shield his eyes just to look straight at her. He swallowed again.

She sighed. "Arthur, I'm not going to bump you off... I'm asking if you'd like to talk in private." Something about the level-headedness of her words brought him back to earth and the music came crashing back in, her dress dimmed, and she shrunk back down to size.

"Talk?" he asked, knowing he sounded like a fool.

"Sure," she offered, bending her head down but keeping her eyes fixed on him, as if she was shy.

"Well, I suppose that wouldn't be..." Henry's words and George's history with her pulled him in one direction and her sweet scent and body pulled him in another.

She grabbed his hand before he could finish, hungry, as if she might lose him if she didn't act. "Come on."

She pulled him in toward the back, keeping a firm grasp on his hand. Her hand felt cold and stiff, not warm and soft like the brushes against Sophia.

His body felt as if it wasn't his own; her magnetism was dangerous, exciting, and impossible to resist. He knew that Margaret didn't offer herself to many men and she chose him. The desire to be special, to be chosen above all others, to be wanted and needed, filled his stomach and chest and oozed through his entire body. A woman like her had never shown interest in him before. Henry had been right—no was not an answer to easily come by.

Margaret led him down a long hallway and then parted the long dark purple curtains at the very end—her private room, saved just for her and whoever she decided was worthy of joining her.

Inside there was a one-sided booth at the back, covered with velvet fabric and a small round table in front of it. To their side was a small table with a mirror and a chair tucked underneath—a place for her to put on her make-up and fix her hair. A single light, like the light that hung over the microphone, dangled over the table. Arthur had to strain his eyes to see clearly, it was even darker than the bar.

Margaret flipped off her shoes and then tucked her feet under her as she sat in the booth.

"What do you say, honey? Would you like a drink?" she asked.

Arthur shook his head, trying to shake away the alcohol he already consumed. His head was fuzzy and she was hard to keep in focus.

She patted the space next to her. "Have a seat. I won't bite."

Arthur didn't believe her but slid next to her anyway. She tilted her head toward him again, this time batting her eyelashes. Suddenly, it all felt like a show, rehearsed and perfectly choreographed.

Arthur had no idea what to do or how to get out. He felt trapped, not only because he didn't want to upset her, but also because he wanted to know what was underneath her dress. He had never been so curious and near to closing the gap between him and his desires. Margaret traced her fingers over Arthur's cheek and then through his hair.

"Arthur?!" He heard Henry's voice shout from behind the curtain.

Arthur shifted in his seat but Margaret answered for him, "We're busy, scram!"

Ignoring her, Henry tore through the curtain and landed in front of them. He reminded Arthur of William in that moment, parental and stern.

"Arthur, we're leaving," he said, his voice dripping with displeasure.

"I was just..." Arthur tried to defend himself but didn't have an explanation for what he was doing. He was a fly drawn into a web.

"Let's go," Henry demanded again. Arthur stood obediently.

"Oh, Henry, you always ruin all the fun," Margaret whined.

Henry ignored her and grabbed Arthur by the elbow to pull him out of the room, knowing that Arthur didn't have the ability to himself do it. He let go when they were halfway down the hall.

"Do you have any idea what George would do if he knew you were in there with her?" he asked, shaking his head. "I lied and told him you were in the restroom and I was coming to get you. He's waiting for the car out front." Henry led him through the room and then to the stairs.

"I thought you said not to be afraid of him?"

Henry stopped mid step and turned around to face Arthur. He was two steps higher and towering over him.

"I said you don't *always* have to be afraid of him. I didn't say you should never be," he corrected. Then he walked up the stairs and Arthur trailed behind, feeling lustful, confused, and caught in a strange trap he had unknowingly set for himself.

The driver was there waiting for them when Henry and Arthur exited into the cold night. George was already sitting in the front seat. Henry opened the back door then slid to the other side, making room for Arthur.

"Long piss," George called back to Arthur as he shut the door.

Henry shot Arthur a look to say *never tell him the truth.* Arthur didn't reply.

"Maxwell, my good man, let's drop Arthur off first," said George, turning his head to the backseat, "his house is first on the way." George and Henry both owned places in the city and spent late nights there instead of going all the way back to their estates. Arthur didn't want to take it as a slight, but the only reason Arthur's house was first was because Henry and George's were on Park Avenue and his was not.

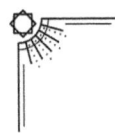

CHAPTER

SEVENTEEN

"It's almost Thanksgiving!" Betty announced as she placed Arthur's mail in front of him. She had been humming to herself when Arthur paused her to express his displeasure at her song.

"Thanksgiving, not Christmas. It's too soon for Christmas carols."

"Oh pfft," Betty said, waving him off cheerily. She'd seemed more carefree over the last few weeks.

"What's all this commotion?" William asked; he'd been in the storage room and emerged to find Betty dancing toward his desk with his mail in her hand.

"I'm telling Betty it's too soon for Christmas songs."

"And I say that it's almost Thanksgiving so it's perfectly acceptable."

"I'm not taking sides," William replied as he held up his hands in retreat. "But I have learned to never question what makes a woman happy."

Betty beamed in victory.

Arthur scoffed, turned his attention to his mail, and shuffled through it to find not much of anything. He found over the last few years that people stopped doing as much business over the holidays. He spent many hours at work gnawing at erasers and staring off into space.

"Are you coming on Thursday?" William asked, but Arthur was off somewhere else.

"Arthur!" William snapped, which brought Arthur to attention. "Are you coming to my parent's house Thursday for Thanksgiving?"

"Oh, yes. Yes. I plan to."

"Swell." William replied, doing the math in his head. Thanksgiving was two days away and his mother was finalizing the details of the meal.

"Can I assume that you don't plan to bring anyone?"

Arthur looked at him but didn't reply, insulted by the question even though he knew William hadn't meant it with any cruelty. Arthur hadn't seen Sophia since the day they went to see the Christmas tree. He felt ashamed of the article and then of being alone with Margaret. Even though he didn't belong to her, he felt as though he'd betrayed her somehow.

The phone rang and Betty answered, her chipper voice greeted the person on the other end.

"Of course," she obliged in a singsong voice.

"Arthur, George Carlyle is calling for you." Arthur hated that she simply covered the mouthpiece and shouted across the room, but he refrained from lecturing her again. Instead, he took the call.

"Hello, George," Arthur answered.

"Arthur, I'm not calling on business, but I first wanted to tell you that my father and his associates were very pleased with our meeting last week."

"That is very good to hear, George. We're delighted to be working with you." He hoped William was listening in so that he would assume it was a simple business call. William became oddly rigid when George contacted Arthur in a social manner.

"Yes, yes," George said, sounding as if he was in a rush. "Anyway, I wanted to invite you to a Thanksgiving dinner I'm having."

"Well, actually on Thursday..."

"No, not Thursday. Gosh, no," George laughed. "Obviously that's just for family. Friday. I've decided it would be nice for all of us to celebrate together Friday. Solidify plans to sail in a week. What do you say?"

Arthur glanced over to William whose eyes were turned down at his desk but was no doubt eavesdropping into the conversation. To his credit, it was his business deal too and he had a right to know.

"Oh. Well then yes. I can do that."

"Swell, we will see you soon."

Arthur placed the receiver down and turned his attention to his desk, trying to ward off any questions that were coming. Strangely, they didn't.

***

Two days later, Arthur sat in the living room of the Henly family. They still lived in William's childhood home despite William's insistence that he could buy them a better house in a better neighborhood. His mother refused the offer, asserting that she could never see leaving the house she had made a home. Although Arthur didn't understand it, it was comforting to be in a place that was closer to his childhood home.

Dorothy Henly approached Arthur with a drink as he sat on the couch. "Arthur, dear, it is so nice to see you again. It's been far too long." Arthur stood and wrapped his arms around her. It felt good to embrace her. She was soft and soothing and the closest thing he had to a mother.

"Thank you, Mrs. Henly," Arthur said as he accepted the tea.

"Dinner will be ready in just a bit. And I can't imagine where that son of mine is."

William had a sister, but Arthur had only met her a handful of times. Once she turned 18, she fled to San Francisco and hardly ever returned to visit. Arthur refrained from asking about her because he knew it was a source of family pain.

William declined Arthur's offer to ride together and still hadn't shown even though Arthur was certain he was an hour later than William told him to be. Arthur sat back on the couch across from William's father, who was lost reading the newspaper.

"That woman can cook, you smell that?" He lowered the paper and sniffed the air.

Arthur nodded but Mr. Henly couldn't see him because he again covered his face with the paper. An article on ship trade and immigration stared back at Arthur, but he was too far away to read the small print.

The front door flung open and William stood on the other side as if he was about to make a triumphant entrance.

Mr. Henly stood and greeted him with a handshake and then a hug. Arthur's father had never been an affectionate man and seeing Mr. Henly with William always made Arthur quietly jealous.

"She's on her way. She had to convince her parents it was appropriate for her to spend it here." William answered a question Arthur hadn't heard as he pulled off his hat.

Mr. Henly slapped William on the back and then William approached Arthur.

"Happy Thanksgiving!" He greeted Arthur with a wide smile. William was unusually thrilled about a holiday he usually found lukewarm.

William sat next to Arthur on the couch as Mr. Henly again lifted the newspaper over his face, but William didn't sit back. Instead, he stayed perched on the edge as if he might have to jump up at any moment.

"Who else is coming?" Arthur asked, but as he did, the doorbell rang and William did jump and pounce toward the door.

"Betty!" William exclaimed as he ushered her in. She was dressed nicer than she did at work, a burgundy dress with stockings covered by a black coat trimmed in fur. In her gloved hands she held a pie. Mrs. Henly came rushing into the room.

"Oh Betty! Happy Thanksgiving!" she said as she tried to work her way around the pie to give her a hug.

When she pulled away, Betty offered her the pie. "My mother sent it, she makes the best apple pie in the city, I swear it."

Mrs. Henly accepted it, her eyes gleaming. "Why thank you so much, Betty. We only have pumpkin, so this is wonderful."

Betty smiled, her anxiety relieved a bit at having made a good entrance.

"Let me take your coat," William offered and she allowed him to help her out of it.

William's father also stood to greet her and so Arthur did as well, feeling uncomfortable at seeing her in such a casual setting.

"Betty, hello." Arthur greeted her but didn't offer a hug.

"Mr. Malcolm," she nodded her head as she said it. It was still incredibly formal, both of them unsure of how to act around one another.

Mrs. Henly was still standing with the pie in her hand and Betty looked at her. "Is there anything I can do to help you in the kitchen?"

Mrs. Henly waved her free hand. "No, no. In fact, it's almost finished anyway, so we can all move to the dining room." There was a frantic energy in the room that Betty brought when she walked through the door.

Arthur still hadn't gotten a chance to ask William why Betty was at his Thanksgiving dinner when the prayer concluded and William's father rose to carve the turkey. Steam escaped and revealed a juicy inside as he cut through the perfectly browned skin. Mrs. Henly's talent for cooking exceeded most other people.

The meal was classic and comforting, reminding him of his childhood when they had the money to indulge in Thanksgiving properly. Overly buttered mashed potatoes, creamy gravy poured over salty turkey, sweet and tart cranberries, and yeasty rolls that hit his nose with nostalgia.

Mr. Henly sat at the head of the table with Mrs. Henly at the other end. William and Betty sat across from each other and Arthur sat opposite an empty chair whose place had been set with a plate to make the table look balanced. It stared at Arthur and he heard it mock him much like William's question about bringing a guest.

No opportunity arrived for Arthur to interrogate William about Betty's presence because he never got up from the table during the meal and there was no way to ask without being overheard. William behaved as if her presence didn't need an explanation and never offered one, which perplexed Arthur further. Several times he attempted to send William an inquisitive look, but William had been too focused on his meal.

"Time for pie?" Mrs. Henly asked when they finished their meals. They moaned but all nodded anyway, knowing they were about to stuff even more into their stomachs for the sake of the holiday.

"Actually, Mother, can you sit first? I'd like to say something," William said.

Mrs. Henly sat slowly, her face turned into curiosity.

William took a deep breath. "I have never been so grateful as I am today, sitting here with the people who mean the most in the world to me, celebrating the success of this year and our prosperity with this wonderful meal." He turned to his mother and added, "thank you. And I would like to share some wonderful news with you all."

Arthur scanned the table to read the faces of the others, hoping for clues, but they all fixed their eyes on William.

William continued, his grin wide. "I am the luckiest man in the world because Miss Elizabeth Farris has somehow, against all her senses, agreed to be my wife."

Mrs. Henly leapt from her chair and threw her arms around William.

Mr. Henly slapped his leg and exclaimed. "Well how about that?!"

Mrs. Henly then turned toward Betty, who stood from her chair, giggling and smiling, and embraced her too. Arthur stayed seated in shock.

William looked down at him and Arthur stared back up with confusion on his face. He came to his senses and finally, stood, hugged William and congratulated them both. Mrs. Henly quickly went to fetch the pies, insisting they celebrate with dessert.

Betty and Mrs. Henly spent the rest of the time talking excitedly over the table about wedding details while William beamed with happiness.

After the excitement calmed and Betty went with Mrs. Henly to clean up in the kitchen, Arthur cornered William in the living room.

"How? I mean..." Arthur stuttered, "I had no idea."

William smiled. "We were pretty good at keeping it secret huh?"

"I would say so," Arthur replied, shaking his head. "How long?"

"Few months," William answered. "I asked her today. Went over to her parent's house last night to ask her father's permission. Can you believe it?"

"Not at all," Arthur responded. "I can't believe you didn't tell me."

"Well, you haven't been around much."

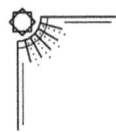

CHAPTER
EIGHTEEN

"I have never been so insulted in my life!" Trixie's wine almost spilled as she enunciated her words with dramatic flair. "The man thought I was a prostitute!" she said as laughter resounded around the table.

Arthur sat across from her, so he could see her every move closely. She moved as though her body had been scripted, like she was playing a character she thought everyone wanted her to be. It was working thus far because everyone was amused.

Elizabeth sat to Arthur's right and had not looked him in the eye since he'd been there. He imagined that she was embarrassed of her behavior the last time he'd seen her. Henry sat across from Elizabeth and Sophia opposite George. Because of Benjamin's absence, George opted not to take the head of the table so that it wasn't lopsided.

Trixie sat breathlessly and sipped at nonexistent wine. She lifted her glass in the air and it was promptly refilled by George's staff. Then clinks of forks on their plates filled the conversation-less air until the salads had been eaten.

Thanksgiving dinner among them was less traditional given that all of them had just eaten one the day before. Instead, George provided light salads, followed by green beans and a honey ham. It was remarkable and refined, the tastes achieving depths Arthur didn't know could exist with such simple foods. Accompanying the meal, of course, was copious amounts of alcohol, which they delightfully imbibed.

As they ate and drank, the formality of the holiday spent with family began to dissipate. The promise of a Christmas away also loomed in their minds. Sophia had excited them all with her proposition and although he was conflicted at why he ended up accepting her offer, Arthur was nevertheless excited.

They would be crossing the Atlantic on the *Aquitania*, an ocean liner operated by the British company Cunard, and landing in Liverpool five days later. George selected it because not only was it luxurious, but it was also foreign owned, which meant they could drink aboard, even though not a member of the group would have faced any serious consequences otherwise.

Arthur squirmed in his seat, anxious to move away from the table so he could more freely interact with Sophia. He wanted to ask her about the newspaper, for her to understand that he didn't have anything to do with it being published. He had no idea how he'd manage such a thing, but he imagined stories were planted all the time.

"Arthur," George called at him from the other side of Elizabeth after the meal was finished and the plates had been cleared. He leaned forward to look his way. "Why don't you make a toast?"

"A toast?" Arthur asked, confused.

"Why yes! You're the only one of us here who hasn't had to do it yet. It's sort of a rite of passage."

Arthur didn't know if he was lying but he didn't want to lose face, so he tried to swallow the lump in his throat. He stood from his chair as all of their eyes followed him expectantly. He lifted his glass.

"The first time I met all of you, I assumed that you were all self-important elitists." Henry let out an amused laugh as he continued, "I'm not often wrong. So thank you, George—" he motioned his glass around the room as he met their cautious smiles "—for making sure I got one out of five right."

The group burst into laughter as they raised their drinks. Then they clinked their glasses together. George smiled widely at Arthur and tipped his glass toward him.

Arthur paused to let them contain themselves and then said, "Oh, and for inviting us all over to share this wonderful evening."

When they regained their composure, they all lifted their glasses and exclaimed again, "To George!"

***

After dessert had been eaten, more drinks consumed, and the fire lit, they all moved to the den. The dimly lit room danced with light from the fireplace and gave the den a cozy feel that even Arthur felt himself giving way to.

"That was some toast." George approached Arthur with a wide smile on his face. Arthur started to believe that his question, about George and Sophia, was at least half-answered with George's good nature to him and increase in requests to be in his company.

Arthur swallowed his whiskey and turned his attention away from Trixie who had been delighted to hear his story about William and Betty.

"Thanks," he replied, confident that George had taken no offense. Every time they interacted, Arthur was warming to him, and although his confidence in certain things was increasing, he was never quite sure if George might suddenly change moods again.

"It was brilliant," Trixie said as she fished an olive out of her glass and popped it into her mouth. "Just brilliant."

"Have you heard? We're taking the *Aquitania*," George said.

They both nodded. George bragged about it any chance he got like he had been the one who built and would captain the ship. Arthur wouldn't have been shocked to find he somehow took over while they were at sea.

"They only have eight first class cabins," he continued, giving them information they already knew, "and we have five of them. Those poor fellas who have the other three." He laughed.

Trixie shook her head. "We have four of them."

George tilted his head in question.

"Well Elizabeth and I wanted to share a suite," she said, sensing that she had crushed George's hopes of taking over the ship, "and we thought that you and—"

"No," said George.

Arthur wanted her to finish. The confidence he had just been so assured of lived on a flimsy surface and it cracked with a simple sentence.

George scowled as he went to find Sophia.

"Who was he going to share with?" Arthur asked Trixie.

"Apparently no one. The suites all have more than one bedroom." She rolled her eyes. "He can be so dramatic sometimes." Arthur was amused at her hypocritical accusation.

The fire was roaring higher in the fireplace as Arthur took a seat on the large leather couch. No one else was sitting, but he was starting to feel the whiskey and needed to sit before he got too dizzy.

Sophia, George, and Henry had been politely discussing something in the corner and when they were finished, Sophia glided her way to sit next to Arthur. She sat with her back straight as usual and Arthur had to keep himself from pulling her back and making her relax.

"Is everything sorted out with the cabins?" he asked.

"Well, I have been tasked with asking you if you'd be comfortable sharing a suite with Henry. Obviously the two of you could split the cost. Unless of course you want your own."

Arthur shook his head. "I'd be more than happy to. I don't need all that space myself."

She smiled. "George and I are a bit ritzy, aren't we?"

"No, that's not what I meant..."

"I'm just teasing you, Arthur. Thank you for being so accommodating." Then she turned toward him and smiled, saying what had really been on her mind. "I am guessing you saw the newspaper a few weeks ago?"

His eyes flashed with concern and he sat up to join her in her posture. "Yes. I did. I had no idea... I mean, I didn't think..."

She stopped him. "It's ok, Arthur, really. It is not the first time that an article like that has been published about me."

"Oh," Arthur replied and slouched a little, feeling unexpectedly disappointed.

"If I had a dime for every man they've had me marrying... well I'd be richer." She laughed.

"I was quite concerned."

She turned to him and the smile vanished. "Why?"

"Well because, I imagine that it is not amusing for people to be so prying, so intrusive into your personal life."

"It was your personal life too."

"Yes, I know, but..."

"But what?"

"But I was out with Sophia Kingsley." He smiled, reminding her what a compliment it was.

She blushed. "I wouldn't be so sure that it's not a compliment the other way too."

They both sat stiffly next to one another, unsure of who might make the next move. It was the closest either had ever come to actually admitting their feelings.

Arthur took a deep breath. "Sophia," he said, sounding more formal than he'd intended.

"Yes?" she replied with the same tautness in her voice.

"I, um, I was wondering, well hoping, if perhaps you might want to have lunch, like that, like we had a few weeks ago, again." He chastised himself for losing his cool and stumbling over his words.

Her throat tightened and she tried to respond as eloquently as possible. "That would be nice, Arthur. Thank you."

They sat again in silence, both unsure if they decided it was a date. He wished he could rewind time and ask her to dinner, to anything more romantic than a lunch spent standing and slurping soup.

"You know, we are going to be leaving in just a few days, so we might not have the time."

His stomach twisted, feeling her impending reconsideration.

But she continued, "Perhaps instead we might spend some time together on the ship?"

"Well I thought we might anyway." He shut his eyes tightly and internally scolded his stupidity. "But, perhaps some more intentional time."

"I'd like that. You know, I—" But George interrupted and motioned for Sophia to join him in the doorway. "Oh, please excuse me," she said to Arthur as she stood.

Arthur released his breath as soon as she was far enough away that he was sure she wouldn't hear. Henry was watching him from the other side of the room and approached once Sophia was out of earshot.

"May I?" he asked.

"Of course." Henry took his seat but stayed stiff and appeared nervous. Henry could be cool, sometimes even aloof, and he could be quite the opposite too, but Arthur had never actually seen him nervous.

"If I asked you a question, do you think you could be honest in your answer?" Henry asked seriously as he settled into his seat. He leaned forward toward Arthur to close some of the space between them.

Arthur's mind quickly flipped through every question he could think that Henry might ask but settled on none.

"I suppose that depends on the question," he replied honestly. There were several pieces of information he might never divulge to Henry.

Henry nodded, satisfied enough. "Have you..." he paused to check and make sure no one else was listening. "Have you seen George with anyone, anyone unfamiliar?"

Arthur frowned. "Unfamiliar?"

"You're around him during the business day a lot, right?"

"I have been recently, yes."

"And you haven't noticed him with" he paused and then repeated again, "anyone unfamiliar?"

"I'm not sure what you're asking me."

"I just need you to answer the question," Henry said, almost desperately.

Arthur scanned his memory. "No, not that I can recall. Apart from his father..." he thought aloud as he responded, "the business partners, me, William..." he said, trying to remember his recent interactions with George. "That's all I can think of, Henry. Why?"

Henry shook his head and peered down into his glass. "I have been a little worried about him is all."

"From a business or personal standpoint?"

"Maybe both. I am concerned he may be spending time with people who," he drifted off for a second, "people who aren't good for him."

A memory snapped into Arthur's mind. About a week prior, Arthur met George at the *1913 Room* for lunch. This time William had joined them. The intention was to go over the financials for a particular part of the sales sector and decide what could stand to be cut. Mr. Carlyle insisted that that sector was draining more resources than it warranted and so they were tasked with combing through it.

When they arrived at the restaurant, George was already there, but instead of sitting at the reserved table, he was standing at the bar with a man Arthur didn't recognize. Arthur found it peculiar, not because he'd never seen the man, there were plenty of men in the *1913 Room* he didn't know, but rather because he looked as though he didn't belong. His suit was made to look expensive but it clearly wasn't, and the man seemed nervous, but more nervous than a man conducting a business meeting for the first time. When George spotted Arthur and William, he said goodbye to the man and told them that he was a former business associate.

He told Henry the story and Henry's gaze returned to his glass with a sort of sadness behind his eyes.

"Henry, I don't understand, who was that man and why are you so concerned?" He feared he ratted out George but was unsure for what.

Henry took a breath, trying to shake it off and feign indifference.

"Do you remember how I told you that when you live in this world, especially for those who have always lived in it, it gets more and more difficult to find things that make you feel alive?"

Arthur nodded, recalling.

"Well I'm afraid that's what our friend George is doing."

"But with what?"

"Listen, I don't want to spread rumors, so I can't say for sure. All I know is that there are certain men who hang around there."

"You don't think that he could be... dope?"

Henry looked back down at his glass and Arthur took that as silent affirmation of the possibility.

"Please don't say anything," Henry begged. "I'm sorry I even asked you but I needed to know. I will figure it out and take care of it if it's true."

"Ok," Arthur replied, feeling helpless. He was comforted by how much they, though always giving each other a hard time, seemed to truly care about one another.

Henry looked regretful, like he wished he could take the information back from Arthur.

"I saw you speaking to Sophia," Henry changed the subject, trying to pull his mind away from worry and into more titillating conversation.

"Mostly about the vacation," Arthur lied.

"Arthur?"

"Yes?"

"Will you just admit that you're in love with her and make us all happy?" He was staring straight at Arthur, not a trace of joke in his voice.

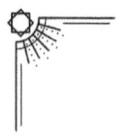

CHAPTER
NINETEEN

Arthur awoke the morning that the *Aquitania* was to embark with a lump in his throat; it'd been there ever since the Friday after Thanksgiving when Henry asked him the question. He tossed and turned at night replaying it in his mind; anxiety would wash over his body as he tried to push it away.

That night, right after Henry asked, Arthur was so taken aback that he froze and before he could mutter any words, Henry stood, placed a hand on Arthur's shoulder, squeezed it, and walked away. The rest of the night passed in a blur, Arthur trying to maintain his composure but was hyper aware of every move he made around Sophia, every look he sent her way, every motion that might give him away.

He rolled over and saw the packed trunks lying next to his bed. He felt sick at the idea of being trapped aboard a ship with everyone, unable to escape any further questioning.

"Mr. Malcolm." His butler quietly rapped on his bedroom door. "It is time to get up, we have to leave in a few hours."

Arthur had never been away from work for more than a day or two; this time, he would be spending almost the entire month of December aboard a ship and in England. They would dock in Liverpool around December 5th and then stay through Christmas day. The day after Christmas, they would load back onto the ship and return in just enough time to celebrate New Year's Eve at home. Sophia wanted to stay longer, but the rest of the group vetoed her, and demanded that she hold a New Year's Eve party at her estate.

She left her staff with the plans so that they could have it all prepared when she returned. She had always been there to oversee their execution, but to her surprise, felt relieved that she could spend her Christmas without worrying.

Her car pulled up last, in typical Kingsley fashion, and her staff unloaded her many trunks from the car. Sophia looked up at the *Aquitania*—it was massive in size, even more overwhelmingly so in person. Several people were already boarding, lugging their trunks with them. Employees from the ship greeted Thomas, who ordered them to take her trunks to her state room. Although she felt a little silly, she declined the offer to share a suite with Elizabeth and Trixie. She enjoyed them but often needed her own space to relax.

The five others already had their belongings loaded onto the ship and were standing in a half-circle, necks craned up. She approached them from behind and George, upon seeing her, scooped her up in his arms, delighted.

"Sophia!" He exclaimed as he set her down.

She straightened her clothes and then messed with her hair, checking to make sure he hadn't displaced anything. Seeing this, he rubbed the top of her head with his hand, teasing. She scoffed at him and stepped away, again attempting to fix the damage.

Arthur watched their interaction. He hadn't been able to shake several things Henry said to him and they'd clouded his mind since. He noticed that Henry seemed disinterested in George; perhaps the vacation was a clever way to remove George from his usual circumstances.

"I think it's about time!" Trixie said, as she clasped her hands together. The energy was high as they walked the ramp to the *Aquitania*; the first-class passengers were allowed to use one all their own, so as to not confuse them with those who could not afford such luxury. Several onlookers cheered and waved as they boarded.

"Oh this is so exciting," Trixie exclaimed, spinning around to those behind her. Her face was lit with joy.

"Let's just hope we fare better than the Titanic," George replied blithely.

"George!" Both Elizabeth and Sophia scolded him at once.

Arthur tried not to think about the fate of the Titanic and had been successful at pushing it out of his mind until George uttered its name again. He felt uneasy putting his fate into the hands of the ocean and the men who could be careless in handling her.

George smirked and looked down and then out of the corner of his eye toward Henry, who was trying to hide his amusement.

The first few hours aboard the ship were a whirlwind for Arthur—waving goodbye to the scores of people below as they departed, pushing up against the railing, while others tried to squeeze in behind him; he even saw William and Betty waving their hands vigorously to make sure Arthur caught sight of them. Then they were escorted to their rooms, the staff of the ship pointed out the amenities along the way—the garden room, the dining room, the smoking room, the library that held hundreds of classic and new books. They explained how the architect, Arthur Davis, modeled several of the rooms after famous landmarks in London and Paris. Then of course there was the tour of the cabins themselves.

Arthur laid in his stateroom on top of the unfamiliar sheets and wondered how, in just a few short months, he had gone from being relatively unknown to traveling aboard the 'Ship Beautiful' with some of the most infamous people in the city.

Several years before, before the war and before she made her maiden voyage, Arthur recalled his mother talking about the 'ship that was faster than any other.' And she proved to be when she crossed the Atlantic faster than any other ever had. Arthur scanned the grainy images in the newspaper and dreamt of what it would be like to simply be welcomed aboard. At the time, even third class felt inaccessible to him.

He heard a small knock on his door.

"Arthur," Henry's voice said quietly, afraid he might wake him. Arthur stood and pulled open his door to find Henry standing in the corridor between their bedrooms. He looked even paler than usual.

"I'm not feeling very well, must be the sea, so I'm not going to make it to the garden room."

They all agreed to find their way to the garden room, the most popular lounge, to start their journey and decide how they wanted to spend the next five days aboard.

Henry continued in his nauseated voice. "George appears to be asleep; I knocked but he didn't answer, so it may just be you and the women."

"That's alright, I'll let them know," Arthur replied as he grabbed for his hat to leave the room.

When he reached the garden room, decorated in light wood, wicker chairs and adorned with greenery in keeping with its title, he saw that Sophia sat alone at one of the tables. When she saw him, she smiled. He slid out his chair and took his seat as she greeted him.

"Henry isn't feeling well and George is asleep, so it's just me."

Sophia nodded. "Well, Trixie isn't feeling well. And Elizabeth claimed she was tired and needed to rest before meeting."

"So I guess it's just the two of us?" Arthur asked, nervous but hopeful.

"It seems we might get that lunch after all." She smiled.

After ten minutes of discomfort and anxiety, they both relaxed into themselves. Whether it was the tea, the conversation, or the gentle sway of the ocean, neither of them could tell, but it again felt like the moments they spent together on the bench.

"Arthur, I would love to walk around the ship and take a look around. Would you like to join me?" Sophia asked when they both finished their tea.

"I would. I've been very curious about the other side, I haven't ventured over there yet, have you?"

She shook her head. "To the port side?"

"To the port side," he agreed as he helped her from her chair.

***

They lounged on the port side deck chairs and turned their faces to the sun. Although the air was cold, they both dressed in coats and the sunshine was enough warmth to keep them from returning inside. It was also the heat from each other's company preventing them from moving lest it be lost.

Arthur squinted toward Sophia who pulled her hair up into several barrettes. A piece wriggled loose and fell alongside her face. He stared at it swaying in the slight breeze.

She felt him looking. "What is it?"

He sat up and swung his legs to the side of his chair, then leaned toward her, reaching his hand to her face. She flinched nervously but didn't move away, and he tucked the piece back into its place. Satisfied, he again leaned back and lifted his feet.

"There."

"Oh," she said as she reached to the side of her head.

She glanced over at him again to find that he had closed his eyes and was basking in the moment. Suddenly, she had a feeling in the pit of her stomach that she couldn't place. The freedom she felt just moments before, being on the open ocean with him by her side, fled and in its place landed dread. She leaned back in her chair, trying to chase it away, but it merely grew.

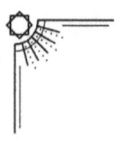

CHAPTER
TWENTY

The following night, after the rest had slept, felt rejuvenated, and became accustomed to the movements of the sea, Trixie suggested that they all go to the garden room, which was cleared of tables at night to make space for dancing. Trixie could always be counted on for wanting to dance, and Arthur could always be counted on for wanting nothing less. He dreamt of dancing with Sophia, of feeling their bodies pressed together, of sliding around her, being able to put his hands in places he hadn't dared, but he knew that once that happened, there would be no returning to his even slight ability to pretend he didn't desire her.

Thankfully, Sophia had protested as much as he, and even though he wished he could know if she shared his secret desire, he was happy to have an ally. Unfortunately, they were outnumbered and outvoted.

After dinner and a few drinks, they all returned to their staterooms to change clothing. Trixie came out looking as she usually did—short, loose, bright sequined dress with mismatched lipstick and hair tucked into her headband. Elizabeth, always a bit more reserved, emerged in a navy dress with black tights, heels, and a simple gold necklace with a diamond charm. Henry and George appeared as though they hadn't changed, still dressed in a grey suit, for Henry, and a black suit, for George. Arthur's suit collection had been growing, but he packed only the newer ones for the trip and they came in three colors: black, dark grey, and navy.

Sophia, in her classic fashion, dressed in a beaded black dress framed with fringe at the bottom that swung around her knees. Black tights covered her legs, and she selected a gold headband, a gold necklace and diamond earrings. She was always the perfect mixture of elegance and understated class, Arthur thought.

Also in her classic fashion, she emerged from her room last, so they had all been waiting in the hall for her. Arthur twisted at his sleeve and wondered how he would keep from embarrassing himself all night—whether from incoordination or too obvious lust.

Sophia and Arthur trailed behind the rest of the crew, both wondering how they might slip away unnoticed. It had been a day and a half of rest, drinking, laughter, and eating more food than they needed and they were all a little tipsy on the experience itself. Arthur feared he might cross over into drunkenness if he moved around Sophia's body much more. Bounding down the promenade, they passed by a small room whose door had been carelessly left ajar. For a moment, Arthur imagined he might push Sophia into it for a quick escape.

When they arrived at the garden room, it had transformed.

"Oh how marvelous!" exclaimed Trixie, as she stared at the ceiling above that had been strung with lights. Candles lined the bar and tables were arranged at the side of the room. The twinkle of them left the light of the room dim and romantic. Dark enough to erase any flaws but light enough to see each movement.

"It really is quite pretty isn't it?" Sophia commented, looking at Arthur. He nodded. "You would certainly never know what it looked like by day."

George grabbed Henry by the arm and pulled him toward the bar for a drink. They had both been quieter than usual since they boarded, perhaps trying to keep their lingering seasickness at bay and hold onto the masculine persona they wanted to portray. Vomiting over the side of the ship certainly didn't fit with the image.

Elizabeth looped her arm through Trixie's. "Shall we drink or shall we dance?"

Trixie laughed. "I intend to do both, I assure you."

Arthur eyed the tables at the side of the room and wondered if he could get away from them unnoticed. An evening spent sitting at one, even alone, was more appealing than what the others planned.

He stood next to Sophia in silence as he watched her look around the room. Couples were already dancing as the band turned out music. It was upbeat but not harsh like the music at the speakeasy could be. And despite its volume, there was something strangely comforting about it.

"Would you like to dance?" Sophia asked, fearing he never would.

Arthur wanted to say yes, and Arthur wanted to say no. In the end, he said nothing and simply offered her his hand. He was not in a mind to refuse Sophia anything she wanted.

She smiled and accepted it. His hand tingled with her touch and he realized how long it had been since he'd touched her with any duration. When they reached the floor, the song was surely halfway through, and so he considered it a compromise. He would dance, but only for exactly half of a song.

He reached his hand to her waist. They had looped arms, brushed shoulders, he'd graced her cheek with his fingers, but he had never touched her so intimately. He swallowed hard and attempted to maintain his balance.

Sophia was very aware of Arthur's hand on her side. At first, he was reticent and stiff, but after a few moments, his hand relaxed and she felt how naturally it wrapped around her. As they moved together, things became more fluid; he reached for her hand and spun her around, she fell back into his hand with ease, they came together, and then apart, and then back together again. Touching, not touching, touching again. Every time, Arthur's hunger grew and when the song ended and the next began, he was far too hungry to let go.

The next song began with a similar beat, slow then fast, then slow again. They talked and laughed, he commented on the lighting in the room, she joked about Trixie's prowess toward any single man. But after a while, nothing seemed particularly funny. Nothing seemed necessary to say. The silence reflected nothing of all that was being communicated between them.

Arthur pulled her out into a spin, and then back toward him, so their eyes locked for a moment. He twirled her again and when she came back, she lingered. She willingly pressed herself against him and tilted her eyes up to his as they swayed together.

It took everything in Arthur's weakening power to keep from leaning down to kiss her, and though his body told him that she wanted the same, his mind refused the thought; he could not bear assuming Sophia wanted him too, only to be humiliated and rejected in such a public place.

The music stopped and they stayed pressed together for a little too long. Then, they parted and clapped, all while keeping each other's gaze. Arthur leaned toward her, remembering something she said to him the first night they met.

"What do you say to escaping?"

She lifted her eyebrows and smiled then music started again. He glanced around to find the rest of their party occupied on the dance floor.

He reached for her hand. "Come on."

He led her quickly out of the garden room, hoping for no reason at all that no one noticed. They surely would notice eventually that they had disappeared, but that was a distant thought in his mind.

When they spilled out into the hallway, the music dimmed behind them and he could hear that she had been laughing.

"What are we doing?" she asked with childlike excitement in her eyes.

Arthur looked around and then without any particular plan, grabbed for her hand again and pulled her down the hall. Eventually, their pace quickened to a run and they ran side by side.

"Don't let anyone see you! Whoever gets discovered loses." he said to her in a loud whisper, thinking of a game he used to play as a boy with his neighbors. They'd run around the neighborhood, trying to go unnoticed and inevitably end up laughing so hard they'd draw too much attention to themselves.

Without a question, she spun around to scan the hall. Arthur realized that money or no money, some parts of childhood were the same.

They were alone. She turned back toward him with delight in her eyes and reached for his hand. He squeezed it and then pulled her down the hallway in a light run. She maneuvered her heels with ease and her hair tumbled around her face.

She squealed and clapped her hand over her mouth when she spotted someone in the distance. Arthur snapped his face to her and laughed then pulled her to his right, down another hall. She tripped over herself as she followed him, then stopped and attempted to tuck a hair back into her headband. He stopped and heard a door open as a staff member emerged from a passenger's room. Arthur grabbed her hand again, pulling her away from her task. They slid behind a partition until the footsteps disappeared. He smiled, glanced to her hair, and whispered, "I assure you, your hair looks fine."

Her heart rate quickened; she could feel his breath on her as he spoke. She leaned out from the partition and then waved her hand. "The coast is clear!"

They continued like this, ducking, running, pulling each other in opposite directions. They dove under a table in unison when they spotted another passenger, she pushed him behind some deck chairs so passersby wouldn't notice. Once, he hunched over behind a fern, trying to take its shape. Upon seeing him like that, curled over and acting as if it made him less noticeable, she burst into laughter.

"Shhhh." He covered his lips with his finger but laughed back at her. If anyone saw them, they surely would've thought they were mad.

When the person left, he stood and ran the other direction, leaving her to catch up with him. He looked to her, wondering if he'd erred and acted too much like a friend, or worse, like a brother. He wondered if he should've stayed and pressed up against her, making his intentions known. Instead, he had pulled her into a childish game.

Somehow, they lapped the entire ship and found themselves again in one of the halls that led to the garden room. Both tired from laughing and running, they paused and grinned at each other. He wanted to find a way to check in with her, to see if she would still look at him like she did on the dance floor, but then suddenly, a door swung open ahead of them. Seeing the room they passed earlier, the door still ajar, Arthur pulled Sophia into it.

He put his finger over her mouth. "Shh," he whispered as they paused motionless. He removed his hand when he was sure she wouldn't make any noise, and then he peeked carefully around the doorframe just in time to see an ankle disappear around the corner.

He leaned back into the room, his hand still grasped around her arm. They both laughed until they realized the position they held. The room was small and dark; it appeared to be a utility closet. The light from the hall filled it enough so that they could see each other, but made it difficult for anyone to see them.

He stood in front of her, his body inches from hers, and didn't release his hand from her arm. He told himself to move, to back away, to let go, but his body wouldn't allow him to budge. He swallowed as they both stood there frozen, alone and hidden from the outside world.

He searched her eyes and felt his heart pound in his chest. He was unsure if it was his alone or if he could feel hers beating just as rapidly.

He released his right hand and reached to hers, his gaze first following his movements, then back to her eyes. He traced his fingers along her palm and then entangled their fingers together.

It was in that moment that all of her senses, all her energy, became fixated on one singular object: him. She didn't dare close her eyes for fear that she would lose the sensation that she was not of herself, that she expanded into the entirety of time and space. She felt, standing there looking into his eyes, that the whole of the universe was contained inside of her.

He reached his other hand toward her cheek and brushed her skin with the back of his fingers, slowly tracing them down along her face and then through her hair until he held the back of her head in his hand. Then, he pulled her to him just enough so that there was barely any distance between their lips.

The tension hung suspended in the air, their desire for each other crashed into the space between them and then swooped them up into its force.

He searched her eyes again, asking without words. She nodded so slightly he was unsure if he'd imagined it. But the pulse of energy radiating from her and the longing he recognized in her eyes meant that none of his questions remained unanswered.

After what felt like eternities, he pulled her face to his and closed the space of longing between them. At first, their kiss was gentle and sweet but then it grew, hungry and ravenous, making up for the months they had gone without satisfaction. He released her hand and ran his up her side, then wrapped it around her back to pull her body against his. She reached hers to the back of his neck, trying to get closer even though there was no space left to be closed.

When finally, there was nothing else to do but stop or fall into it forever, he pulled back but kept his arms on her, both around her back. She didn't move hers either. They looked into each other's eyes and then smiled, out of happiness, out of excitement, out of relief. The burden they both bore for months finally felt released.

In the next instant though, the relief subsided and then the hunger intensified even more. He pulled her in again, his lips finding hers in a still unfamiliar kiss. He ran his hands up her side again, this time finding bare skin at her back. She gasped at the touch and he pulled back.

"Sophia," he whispered into her ear.

"Yes?" she asked, barely audible.

He pulled back so that he could look her in the eyes with softness and longing, a look she had never seen from anyone before.

"Sophia, I, I..."

"Arthur," she whispered back before he could finish.

He studied her face, waiting for her to finish, wondering if she was about to return the sentiments he felt.

"Would you like to go to my room with me?"

He stopped and pulled away from her; he had not expected the question. But her face was serious.

She grabbed his hand and pulled him out the door, only releasing it when they exited, glad to find that there was no one on the deck. She turned back to him and smiled, trying to tuck in errant strands of hair that fell in their passion.

The journey to her cabin was a blur, both trying to walk slowly and casually but wanting the moments to pass as quickly as possible. When they reached her door, she glanced down the hall both ways until she was sure that no one was coming. Then, she slid her key into the lock and turned the knob, opening it to a room not unlike his on the other side.

He entered behind her and closed the door so that it was again the two of them alone. This time, there was no way they could be discovered, they were free to do as they wished without fear of being caught. Arthur swallowed and stepped toward her but she hesitated.

"What?" he asked, not wanting to push her farther than she was comfortable.

"I have never done this before," she admitted as she played with the ring on her finger nervously.

He shook his head. "Neither have I."

"You haven't? But I thought..."

He smiled at her assumption that he had ever been so wanted, or so wanting. "No," he reassured her.

She swallowed. "I'm nervous."

He took another step toward her and kept his eyes on her. "So am I."

***

Arthur awoke the next morning around five a.m.; he hadn't intended on staying the night with her, but it proved to be too difficult to leave. He watched her drift off to sleep, and then not wanting her to awaken feeling abandoned, decided it was best for him to stay. Besides, any more time spent near her felt like a gift. He gently shook her arm to wake her.

"Sophia," he whispered.

"Mhmm," she replied in her half-awake state.

"I think I need to go back to my room."

Her eyes slowly opened. "Why?" she asked in a soft voice.

"Because others will wake soon and might see me leaving your room."

"Oh," she hesitated, "ok."

She watched as he dressed and then he leaned over the bed and kissed her gently on the forehead. As he exited her room and she watched him walk away, the sinking feeling returned and she willed herself back to sleep, unsure of why or what it was trying to communicate with her.

Arthur gently shut her door behind him and turned down the hall. He walked past a few doors and then turned two corners. The door to his suite was just around the second bend. When he rounded the corner, he stopped suddenly. Henry stood at their door, squinting as he tried to shove his key into the lock.

"Arthur!" Henry exclaimed, both too tired to process the encounter. "What are you doing up so early?" He then looked over Arthur's clothes and disheveled appearance, registering the direction from which he had come.

"Oh." He smiled. "Never mind."

Arthur turned his eyes away, fearing what Sophia might think. But then he looked over Henry who looked much like him. His hair was a mess and his tie hung undone around his neck.

"Looks like you might have had a similar night." Arthur smiled.

"Ha," Henry replied, "not quite. Trixie has been up sick from drinking all night. I'm finally getting back to my room now."

"Oh," Arthur replied, embarrassed.

Henry waved him off and then opened the door. Arthur shut it behind them as Henry walked toward his bedroom. "I am off to bed. Good night!"

Arthur stood for a moment and then called after him, "Henry?"

Henry spun around. "Yes?"

"Don't, um, say anything ok?"

Henry smiled and then drew his fingers over his lips to mime sealing them, then turned around and went into his room.

***

When Arthur awoke again, it was nine a.m. He rolled over, momentarily forgetting what had happened the previous night. It hit him with a force of joy so powerful that he felt like he might disappear into it.

Nothing mattered after that, especially time. Morning, evening, time spent alone, time spent with friends, whiskey, food, dancing, worries about George, they all faded into a cloud of lust. Arthur and

Sophia spent the rest of the outbound journey falling into each other's laughs, into each other's smiles, into each other's bodies.

Arthur was never sure if he had consumed too much liquor or if it was his lust causing him to feel drunk. He was uncertain whether they were too obvious with each other or if everyone else simply thought he'd gone mad. In a way, he had. His desire for her grew in monstrous proportions with every glance she sent and every kiss she snuck.

Sophia, unknown to Arthur and everyone else, felt herself falling. Both in love and into a deep despair. There were moments in which Arthur touched her bare skin that she felt alive and then when he walked out of his door to pretend he had been in his room all along, she watched him carry it all away with him. There were the other times in which she felt as though she wasn't connected to the floor, sometimes out of elation, but others when she would feel lost and confused as if she had just woken while sleepwalking. She walked around like this, detached and void until he might come along and brush her fingers and she'd realize she was still on the *Aquitania* with all of them.

The final day of the journey, only a few hours before they docked, it was late morning and no one had yet seen her. It was usual for Sophia to be right on time as to be almost late, but she was never one to not show.

They sat around the dining table, waiting for her so they could have their final breakfast.

George looked toward Elizabeth and Trixie. "Have you seen her? This is quite unusual."

They both shook their heads and then he glanced at both Arthur and Henry who did the same. Arthur last saw her after dinner, when she informed him she was tired and needed to take a night to herself. He felt rejected but noted the exhaustion in her eyes, as if she'd been wrestling a demon.

George pushed back his chair to stand but the women stopped him. "We'll go get her," they assured him.

What they found when they made it to her room was someone neither of them knew. She had not yet gotten out of bed and had slept in her clothes from the night before, sending the maids away when they tried to get her ready for bed. Her hair was pulled into barrettes but falling out at all sides and frizzed from not being properly pulled back for sleep.

They scurried back to the table and as soon as they got close enough, Elizabeth called to George.

"She's asking for you," she said as they both sat. He frowned in confusion to ask what the matter was but Elizabeth replied, "just go."

By the time George returned to the dining room, they had finished with their breakfast; Arthur mostly just moved things around his plate, too worried to eat.

"I think she might just be a little seasick," George said, "It'll be good for her to get off the boat onto dry land." He reached over the breadbasket and pulled out a roll no one had touched. "Henry, can you hand me the jam?"

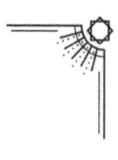

CHAPTER
TWENTY-ONE

The next two weeks passed by with Sophia's inconsistency. One day she would be up early, ready to explore, chipper and acting like her usual self. The next, she'd barely leave her bed and they'd have to leave her behind, one of them usually electing to stay just in case she needed help. No one could figure out what ailed her and each time it got better, they all collectively sighed with relief hoping it had lifted.

On one afternoon, when she was feeling well enough to venture out, she and Arthur sat on a bench near a market where the others wanted to shop. She asked to rest and like often happened, Arthur volunteered to stay with her.

"I fear I might be losing my mind." She glanced toward him. It was the first time she expressed anything other than hope. Most days, she would dismiss their worries. But her eyes were filled with concern and confusion.

"Maybe you're just not used to all the difference?"

"What do you mean?" she asked.

"Well," he continued, wanting to believe himself, "perhaps it is just all the strange foods, the strange smells, different air."

"I suppose it could be." She twisted her mother's ring around her finger. She had been doing that more, trying to find comfort. "The thing is though, I find all of this so exciting. I can't imagine what might be the matter with me."

"I think you're ill, my dear. You will heal. I would gamble by the New Year, you'll be back to normal." He grabbed her arm and gently squeezed it, reassuring her and himself.

"I hope so." She sat back on the bench, the tip of her nose red in the cold air. "I do feel much better over the last few days."

"See?" he asked, as if he was confident in his prognosis.

"Do you want to join them?" she asked; she felt guilty every time he stayed behind with her.

Arthur shook his head. "Not unless you would like to."

"Maybe we could walk down this street?" she suggested, looking down the street at the shops that were decorated in garland and had windows full of Christmas items.

"Sure." He offered her his hand as he stood. She accepted it and rose from the bench, feeling stronger than she had in some time.

Snow gently fell over the cobblestone streets; the old storefronts were just as Arthur had imagined, especially for the holidays. He hadn't been able to stop using the word idyllic and the rest of the group began finishing his sentences for him when he started to describe anything.

The town they chose for their holiday was nestled outside of London so that they could take the train into the city when they wanted, but they could also hide away in the quiet of the countryside. In particular, George and Sophia enjoyed going unrecognized. It freed them in ways that no one had ever seen. In fact, outside of Sophia's occasional mysterious illness, it was the happiest either of them ever seemed.

Sophia and Arthur barely even kissed since they'd been on the ship and though he understood, he also tossed and turned at night, going through withdrawal from her body. Others noticed the strange inconsistencies between them but no one mentioned it. Henry, more perceptive than the rest, sent Arthur some pained glances.

As they walked down the street, Sophia looped her arm through Arthur's and her warmth felt familiar and soothing. She stopped in front of a store; behind the window were trinkets and figurines, antiques, mostly items that people would pass by unnoticed because of their little value.

"Oh look." She pointed. "Look at that necklace."

Arthur peered into the window. Laid upon a display board was a gold necklace studded with blue and red gemstones.

"It looks like one my mother used to wear."

"Should we go inside?" he asked, starting to pull her toward the door.

"Oh no, no," she declined, "we shouldn't." She smiled and looked back at the necklace. "I can't believe how similar that one is, though." She sighed, gently and happily lost in reverie. Arthur was pleased to have his Sophia back. Sometimes when they were alone, he felt her return to him.

They walked a few more steps and she paused again, looking into another window and admiring more items no one could ever need.

"You know," she said, "I've been thinking."

"Oh? What about?"

"Do you remember when we disembarked the ship and all of those men were toiling away with the ropes, securing it to the dock? There was so much commotion, so many men dirty and covered in sweat. And then there were the women who were greeting the men coming off the ship, so happy with children in their arms."

Arthur squinted, trying to recall. He had been so worried about Sophia that he hadn't paid much attention. "I suppose," he replied.

"And the men who were selling things by the water, trying to get us to buy nuts and souvenirs."

Arthur had found them to be obnoxious but she seemed to be lost in some nostalgia over them, so he nodded anyway, curious as to where she was going.

"And the house! It's so quaint!"

Arthur smiled and then tucked it back away. The house they were staying in was at least twice the size of his and no reasonable man would've called it quaint, but he didn't dare argue with her.

"I wonder what it's like, you know?"

"What what is like?" he asked.

"That life. The life of the sailors, of the vendors. What it would be like to move without expectation," she answered.

He paused, both in conversation and on the street, halting her in her tracks. She still had a hold of his arm and it jerked her back when he did.

"What?" she asked, seeing she may have offended him.

"You don't know what you're saying, Sophia," he replied.

Arthur, in his different upbringing, had lived in such a way and knew that romanticizing it was a disservice to those who labored long hours just to put food on the table. Though as offended as he might have been, Arthur also understood the longing for simplicity, for the finer things in life to be kisses, sentiments of sweet dreams, and moments spent with those who would endure the hardship with him.

He shook off the memories of his childhood, reminding himself that only those who had no promise of upward movement sold themselves the story that the simpler life was the better one. He thought of the lavish meals he'd been eating, the comfortable bed he'd been able to pass out on after imbibing the finest liquors, and remembered the ache of dreaming for such luxuries when they all seemed like an unattainable dream. He almost felt angry with her for being so deluded.

She shied away, but only slightly. "I think it must be kind of nice," she said, "to be free to see the world in whatever way you want. To wake up in the morning and not have to be anybody. It's been nice here."

His irritation grew because she was speaking of things she didn't understand. "You think those people are free? Trust me, Sophia, they are not. They wake up and are nobodies to anyone."

"That's not true," she countered, "they're someone to the people who love them."

"Not to anyone who matters."

She stepped back, a sort of horror in her eyes. "Those people don't matter?" She let go of his arm.

"That's not what I meant." He shook his head, trying to correct himself. "All I meant is that you have no idea what it is like to have so little."

"I just wish I could see the world that way," she said, quieter now.

"But you are seeing the world!" He threw up his arms to motion to the scene around them.

"Am I?" She looked at him intently and the seriousness in her eyes took Arthur off guard. He knew he could never make her understand the life she dreamt of was one most were trying to escape.

"You are!" he shouted, spinning in the street. "Darling, I could have never seen the world in such a way before you! You have ships and carriages at your service. Why it's more than even *I* could've dreamt of!" He was impassioned, trying one last time to make her see his side, but he knew that he had been the only one of them to live on both ends of it.

"You're right, of course you are," Sophia conceded. "I have been wanting to spend Christmas here for years! I should be so grateful for this." She looked around at the gently falling snow and breathed in the unfamiliar scents.

Arthur wasn't convinced she believed herself, but he didn't want to argue with her anymore. She was unaware of the life that existed beyond the walls of her privilege.

They both turned to see Elizabeth waving her hands in the air; the four others were walking toward them, bags in their arms.

"We are going to drop these off to our driver and then thought we should get dinner? How do you feel about a restaurant instead of eating at the house?" Elizabeth asked, trying to balance her things against her tiny frame.

Arthur leaned forward to help her. "Sure that would be fine with me," he replied. Sophia nodded as well. They both wondered who could feel the tension they had just unsuccessfully tried to break.

***

Around the dinner table at an upscale restaurant, they enjoyed drinking in public without the threat of being caught. Arthur was becoming accustomed to throwing his money around with ease, starting to feel more comfortable in its security, like perhaps it didn't have an end and no matter how much he spent on a plate at dinner, it would come back twofold in business in no time. The past year had certainly proven that to be true.

"I want to dance!" Trixie shouted to everyone at the table, causing a few older patrons to turn their heads in disgust at the tourists who were disturbing their evening.

"Sshhh." Henry laughed as he attempted to quiet her, but he was having too much fun to truly care.

"Should we?" Elizabeth asked, already knowing her answer. Things between Elizabeth and Arthur had returned to normal and Arthur was left wondering if she even remembered her attempt to kiss him. She never mentioned a word of it and so he pretended as if he didn't either.

"Come on, I didn't put on my glad rags for nothing! I talked to that fella a few nights ago and he told me there is a hip joint just a few blocks away. We could ankle there easily." Trixie goaded, looking around the table.

"I'd go," Sophia replied. Her assent surprised them all but they thought better than to question it.

As they stumbled down the street, six young, rich, tourists, they looked less like refined socialites and more like teens who had just been released from under their parents' rule. Perhaps that was the appealing part of the vacation; that for a brief period of time, each of them could pretend that life and its realities didn't await their return.

Henry selected a table near the bar and was the first to sit. Arthur sat next to him, the sound of music was already blasting out of the instruments in the corner opposite them. George took the other side of Henry and promptly lit a cigar to protests by Trixie, who when realized she had lost, sat down with her arms crossed defiantly over her chest.

Sophia sat next to Arthur and Elizabeth next to George.

"Maybe we should just stay here and not go back." Sophia smiled as she looked around.

"Ah yes, delightfully sitting around here drinking and eating all the time." George smiled, pulling his cigar out of his mouth.

"Sounds wonderful." Elizabeth dreamed.

"Let's daaaance." Trixie whined.

"I'm not sure any of us are bent enough for that yet, Trix," George replied.

She shot him a disapproving look and then stood up. "Well then, let's get bent enough."

George stood. "Please, why don't you let me?" he offered sarcastically. "What would everyone like?"

They gave him their drink orders and then he motioned for Arthur to help him so that he could carry them all back at once.

George pressed his cigar in the ashtray on the bar, extinguishing it.

"So, Arthur, what do you think?"

"It's beautiful here," he answered.

"No, no." He shook his head. "About Sophia."

Arthur turned to look at her and found her gazing in their direction. She snapped her face away when he caught her eye.

"I'm worried about her."

George nodded. "She seems alright tonight though."

"That's true. Hopefully it sticks this time." The bartender slid their drinks one by one toward them.

"And what about you know, you and Sophia?"

"I imagine you know what I think, George," he replied, wondering why he still couldn't admit what was obvious.

"Finally." George smiled as he grabbed his drink. "I have been rooting for the two of you."

Arthur studied George's genuine smile and allowed one to cross his face too.

"To you and Sophia." George lifted his glass toward Arthur.

Arthur clinked his glass against George's. "To new friends."

"I might go dance." Sophia glanced at Arthur, waiting for his reply. He lifted his eyebrows in disbelief.

"Really?"

Sophia looked out over the crowd; the other four were already laughing and moving around the dance floor, fueled by alcohol and freedom.

"Do you want to come?" she half-asked, half-begged. But he shook his head.

"Fine," she said abruptly, "but I am going to dance with our friends." She handed him her empty glass.

"Wait." He stopped her as she started to walk away. He reached to her hair and fixed a piece.

"There," he said, satisfied.

George watched from the dance floor as he moved and spun Trixie around, trying to keep her from falling. Heels and the amount of alcohol she drank were a dangerous combination.

Sophia made her way toward them; George let go of Trixie and grabbed onto Sophia's hand, spinning her around. He caught her with his other hand and wrapped it around her waist, then spun her back around the opposite direction until their arms were extended but their hands were still joined.

The music stopped and they all clapped. George took a step closer to her as the next song began to play. Sophia had her hair pulled up tightly in a barrette on each side, revealing her earrings that swayed around her face as she moved.

He reached up to the piece of hair Arthur had just fixed and, as if he'd done it a thousand times before, unclipped one barrette, sending her hair spilling forward. She screeched and reached for her head then demanded her barrette back.

George shook his head, teasing her and refusing to comply. In his left hand he held it out and then as she was distracted, he reached with his right to pull out the other one, causing the same thing to happen.

"George!" Sophia screamed at him over the music. "Give them back to me!"

He shoved them into his pockets and then took his hand and messed the top of her head, making her hair even more disordered around her face.

He then grabbed her and spun her around again and when she moved, her hair whipped around, free and loose. She laughed and stopped caring when she realized that no one had even noticed her change in appearance.

Arthur, watching from the sidelines, moved to fetch her, but sat back down when he saw the smile on her face. He watched the way that Sophia looked at George and the assurance he'd felt so strongly while standing with George at the bar cracked slightly.

Sophia wouldn't be so intimate with a man she didn't intend on marrying, he assured himself. But then William's words flashed in his mind and he swallowed the thought – *"have their fun while they can before they have to succumb to expectations."*

***

On Christmas Eve, they gathered together in front of the fireplace and talked about the Christmases of their pasts. Henry was lost in a story about his childhood, where his mother and father would hide treats in their shoes so that when they awoke, they would discover candies had appeared in them. Sophia received a horse one Christmas, George spent one in the Swiss Alps with his parents, and Elizabeth recalled feasts of more than twenty guests on Christmas Eve. Even Trixie, who was several years younger than Henry and experienced life before Henry made his fortune, had stories of elaborate gifts and parties.

"What about you, Arthur?" Sophia asked.

He shook his head. "I don't have much to tell."

Sophia and the others groaned, but he wouldn't budge.

"But, I do have something I'd like to share."

Arthur got up and reached into his coat pocket that hung by the door. The other five watched him diligently. He pulled out a small wrapped present and handed it to Sophia. "Hopefully we can make some even better memories, starting with this."

The gift was about the size of a novel, wrapped in green and white paper with a red ribbon fastened into a bow in the center.

"You didn't have to!" she exclaimed as he sat back into his chair. She settled in next to him to open it. "Did you wrap this too?" she asked in amazement.

"I did. My mother taught me well."

She pulled at the bow while everyone watched. Then she ripped open the wrapping paper and threw it to the ground. Inside was a dark blue velvet box held together by small gold hinges on one end. She lifted the other end and gasped.

"Oh, Arthur, you didn't." She put her hand over her mouth and then without thinking, grabbed him and kissed him.

"What is it?" Elizabeth wanted to know.

Sophia spun the box around to reveal a sapphire and ruby necklace not unlike the one Sophia pointed out in the street days before. The women gushed over it.

"This must have cost you a fortune!" Trixie exclaimed as she ran her fingers over it.

"Trixie!" Sophia scolded her but Arthur shook his head.

"It's ok." He smiled. "Of course it did. It's like the one that you pointed out to me in the shop, remember? Except nicer."

Sophia frowned slightly and snapped the necklace box closed. But then she rearranged her face back to a smile. "Thank you. It's so lovely."

Arthur caught George out of the corner of his eye; sitting back into his chair and crossing his arms tightly over his chest.

"I didn't know we were doing gifts," Trixie said with concern.

"No," Arthur comforted her, "I just wanted to give this to Sophia."

"It was awfully nice of you," George quipped in, but his voice was hard and unimpressed.

"It was," Henry interjected as he shot George a look.

"Why don't you put it on so everyone can see it?" Arthur requested.

Sophia shifted uncomfortably in her chair. "Oh, I don't know that it goes with these pajamas."

"Nonsense," Arthur countered, "it goes with everything."

"That's true," agreed Elizabeth.

Sophia conceded and let Arthur clasp it around her neck. She reached up to touch it and saw him admiring it. She couldn't shake the feeling he was putting on a show and she was the lead actress.

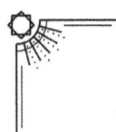

CHAPTER
TWENTY-TWO

The *Aquitania* docked stateside six hours later than scheduled, which meant they all had to rush home, bathe, and change before Sophia's New Year's party began. Sophia hoped she would have the entire day to settle in, but her estate was abuzz when she reached it, the staff flawlessly executing the plans. She'd left them with a skeleton of plans and left her most trusted staff to fill in the details. She saw they'd done a marvelous job so far.

Violet helped her change into her evening gown—an embroidered dark green silk dress with a drop waist. Violet then pulled her curls into the matching headband fastened around her head.

"You look like a real flapper," she said as she stepped away.

Sophia took her place in front of the mirror, she was as, if not more, glamorous than any star.

"Well I am one, but please don't tell anyone that." She laughed and Violet followed, relieved she had not offended her.

Dressed in a black tuxedo, Arthur watched Sophia descend the stairs; he arrived early upon request so that he could accompany her throughout the party. He wanted to sweep her away and back up to her room; they had spent the night together twice more on the way home, but she felt colder during those times, more distant.

"Arthur," Sophia greeted him as she reached the bottom of the stairs, "don't you look–"

"Not nearly good enough to be standing next to you." He smiled.

The knot in her stomach untwisted and she felt like she could breathe for a moment, but as soon as the guests began to arrive, it returned.

***

The New Year's party was nothing less than expected. Even more guests than usual poured in, anxious to see what extravagance awaited. Arthur stayed near Sophia's side as they greeted people, helping to fix her dress and occasionally her hair when it fell out of place. No one appeared all that surprised to find him by her side all night, but he imagined there were whispers when they walked away.

Sophia was different when she wasn't drinking; less relaxed and her interactions with her guests felt formal. It was a relief when someone like Henry or Elizabeth came to speak to them because she let her armor off for a moment. Arthur was proud of her for carrying herself with grace for so long.

Unlike any of her previous parties, a stage had been constructed and placed at one end of the room. On it was a microphone and a place for a band. Over it, even more balloons and streamers.

"Ladies and Gentlemen!" George took the microphone and his voice boomed across the room. "Welcome, welcome. First let me thank our gracious hostess, none other than Miss Sophia Kingsley." He raised his glass to cheers from the crowd.

"Now, I'd like to introduce tonight's entertainment, who are going to carry us into the new year with music and dancing." The crowd was still cheering and Arthur understood why George and his deep voice had been elected to speak.

"Please give a round of applause to Miss Margaret and the Jazz City band!"

The crowd erupted and the entertainers walked onto stage. George handed her the microphone and if they had any reaction to each other, it was undetectable.

Arthur felt his chest tighten and Sophia grabbed his arm as Margaret opened her mouth to sing. "Wow, she is stunning."

Arthur didn't reply. Sophia was still staring at the stage when Arthur caught Henry's eyes from across the room. Henry mouthed, *I had no idea* with a pained expression on his face.

Arthur pulled Sophia onto the dance floor and pretended as though the voice carrying them through their moves didn't make his hair stand on end. Sophia laughed as he twirled her and it delighted him to see her so lighthearted.

After a few songs, tired and thirsty, Arthur excused himself from the dance floor. Sophia began to follow him, but George caught her and dragged her back into another dance.

Arthur stood at the bar waiting for his next glass of whiskey when a familiar voice appeared beside him.

"Suppose I was right about you and Miss Kingsley, huh?" James' face beamed at him. "Perhaps I should be a psychic."

Arthur laughed, too happy to be annoyed. Besides, a newspaper article had already run anyway.

"I can't say I'm upset about the way things turned out, James."

James nodded excitedly. Arthur tuned him out while he watched Sophia and George dance to a slow song. He saw her tilt her head back; George was laughing. Then he saw George hug her and excuse himself. George walked toward Henry and lifted his glass to him.

"Excuse me, James," Arthur said to him as he collected his whiskey. "I need to return to my lady."

James stopped speaking mid-sentence and vigorously shook his head. "Of course, of course."

Sophia caught sight of Arthur and walked quickly toward him as she reached her hand out to his. "Arthur, come on. I want to thank her while she is on a break."

Suddenly, Arthur realized Sophia was pulling him toward Margaret, who was standing near the bar, sipping water.

Henry noticed the trajectory in which Sophia was dragging Arthur. He grabbed onto George's arm and pulled him that way as well. They all landed in front of Margaret at the same time.

"Hello." Sophia extended her hand and Margaret accepted it. "Thank you so much for being here; you have such a lovely voice." Margaret shook her hand in return and smiled, but she looked at George, then to Henry, and landed her eyes on Arthur.

"Thank you for having me; it's such an honor," she said as she briefly looked at Sophia again, but then her gaze turned back. "And Arthur, how nice to see you again." She let go of Sophia's hand. Sophia frowned and looked at Arthur, who had gone pale.

"You've met?" Sophia asked.

Henry tried to jump in. "We all have met actually—"

"That's right, we all have met." Margaret looked over George and Henry. "Henry, nice to see you... and George," she finished flatly.

"Oh, I hadn't realized," Sophia said, pulling back.

Arthur swallowed, hoping Margaret would leave it at that.

"But Arthur... I know a little better," she said, looking directly at him, "so the newspaper article was true huh?"

Henry interrupted again and George looked just as confused as Sophia. "We've heard her sing before, right before Thanksgiving, I think, right? It was after that silly article in the newspaper." He looked at Margaret with a stern face. George was staring at Henry like he didn't know him.

"Oh, Henry, you're a doll." Her tone was patronizing, amused he thought he could stop her from using her ammunition.

"I wouldn't have been so... personal with you had I realized it was true. I always just assume those things are garbage," she said looking directly at Arthur, lingering over the word personal.

Arthur swallowed. Sophia's expression had not changed, but she straightened her posture and clenched her jaw just slightly.

"Nothing happened," Henry jumped in, though he wasn't sure why. He felt some desperation to save Arthur, who he feared might crumble in the next few seconds.

"Nothing," Arthur directed at Sophia, trying to make the word land again.

"Well, I suppose that is true but we were interrupted before we could see, weren't we?" Margaret tilted her head.

Arthur detected a hint of confusion on Sophia's face. He knew she wasn't familiar with the back rooms of speakeasies.

"Come on, Margaret, you know you dragged him back there. If I hadn't pulled him out, he certainly would've done so himself," Henry tried again in defense.

"You what?" George asked, throwing an accusatory tone at Henry. Henry took a deep breath.

Margaret's eyebrows shot up as if to again say, *we'll never know for sure.*

"Back where?" Sophia asked, just slightly above a whisper.

"Oh..." Margaret spoke to her like no one ever dared, but she knew she had her in a place no one ever had. "We just have these rooms in the back where we can take gentlemen for a little more private time, if they like." As she finished, she reached forward and brushed Arthur's arm, having no regard for her own reputation.

"Well it was nice to see you all, but I have to get back," Margaret said, and then left them standing there in shock.

"You what?" George asked Henry again.

Henry sighed, and then answered hesitantly, "You were out getting the car."

"Is that true?" George's eyes seared into Arthur.

Arthur kept his eyes fixed on Sophia, who still stared straight ahead into the empty space Margaret left.

He swallowed and George got louder. "Arthur, is that true?"

"Yes, but..."

George grunted in derision, interrupting Arthur's attempt at an explanation.

Without a sound, Sophia turned around and walked decisively in the other direction, making her way toward the back terrace.

Arthur turned toward her and then back to the men, Henry regretful and George angry and confused.

"Arthur, how could you?" George accused.

"I know, I know. But I have to... Sophia," he replied in fragments as he turned and followed after her, trying not to run and make a scene. He pushed through the doors that had just closed after her. People were still inside laughing and dancing, not noticing the drama that had just unfolded.

"Sophia!" he called after her as she was just about to make her way down the last step off the back of the terrace.

"Sophia, stop!" he pleaded, running toward her.

She walked three strides away from the last step and then stopped and spun around.

"Is it true?" she asked, trying to pull back the tears that were forming in her eyes.

"Sophia," he said again breathlessly as he stopped in front of her, "I can explain."

She waited, her eyes boring into him.

"I went back there with her, yes," he paused, desperate for her to understand, "I didn't know that this"—he motioned his hand back and forth between them—"was something."

"This was after the Christmas tree and the lunch, right?" she asked, tilting her head. He swallowed, realizing that it meant just as much to her and he had been a fool to doubt himself.

"Yes, but, but nothing happened. Henry said so." Arthur pointed back to the house as if to make his point stronger. "He was there."

"Pulled you out," she said calmly, her arms across her chest.

"Yes," Arthur confirmed, trying to emphasize the point.

"So, tell me," she said harshly, "had Henry not been there, would you have...?" She looked to the side unable to finish the question, and he saw that she was fighting a losing battle against tears.

"I... I, um," he stuttered, unsure himself what might have happened had Henry not intervened. "Sophia, I never wanted her."

She nodded slowly. "I see."

He stood in front of her and felt her fading away, felt her retreating back into herself, her edges becoming harsh again.

"I have to get back to my guests," she said quietly.

"Sophia, please," he begged as she passed by him. He reached out his hand and grabbed her arm.

"Don't touch me, Arthur," she said as she moved away. Arthur looked toward the back doors to see George standing right outside them holding Sophia's coat in his arms.

He gestured it to her but she shook her head, and then he followed her back inside, leaving Arthur in the quiet night with the sounds of elation and celebration muffled inside.

Arthur sat down on the steps and stared off into the gardens. His breath swirled around his face, but he couldn't feel the cold; the only sensation was a piercing regret that had stuck in between his ribs and lodged itself there.

"Here." He looked up to see Henry standing over him handing him his coat.

Arthur took it and put it on. "Thanks."

Henry took another step down and then sat next to him on the cold stone. He took a deep breath and joined Arthur in staring out into the darkness. Then he pulled a pack of cigarettes from his pocket, retrieved two and handed one to Arthur.

"No thanks," Arthur declined.

"It's for pretense. Here." He lit Arthur's cigarette for him.

"Is George upset with you?" Arthur asked, not lifting the cigarette to his mouth. The ash fell off the end as it hung from his hand.

Henry shook his head and took a drag. "No, I don't think so. Taken off guard, I think. He's not used to being taken by surprise."

They both sat in silence for a moment and then Henry continued, "I'm sorry, I was trying to help."

Arthur shook his head. "You didn't do anything wrong. Who knows what would've happened had it just been up to Margaret to paint the picture of that night."

"You understand why I was so adamantly against it, against her?"

"Yes," Arthur replied, regretfully.

"She loves drama. Nothing even happened with George and she's carried that one along for almost a year."

"You think she's going to keep this up?" Arthur asked.

Henry shrugged. "I would imagine that she's gotten her satisfaction, watching Sophia Kingsley react that way."

Arthur swallowed. "Is she all right?"

Henry shrugged again. "George took her to her room to calm her down."

Arthur thought of Sophia collapsing into George's arms; the man who was always there to catch her and comfort her. He buried his head into his free hand and then guided it back into his hair. He tugged on it like it might pull his idiocy out of him.

"I don't know how to get out of this mess." He looked at Henry, hoping for advice.

Henry shook his head. "You know you have to go in there and pretend everything is fine."

"What?" Arthur sat up, confused.

"Sophia is the center of this party. Everyone saw the two of you together all night. People will have a lot to say if all of the sudden you're nowhere near each other at midnight."

"She's not going to want me near her."

"Maybe not, but she wants all the gossip less."

"So what am I supposed to do, act like everything's jake?"

"That's precisely what you're supposed to do. Welcome to our world." He stood from the stoop and threw down his butt. "Come on, we've been out here long enough."

Arthur obeyed Henry's command and followed him inside as if he was being led to his death.

"Get that look off your face. It's a joyous occasion." Henry ordered.

Arthur attempted to erase the concern. As soon as he reentered, he noticed James looking his way, no doubt he had watched every move they made.

"Don't worry, he doesn't take pictures at Sophia's parties; he wouldn't dare go that far. Now go find her."

Henry split away from him with a smile and walked toward Trixie and Elizabeth who were laughing with a few young men.

Arthur hurried as calmly as he could through the ballroom. As he exited, he noticed George and Sophia walking toward him, George's arm around her shoulder.

Arthur put his head down and then remembered what Henry said and lifted it again. George moved his arm away as they got closer. Sophia's face was neutral but her eyes were cold.

"I'm going to find a drink," George stated as they met in the middle. He didn't look at Arthur. Instead he sent Sophia a look and then turned to walk away.

"Sophia," Arthur tried.

She looked down at her hands and took a breath. "Let's go back inside, this is not the time."

"But,"

"No, Arthur. If you care about me please, not now," she said, and he shut his mouth and swallowed his words. He offered her his elbow as he would've done if everything were fine. She accepted but her hand was stiff and her body was rigid next to him.

They both smiled as they reentered the party, to the welcome of guests who surrounded them as soon as they did. Arthur caught James looking in their direction.

When the clock struck midnight and everyone shouted, "Happy New Year!" Arthur leaned over to give her a kiss, but she turned her head and offered her cheek, feigning a modest smile.

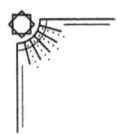

CHAPTER
TWENTY-THREE

Arthur's world collapsed around him, the destruction caused by the slightest and most insignificant moment, and yet, it had taken no longer than seconds for it to happen. Arthur left the evening of her party later than most of the other guests to continue the charade. He only left Sophia, Henry, and George behind, deciding that leaving two men was far less suspicious than one. For the next few days, he returned to work and attempted to focus while William mostly left him alone; William was lost in his happiness and barely took notice of Arthur's misery.

On the third day after her party, the office phone rang. Betty and William had gone to lunch.

"Offices of Malcolm and Henly," Arthur answered.

"Hello, Arthur," George's voice boomed through the other end.

"George, hello! I didn't know if I'd hear from anyone," Arthur replied quickly.

He could almost hear George waving him away at an attempt to interrupt. "I'm calling about Sophia."

"What is it?"

"She hasn't been out of bed since the party. I'm thinking of taking her to the doctor, but I think you need to come see her."

"Me?"

"Yes," George replied impatiently.

"Ok, I can be there this evening."

"How about now?"

"Ok, yes, I'll leave now." Arthur shook his head and scolded himself for not doing it in the first place.

***

George, Henry, Trixie and Elizabeth were in Sophia's den, having halted their conversation when Arthur walked into the room. They greeted him quietly, clearly all exhausted themselves.

George wasted no time. "She's upstairs in her room." He nodded toward the hallway, insisting Arthur go.

Arthur didn't say another word and instead followed George's orders. He found Sophia's bedroom door slightly ajar and he pushed it gently open. Sophia sat on her lounge chair as the fireplace in front of her crackled with heat. He imagined George poking at the burning logs as he watched over Sophia.

"Sophia," he said quietly; she hadn't seemed to hear him enter and he didn't want to scare her.

She snapped her head to him, her eyes lifeless and dull. Her skin had gotten paler so that it was almost grey and her hair was pulled back tightly, making her features appear larger. She sat wrapped up in a long robe with a blanket over her.

"Hi, Arthur," she responded weakly.

"George called and asked me to come see you."

She nodded. "I know. I asked him to."

"Oh," Arthur replied with some relief. He sat at the bottom edge of her chair, just enough to get balance. His heart beat quickly and he kept his body rigid fearing her request to see him might be followed with asking him to leave forever. "How are you feeling?"

"Dreadful," she replied and then looked back at the fireplace. Sweat formed on his back as heat poured off of it.

"Is there anything I can do?"

She shook her head. "I'm not sure. I don't think so, thank you for asking, though."

He leaned forward and put his hand on hers.

"I'm surprised you wanted to see me."

"I always want to see you."

"You do?"

"Yes. I do." She looked straight at him and he knew she was awaiting an explanation.

He took a deep breath. He had rehearsed what he might say a hundred times, but it all fell out of his head as soon as he saw her. "Sophia, about the other night, what happened... I need you to know that I had no interest in Margaret. I was drunk." He paused knowing what a poor excuse he just made. "I was crazy about you. I lived in constant fear of rejection and that night, I guess it just felt good to know I was wanted. I can't say I know what would've happened, but I can say I regret ever stepping foot in there. I never wanted her, never." He was shaking his head, letting his desperation run freely. "I wish that I could take it back–I would, in an instant. If you could just know how I feel for you, how much I've always wanted only you, you would know that it's true."

She listened but showed no reaction. She searched his face, full of desperation and sincerity. Finally, she said, "I felt like a fool."

"I know, I know. But it's me who is the fool."

"Arthur?"

"Yes?" he replied, bracing for her response.

"Never do that to me again," she said concisely and without emotion.

He scooted closer to her and wrapped his arm around her. "I never will. I promise."

"This isn't a game to me," she added.

"It isn't a game to me either, Sophia."

"It isn't?" she asked. Her skepticism stung.

"No, of course not."

She nodded, convinced enough it seemed, though the shame and regret had still not dislodged from his ribs.

"Trust is the most valuable currency I have in this world," she said.

"I promise to do everything I can to prove you can trust me."

She leaned her head against his shoulder and he closed his eyes in relief.

"I've missed you and been so worried these last few days," he said.

"I missed you too. I wasn't sure I wanted to talk to you yet, but I also just felt too tired to do much of anything other than sleep."

"I wish there was something I could do. George mentioned you might be going to the doctor?"

"Yes. It is probably a good idea."

"I think it would help," he agreed.

"Can you do me a favor?" she asked, her eyes closed.

"Anything, yes."

"Can you get George for me please?"

He didn't let go of her. "Is there something *I* can do?"

"Yes, you can send George."

Arthur returned to the den and sent George. George hopped up at once, eager to return to her. Arthur knew he only had himself to blame for driving her away but felt his insecurity transform into jealousy anyway.

Henry, who hadn't said a word to Arthur since he arrived, seemed to feel it all happen. He stopped what he was saying to the women and turned his attention toward Arthur.

"Are you alright?"

Arthur shook his head, feeling the stares and pity of the women boring into him. "I'm worried."

Henry nodded. It was clear that most of them had been at Sophia's house since they returned. They appeared tired and uneasy.

George reappeared after several minutes of silence and brought with him a new energy into the room.

"We've set her up to see Dr. Narudo next week," he informed them all.

"Next week?" Elizabeth asked, concerned.

"It was the soonest we could get her in; Dr. Narudo is away on vacation. His secretary cleared his schedule the day he returns for her."

"Who is Dr. Narudo?" Arthur asked.

"He's an outsider," Henry replied.

Arthur frowned and George continued, "He's far outside of town, discreet."

"And good?" Arthur asked, as if George wouldn't want the best.

"He has seen and cured a few of us in this room," Henry replied.

"Oh, who will take her?" Arthur asked.

"I think that's up to her," George replied. He went to the bar cart and began to fix himself a drink. The rest sat in silence until George walked back toward the sitting area.

"We need to get some joy back into this group." Trixie broke the heaviness in the air. "Look at us! Just a few days ago we were on top of the world!" She stood and attempted to bring the rest with her.

"Well that would be swell, but it's a little difficult under the circumstances, don't you think?" George challenged her.

She put her hands on her hips. "I know, but I think it might be good for us."

George shook his head. "Can't you just pipe down for once?"

No one said a word; Henry, Arthur and Elizabeth froze as George and Trixie's eyes were locked in a standoff.

She kept her hands on her hips. "I don't know what you're in such a lather about."

"For Christ's sake, sit down!" he yelled at her, stunning everyone in the room.

She smirked and dropped her hands by her sides. "Ohhh," she

began, her voice backed by ammunition she knew would drop him at once. "I do know why you're so upset."

He frowned and clenched his jaw as she continued, "Sophia isn't the only one dealing with something she wants to keep secret."

Henry shot up from his seat and charged toward her, stopping a few feet in front of her face.

"Sit down!"

Arthur had never heard Henry so full of rage. Elizabeth gasped and George sat still, his face blank.

Stunned, Trixie did as Henry ordered. She blinked a few times, trying to shake away the attack and reason what had just happened.

George walked toward the fireplace without a word. No one else moved. Arthur sat there motionless, fearing that movement might draw too much attention to him.

Elizabeth was the one who broke the silence. "Arthur, why don't we check and see if lunch is ready for us yet?" She said it in a nurturing tone, attempting to settle everyone down with her composure.

She stood and reached out her hand to break his daze. He reached for it and allowed the five-foot woman to help him up, unable to make it himself.

Arthur was concerned about leaving the three of them in the room, but followed Elizabeth anyway. When they were down the hall far enough, Arthur turned to her. She stopped, anticipating that he might ask.

"What just happened?"

Elizabeth sighed and shook her head. "Well, we're not supposed to say anything, but since it's you." She paused and searched his face as if she could determine whether or not he was trustworthy. "George's father has threatened to leave him nothing."

"Why?" Arthur asked, dumbfounded. In all of their business meetings, there had been no indication Thomas Carlyle wouldn't leave everything to George, his only son.

"Well, he has demanded that George get married. George refused and so Thomas made it a condition to be his heir."

Arthur frowned. "Why would he want him to get married so badly, isn't that odd?" It was not unusual for a woman's parents to demand marriage of her, but most men didn't get the same pressure.

Elizabeth shrugged. "You've met Mr. Carlyle. He's very traditional." She paused and then added, "It's not anything new; he's been pressuring him for over a year now."

"So why has it gotten more serious?"

"With the trip, George always hanging out with single women, drinking. He thinks it makes investors and the older partners nervous. And you've heard the rumors?"

Arthur thought of Henry's concern about George and nodded.

"Those sorts of things fly around quickly, and can easily ruin a man's image and reputation. But do you want to know what I think? He wants a grandson to carry on the family name."

"Why does George want to keep it a secret so badly?" Arthur asked.

Elizabeth started to walk again. "Trixie was just being Trixie. George just found this out a few days ago and she knew it would get to him. She can be such a... well careless, sometimes."

"That was a cruel thing to do."

"We're all a little on edge," she replied, somehow becoming the coolest one of the group.

"I can't believe I didn't know this. I suppose when you don't have parents, you forget how harsh the expectations can be."

"Mhmm, I think that it's times like these that George and I envy you. Not to be cruel, of course."

"Wait," he paused her again, "what about Henry? I thought his father was alive."

Elizabeth shook her head and frowned. "Oh no, Henry's been an orphan since he was about nine or ten years old."

"But what about all those stories at Christmas?"

Elizabeth shrugged. "I don't know. Maybe those were true, but I know that he was on his own very young."

"Did his aunt and uncle take him in?" Arthur asked, suddenly concerned for young Henry.

"Who?" Elizabeth asked.

"Trixie's parents. I imagined that's why they're so close."

Elizabeth frowned again and then laughed. "You know they're not actually cousins, right?"

Arthur felt dumb, he hadn't.

"Henry started working the docks about that time, around nine or ten, and lived on the streets. That's where he met Trixie. She was younger and he took care of her. I don't know why, guess he felt responsible for her for some reason. Anyway, he worked his way up and one of the superiors took notice of him, offered him a place to stay and to be his mentor. It's really because of him that Henry is where he is. He died a long time ago though. Anyway, Henry couldn't bear to leave her on the streets and so he lied, told the man she was his cousin so he'd take pity and let her come too."

"So, Benjamin, is he really Sophia's cousin?" Arthur asked, convinced he had known nothing.

She laughed "Yes, that is true. Benjamin is her cousin." She blushed a bit, a shy smile gave her away. She looked away for a moment, but Arthur recognized it.

"You? And... and Benjamin? But he's so... I can't picture it."

"He's shy, yes. But he's a great man. And we get along quite well."

"I had no idea." Arthur was further persuaded he'd been in the dark all along.

"I wanted to apologize for that night," she continued. "I was upset. He left because he was cross with me and I was worried. I guess I wanted to feel wanted or something. Not that you did that for me." She giggled. "I had no idea about you and Sophia, or I would have never."

Arthur smiled to himself when he realized that he'd been used and too daft to see it.

"Is that why George was so upset? Because he knew about you and Benjamin?"

"Maybe that was part of it. He's been friends with Benjamin since there were kids too. But I think mostly it was about Sophia."

Arthur nodded and recognized he had been going to the wrong places for information. He hadn't taken Elizabeth for the most likely to spill.

"George was really upset that night," he said.

"I imagine," she said, stopping shorter than Arthur hoped.

"He is very protective of Sophia, isn't he?"

"Yes. He is. He didn't trust you for a long time," she admitted to Arthur's pleasure.

"He didn't? Why?"

"Well he doesn't trust anyone at first really. You can't blame him for that. But especially not anyone Sophia is interested in, that's for sure."

"He knew she was interested all along?" Arthur asked, shocked.

She laughed. "Of course. Watching her around you was very different than she'd been with anyone else. It wasn't hard to see."

"Huh," he thought back to all of his insecurity. "So what does he think now?"

Elizabeth swung open the kitchen door. "He likes you, of course. I can't say about trust. I don't think the New Year's drama helped. Besides, he lets Sophia figure those things out for herself anyway."

"What things?"

"If she's making a mistake," she replied as she turned her attention to the cook to ask about lunch.

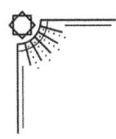

CHAPTER
TWENTY-FOUR

Dr. Phillip Narudo flung open his office door and announced himself haphazardly. Arthur and Sophia sat waiting in the otherwise empty lobby. He ensured that he did everything he could to make her comfortable on the way. She had finally grown tired of his attentiveness and informed him that she would make him wait in the car if he asked her what she needed one more time. Since then, he'd been mostly quiet.

Dr. Narudo was a man of small stature but large presence. His eyes shone with the kind of hope usually only seen in children unaffected by the sufferings of the world. Although they were a dull grey, a gold ring encased his iris causing one to think that he might have magic inside him. Arthur trusted George that Dr. Narudo was good at his trade, but his confidence waned with each passing moment.

Dr. Narudo practically fell out of the door and into his waiting room to summon Sophia. He grasped for his cane to help keep his right side stable. His clothes hung on his body as if he'd lost a hundred pounds and forgotten to have a tailor resize them. Placed unevenly in the center of his shirt was a faded blue tie, the knot loosened over the course of the day. Arthur supposed that he had been wrestling wild animals; it was the only explanation for the man's sloppy appearance and his heavy, labored breath.

Arthur aided Sophia in rising from her chair. Her hair fell loosely around her shoulders. Violet had taken care to curl it so that it cascaded down her back in large rings. Arthur knew she felt exhausted and ill, but he was impressed by her ability to gather herself to go in public. She wore a burgundy dress with black stockings and heels and managed herself with grace despite having barely eaten for days.

Sophia took his hand and rose slowly, barely making eye contact on the way up. But never one to skirt manners, she greeted Dr. Narudo with a smile and a handshake. Dr. Narudo smiled wildly into her and Arthur's stomach lurched. For what, he was unsure, but there was something about the man and his cramped waiting room that made Arthur uneasy.

"Sophia Kingsley, lovely to meet you, dear. Not under these circumstances of course." Dr. Narudo laughed and Arthur saw that his teeth were stained.

He turned to Arthur. "You are welcome to wait here." He motioned to the chair from which Arthur had just come.

Arthur shook his head. "I'd like to go back with her."

Dr. Narudo didn't flinch. "Very well then." He then extended his hand to Arthur and he shook it, surprised by its firmness.

"You are?" he asked.

"Arthur Malcolm."

"All right, Mr. Malcom, Miss Kingsley, this way." He gestured through the door down the long yellow hallway.

The office he led them to was a small windowless box whose walls hung bare. They were painted white at some point in their tenure, but the paint had yellowed and chipped. Arthur looked up at the ceiling and noticed a water stain that had never been remedied.

At the center of the room, there was an examination table and one chair to the side, which Arthur promptly took as his own. A dark wooden cabinet ran along the back wall opposite the door; the doors were solid and closed, giving no clue to what was inside. Arthur imagined them full of vials of potions and concoctions that Dr. Narudo sold as cures and spells. Sophia seemed to have no reaction to the strange set of circumstances.

After Sophia situated herself on the examination table, Dr. Narudo turned his attention solely to her and spoke in a soft and caring voice that surprised Arthur. He anticipated the man being aggressive or pushy, but instead he had the patience of someone who worked exclusively with misbehaved children.

"Miss Kingsley, I understand you have not been feeling well. Please tell me what you have been experiencing," he prompted.

Sophia swallowed and then said, "Well, I have been feeling... different. Unlike myself." Dr. Narudo nodded along as if it made perfect sense. "I have been feeling awfully tired, unable to do even the simplest of things. I have no interest in normal things."

"Normal things?" Dr. Narudo tilted his head urging her to continue.

She sighed with her feet dangling off the edge of the table. "Yes. Like hosting parties, dinners, going out around town. And," she paused again, "I have been dreadfully... dulled." She stopped on the word.

"Dulled?" Dr. Narudo inquired.

She sighed. "Yes. Nothing seems to excite me. It is as if a dark cloud has colored my entire life." She pointed to her stomach and then continued, "and it is as if I have something stuck here that I cannot get rid of." Arthur frowned, he had never heard her mention it.

"When did all of this start?" Dr. Narudo asked.

She didn't have to think. "Around Christmas. I think the day after we started our holiday to England."

Dr. Narudo nodded. "And is there anything that seems to make it better, worse?"

"Well, I suppose I do feel ok sometimes, though that hasn't happened much lately. But I went dancing while we were away. I enjoyed Christmas."

"And what about worse?" He asked.

"Well," Arthur interrupted, causing them both to look in his direction. "It has gotten worse since New Year's Eve."

Dr. Narudo looked to her for an answer.

"Yes," she admitted, "that's true. It has been relentless since then." Unprompted, she added, "I don't feel alive."

Arthur had to admit that she didn't look alive most of the time either.

Dr. Narudo scanned her and noted her well-kempt appearance. The words coming from her mouth seemed disconnected from the woman speaking them.

Arthur interjected again, "Dr. Narudo, please, can you help us?'

Dr. Narudo looked at Arthur as if he was surprised to see him still in the room and then back at Sophia. It annoyed Arthur the way he ignored his presence.

"Miss Kingsley, when you say it has been relentless since New Year's Eve—why?" He tilted his head as he asked. Sophia glanced at Arthur and he braced himself for the answer.

"Well, we—" she motioned toward Arthur, "—had gotten into an argument that night. But honestly, I think it might've had more to do with returning from England."

"I see. England, what was that like?" His eyes were misty as if he was trying to travel through her stories.

Sophia began to explain the sights and the culture, but he stopped her. "No, dear, how did you feel about your time in England?"

"Oh." She frowned, thinking. "I was sick while I was there, which was odd, because I was also freer there. No one knew me, no one expected anything of me..."

"Yes? Go on," Dr. Narudo urged, sensing there was more.

"Well mostly no one expected anything of me."

He nodded again and reached for the cabinet. Arthur's anticipations had been incorrect. Within them lay typical doctor's tools. He fetched his stethoscope and put the ends in his ears, instructed Sophia to take deep breaths and then intently listened. All the while, he was still nodding, as if it made perfect sense.

When he finished, he returned the stethoscope to his cabinet and Arthur stood to be nearer to Sophia. "Are you ok?" he whispered.

Sophia simply nodded but gave him a gentle smile. Arthur rearranged a piece of her hair that had fallen out of place. Dr. Narudo scanned them both and watched as Arthur kissed her hand and then returned to his seat.

"Well," Dr. Narudo broke the silence, "you certainly are suffering from a malady."

"Is it serious?" Arthur asked, his concern growing. He saw fear in Sophia's eyes.

"Doesn't have to be, if you comply with treatment," he assured them. Arthur sighed with relief.

"What do I have to do?" Sophia asked desperately.

"Are you sure you want me to treat you?" he asked her, needing her consent before he continued.

She frowned. "Of course. Why wouldn't I?"

He looked toward Arthur and then back at her. "Well I imagine your friend Mr. Carlyle told you that my treatments can be... unconventional."

"He didn't tell me anything. Just that he and Henry had both seen you with positive results."

"Ah yes, Henry," Dr. Narudo recalled as he looked off into space as if it was a fond memory.

"Dr. Narudo!" She snapped him back to reality. "I am willing to do anything to fix this. I cannot live like this anymore."

"You certainly can't," he agreed, his chipper tone not matching the situation. "Very well then." Dr. Narudo looked well enough convinced. "I believe I know what is causing your discomfort."

"What is it? Anything." Sophia begged.

"Does she need medication?" Arthur asked, still confused. But Dr. Narudo again ignored him as he flipped through her medical chart. When he finished, he looked directly at Arthur.

"How have you been feeling, Mr. Malcolm? I have to admit you don't look well either."

Arthur frowned and Sophia turned toward him.

"Me?" Arthur stammered. "I'm feeling just fine. Worried about Sophia, of course. But Sophia and I aren't suffering the same symptoms, why, I'm not suffering any at all. This has nothing to do with me."

Dr. Narudo shrugged and said, "I wouldn't be so sure about that." But before either could reply, he turned his attention back to Sophia. "No medication is needed, Miss Kingsley. We'll get you fixed up if you'd like."

"Yes," she assured him again, her patience waning.

Arthur nodded but was still fuming in his chair, unsure of what he'd done to cause Dr. Narudo to treat him in such a manner. And then he realized that Dr. Narudo was accustomed to a certain kind of clientele, a kind of clientele he didn't yet know Arthur was too. His feelings of inferiority bubbled up again and he wished he could tell Dr. Narudo just who he was.

Sophia sat in silence and kept her eyes fixed on Dr. Narudo. He stood in front of her, leaned down slightly, and took her chin in his hand so that his face was just about a foot in front of hers. Arthur grabbed the chair arms prepared to launch.

"You are so elegant, my dear." It was an unusual time to compliment her and she frowned at him, signifying her disapproval. He released his hand and stepped back, then positioned himself slightly behind her so that she had to turn her head to see him.

"And your hair is so beautiful."

She frowned again, suddenly feeling that his sanity had broken. But then, clumsy Dr. Narudo of the waiting room vanished and in his place stood a man who moved with the swiftest and smoothest of movements. How he got the scissors without them seeing they would never know, but he held them open in one hand. He reached behind Sophia's head with the other and swept up her hair so that it was all pulled together behind her back. Then, in one quick movement, he pulled the open scissors around her hair and clamped them shut, the loose ends of her hair falling into his hand. What was left fell abruptly and unevenly around her, the blunt ends coming to a halt around her cheeks.

Arthur's face twisted in anger and he leapt from his chair. Someone screeched and he was unsure if it had come from him or Sophia. His eyes darted back and forth between Dr. Narudo and Sophia's cut hair as he caught himself before he tackled Dr. Narudo. He stood frozen, trying to register what happened. Without a word, Sophia reached her hand to her hair and fingered the ends. She was in shock, staring ahead at the wall in front of her.

Dr. Narudo motioned to hand Sophia the hair he robbed from her. She took it from him and stared at it in her hand, trying to fathom how it had become disconnected from her. Arthur stood speechless, unable to move. His confusion paralyzed him and despite desperately wanting to help, the damage had already been done.

Dr. Narudo calmly put down the scissors while Arthur stood mouth agape and wide-eyed and Sophia stared down at her hair. Without saying a word, she dropped it to the floor, watching it fall apart and spread across the ground beneath her in a mess.

Finally, Arthur was able to choke out some words, "What on earth do you think you've just done?!" And then to assert dominance, despite how weak he felt inside, he added, "You will not get away with this, you hear me?!"

Dr. Narudo turned toward Sophia and disregarded Arthur. "You agreed to comply with my treatment."

Arthur let out a "hmph," baffled at Dr. Narudo's insolence and insistence on continuing his charade of madness. "This was no treatment! Why, you've made her feel worse!"

Dr. Narudo looked up at Arthur. "Perhaps you should let the lady decide how she feels."

This statement incensed Arthur and he lunged toward Dr. Narudo. Sophia stood suddenly and caught Arthur in her arms before he could reach him.

Confused, Arthur looked down at Sophia, or the disheveled Sophia who was standing in her place, protecting the man who had just harmed her.

"Arthur, I think that we should just leave," she said calmly as she pulled him toward the door.

Arthur resisted and shouted a few coarse words toward Dr. Narudo, many of which he would've normally not dared to say in front of Sophia. She continued to push him out the door until they were in the hallway. She used her body to corral him toward the front as Arthur tried to fight his way back. Dr. Narudo emerged from the office and stood in the hallway behind them. Arthur walked forward while turning his head back to shout at him. Sophia hushed him until he gave up. When they reached the front door to his office, Arthur shoved open the door. Dr. Narudo followed them down the hallway and was a few feet behind them, as if he was calmly escorting them out after a routine visit. The chairs they sat in while waiting for him were empty, as they paid him for the entire day so no one might see Sophia at his office.

"Arthur, Arthur," she tried to reason, "let's go. Leave him."

Arthur blinked, shocked at her acquiescence. "Sophia, do you know what that man just did?" Arthur wondered if it had all happened so fast she hadn't yet registered it.

But instead, she nodded. "Yes, Arthur. But it is done. There is nothing we can do about it now."

Arthur felt compelled to take off his jacket and place it over her head so that no one could see what Dr. Narudo had just done to her as they walked to the car. He stopped himself, knowing that Sophia already felt enough shame for one day. Arthur helped her into the car and then went in after, shutting the door closed behind him. He watched a couple pull open the door of Dr. Narudo's office and shook his head in outrage. He had lied about blocking out the entire day for their visit.

The ride back to Sophia's estate was a silent one. Neither Arthur nor Sophia knew what to say; they had gone in with such hope and Dr. Narudo made matters much worse. Arthur's stomach twisted as he thought about Sophia having to host guests looking the way she did. Perhaps her stylist could fix it, but her long, lovely hair was gone and there was no undoing that. He glanced over to find her gazing out the window. Since the first day they met, he had been trying to guess what she was thinking, and now it pained him even more to think what it might be.

When they reached Sophia's estate, Arthur exited the car and went around to open Sophia's door. He offered his hand and she accepted, standing up in front of him. He closed it behind her, but before he could escort her to the house, she stopped him.

"Arthur," she said, sounding in pain. "Would you mind terribly just going home for the evening? After today's events, I think I would like to be alone."

He attempted to pull the pained expression from his face; she was the one who had the rough day.

"Of course, Sophia," he lied and tried to offer her comfort. "We will get you fixed up, you'll see. You'll be back to normal."

She flinched.

"Please get some rest and call me when you feel better," he said and pulled her hand to his lips and kissed it, something he had been doing to soothe the ache of wanting to kiss her again while she had been sick.

She turned to walk away and he watched as her staff escorted inside. When the door shut behind her, he climbed back in the car and started it, the turn of the engine turning something inside of him too. It seemed to Arthur that whatever happened was far from being over.

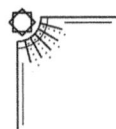

TWENTY-FIVE

"Mr. Malcolm... Mr. Malcolm! ...Arthur!" Betty shouted from the other side of the office.

Arthur finally turned his attention to her. It had been three days and he hadn't heard anything from Sophia and so it had been three nights since he'd slept well.

"George Carlyle just called for you, sir."

"Oh, ok. I'll take it at my desk."

"No, sir. He just left a message. Asked you to visit Miss Kingsley's tonight."

Arthur frowned. "He didn't ask to speak to me?"

She shook her head. "No, just left the message."

Arthur stood and walked to her desk. "Can you get him back on the phone? Call his office?"

She shook her head again. "I believe he was at Miss Kingsley's. But I can call there."

Arthur nodded as she dialed the operator. When they connected, George's chipper tone caught Arthur off guard.

"Arthur, old boy, calling to cancel already?" George heard Arthur shift on the other end and tried again. "Arthur? Are you there?"

"Yes. George, I'm here. And no, I will be there. I just wanted to ask how she is."

George didn't miss a beat. "She's doing well. Better."

"Oh, good, good. Is anyone else going to be there?"

George coughed a little and then cleared his throat. "Sorry, Arthur, I've been fighting a cold. Good news is that Sophia's cooks are the best at homemade remedies. But no, just you and me. She's not up for seeing anyone else yet."

"Have you been there long?"

"Uh, just a few days."

"Oh, ok," he replied, wishing he hadn't asked.

"Oh, Arthur?" George stopped him before he could end the call.

"Yes?"

"You might want to drive here instead of having Andrew bring you." Then George clicked the phone down without another word. Arthur frowned at the receiver in his hand.

***

Thomas ushered Arthur to the den to wait. He sat alone in the enormous room which made him feel even smaller. He checked his pocket watch after sitting alone for some time listening to the clock on the wall tick; he had been waiting for twenty-three minutes.

Finally, George appeared in the doorway. He had a large smile on his face and Arthur stood.

"Arthur, good to see you again! It's strange to go even days now after we spent all that time together," he said laughing. Arthur was confused at how George could be so lackadaisical.

Arthur didn't respond to his comment and instead asked, "Where is Sophia?"

George looked up as if she was on the ceiling. "She's in her room." And then offered nothing else.

"Is she coming down?" he asked, annoyed.

"Well I would imagine. Wouldn't that be funny if she invited you over and then stayed up there the whole time?"

Arthur didn't find it particularly funny and he corrected George. "Well actually it was you who invited me."

George laughed. He was standing over the bar cart fixing himself a drink. "For my sore throat," he justified. "Would you like one?"

Arthur shook his head and watched him in disbelief, unsure of how to move around him. George seemed different too since the last time Arthur had seen him.

"I guess I did invite you, didn't I? But I just follow orders from the lady of the house." He sat on the couch across from Arthur.

"How does she look?" Arthur asked, thinking of her hair and its blunt, uneven ends.

"What do you mean?" George asked, clueless.

"You know. With what Dr. Narudo did."

"Oh!" George exclaimed as if he just remembered. "Isn't that man something?" Before Arthur could give his opinion he continued, "she looks wonderful, as always." He tipped his glass to his lips and took a drink.

"Why did you want me to drive?" Arthur asked.

George looked at him with confusion. "Did I ask that you drive here?"

"Yes..." Arthur replied cautiously.

"Huh, this cold is making me delusional isn't it?"

Just then, a voice came from the doorway. It was soft and gentle, maybe even happy.

Arthur stood and shifted his attention away from George. Sophia was standing in the doorway, dressed in black wide leg pants and a bright blue wool sweater. Arthur had never seen her wear pants or anything but dark and neutral colors outside of the occasional party in which she wore silver or gold. Her hair had been cut evenly around her face and she pulled a black hat over it so the ends were just visible.

He paused to look at her; her cheeks were rosy and her eyes bright again. She smiled at him and walked closer. They met in the middle of the room and she kissed him on the cheek. She smelled of flowers.

"You look well. Different. What is that scent?"

She smiled. "Chanel Number five. It was given to me as a Christmas gift but I hadn't worn it yet. Isn't it divine?"

George hopped up from his seat. "Marvelous! Don't you think?"

Arthur ignored him but Sophia smiled.

"How are you feeling?" Arthur returned his attention to her.

Her eyes got wider and she took in a deep breath. "I feel..." She looked up at the ceiling, making Arthur wonder why they kept turning their gaze up there. "I feel good."

"That's so wonderful to hear."

"I think so," she cooed in George's direction.

Arthur frowned, wondering if Henry had been right about George. They were both acting strangely.

"I don't understand," he remarked, making them both stop and look at him. "Why didn't you want anyone here, want me here, if you were feeling fine?"

She sat down on the couch and looked up at him. "Well I wasn't sure. I was scared it might go away. Like it did when we were in England."

Arthur nodded, he couldn't argue but also couldn't hide his hurt.

"I think I'm going to find out about my soup," George announced and left them alone in the den.

Sophia patted the space next to her, motioning for Arthur to sit. He did so hesitantly, scared of her newfound energy and exuberance.

"Arthur," she said, oblivious to his concern, "I have been thinking, what do you think about Africa?"

"Africa? For what?" he asked, confused.

"For the next trip. I hear that it is unlike anything we've ever seen."

He grabbed her hand and pulled it onto his lap. "Perhaps we should wait to see, to see how you feel? I'd hate to rush into anything."

She looked disappointed. "I suppose that does make sense."

She took in a deep breath and then stood again. "What do you think?" She motioned over her clothes and then spun around.

"Are they new?"

"They are. I picked them out. Fun aren't they?"

"They're... colorful. Different from what you'd normally wear."

"I know." She sat down again. "You should've told me that pants were so comfortable!"

He nodded, unsure of how to react to her, afraid of making one misstep and setting off a bomb of some unexpected kind.

"I'm going to have my rooms redone too. I was lying in bed this morning and thinking, this is all so outdated."

"Your rooms redone?" He was trying to process all the information as it came at him.

"Yes. I am going to have all of this dreadfully depressing décor redone. It's been like this for decades, I think it's time for a change." She stood and walked toward the terrace doors, running her hands over the drapes and then held one out to him. "These are dull."

He stood and faced her. "I don't think so. They're traditional, classic. I think your house is beautiful."

"Sure, but not very like me."

"Since when?" It had always seemed like the perfect backdrop for her.

"Since always, I suppose. I just didn't realize it could be any different."

"Just because something can be different doesn't mean it *should* change, Sophia."

***

The next night before dinner, she appeared in another pair of loose fitting pants with a button-up blouse tucked into them. She wore a red felt cloche hat adorned with a large matching flower on its side, the ends of her dark hair peeking out.

When Arthur met her in the sitting room, he had to admit she looked radiant, sophisticated even.

"I'm still getting used to the pants, but you always look wonderful," he said as he kissed her on the cheek.

"So do you, but we need to get you some more color in that wardrobe! If I'm going to be wearing red, you can't well be wearing such dull colors all the time." She held his hands out as she scanned up and down his grey suit that he had paired with a black tie and pocket square.

He shifted uncomfortably. "I quite like my suits."

"Of course, of course, they're spiffy. Ignore me. You should dress however you like."

"Is anyone else coming to dinner?"

She shook her head and smiled. "Just us."

They hadn't been alone, outside of the moments they argued, since the cruise home. It had been nearly two weeks since he'd been able to kiss her and he felt like he might burst. Her shift in mood, her change of style, her energy, all felt pent up inside of him.

He grabbed her and wrapped his hand around her back, pulling her in close to him.

"I've missed you," he whispered, looking down at her.

"Well I'm right here."

He leaned down and kissed her. It felt familiar, like the Sophia he had always known.

She pulled back. "If we went to Africa, we'd have the entire trip there to be alone as much as we liked."

He laughed. "You are very clever with your ways, Sophia Kingsley."

He looked around the room and then back down to her. "They can keep the food warm until we're ready right?"

"What?" she asked, smiling in intrigue.

She screeched as he scooped her into his arms, one arm under her knees, the other around her back. She reached her arm around his neck for support and laughed, then he carried her down the hall and up the first flight of stairs.

"Ok," he said, putting her down, smiling and breathing heavily. "I can't make it two more flights, but you get the point."

She laughed and took off running toward the next staircase. He followed after, both bounding in the direction of her bedroom. When they arrived, he closed the door behind him and faced her to find her face full of life, full of joy.

He moved toward her and kissed her, then reached his hands toward the buttons on her blouse. Her heart raced from the exertion of energy and excitement as he slowly undid them, one by one. She reached to his tie and loosened it, then used it to pull him back toward her face. He kissed her, hard and hungry as he backed her toward her bed. They fell backward onto it, half dressed. They tore at each other's clothing between kisses, their bodies starved from the days gone without touching one another.

He lifted himself up to look down into her eyes. They stared at each other for a moment until he whispered, "Sophia... I, I love you."

She smiled and lifted her face to him, kissing him gently. Then they gave themselves over to each other, forgetting anything else in the world existed.

She didn't bother pulling a sheet over her when they finished like she had on the ship; instead she lay next to him, naked and satisfied.

"I know you think I'm mad, but I'm still going to redo this decor."

He propped himself to his elbows and looked around the room, then laid back down. "I still like it how it is."

She laughed. "You need to learn how to be better with change."

He rolled over to his side and faced her, then ran his finger up her stomach and over her breasts, still baffled how he'd gotten so lucky to be able to touch her in such a way.

"I think I've done just fine with some changes."

"Yes, it has been quite tortuous for you hasn't it?"

"You have no idea." He leaned forward and kissed her gently.

When he pulled away, she whispered, "I'm hungry. Let's go eat?"

He pulled the sheet over them both, trapping them underneath. She laughed as he climbed on top of her and kissed her all over her face. Then he rolled off.

"Ok fine, I'm hungry too."

Both satisfied and happy, they sipped on wine at dinner. She looked up at him. "I'm having an engagement celebration for Elizabeth and Benjamin."

"They're engaged?" Arthur asked, surprised.

Sophia set down her glass. "Yes, isn't that wonderful? Just happened yesterday. They phoned after to tell George and me."

His stomach sent an old but familiar pang of jealousy through him. "Oh... when are you having the party?"

"Three weeks. I'm thinking not too big, say maybe, twenty? Thirty? Oh I really should ask Elizabeth what she wants, shouldn't I?"

"That's not long to plan a party."

She shook her head. "It'll be casual. Won't take much preparation."

"Casual? That's not what people expect from a Kingsley party. Kingsley parties are always ritzy, extravagant."

She bit her lip, thinking. "That's true, but this isn't about what people expect."

"Of course it is," Arthur said as he buttered his roll. "Parties always are about impressing the guests."

"Funny, I thought they were about celebrating."

He stopped what he was doing and looked across the table at her. "Well of course. But what's the use of having all of this at your disposal if you aren't going to show it off?"

"Show it off?"

"You know what I mean, share it." He looked back down at his roll and set his knife on the table.

"Arthur." She pulled his attention from his plate. "Are you alright? You're acting strangely all of the sudden."

"I'm fine, Sophia. I'm confused, that's all."

"Confused?"

"Or worried. Confused and worried. There has been so much sudden change."

She processed his words carefully. "And it's bad?"

"Just different."

"Different can be good."

"Of course." He took a sip of his wine and picked up his fork. "It's just taking me a moment to catch up."

She watched him cut into his veal and put a bite in his mouth, and even though he could feel her eyes on him, he didn't look up.

***

The rest of the following weeks went much the same way: Arthur visiting her after he was finished at the office, whisking her up to her bedroom when it was just the two of them. They'd laugh and he'd feel comforted, and then she'd start talking about all the change again and he'd feel her slipping away from him. Arthur tried to navigate her, tried to believe in her newfound happiness, but his skepticism remained.

One evening, he'd gotten stuck at his office later than usual and George arrived before him. Thomas didn't answer the door, and so Arthur showed himself in and escorted himself to the den where he was sure they'd be waiting. As he approached, he could hear their voices, George's clearer than Sophia's.

"...Sophia, yes, it was a promise," George said.

Then there was a pause and Arthur heard Sophia's voice, but it didn't carry enough to make out what she said. Still, he could hear a hint of anger or irritation in it.

Then George spoke again, "you aren't going to hurt me. You can—" but again he was cut off by her voice, which grew a little louder as Arthur neared, but he still couldn't decipher her words.

Finally, George interjected again, "I don't think we should be having this conversation right now. He'll be here any minute, I'm sure."

Arthur paused in the hall outside the door, wanting them to finish, but neither spoke. When he was sure they would say no more, he entered the room and both their faces snapped toward him in smiles.

"Arthur! You made it!" George stood to shake his hand then excused himself from the room.

Sophia grabbed his hand. "The fabric samples came today. Come, I want to show them to you." She dragged him to a table where they had been laid out. "Aren't these wonderful? So much more modern. Just the bee's knees."

"Bee's knees?" He lifted his eyebrows.

She giggled. "It does sound silly coming out of my mouth doesn't it? But what do you think?"

He fingered the fabrics and then looked at her with curiosity, his mind still stuck on the conversation he overheard. "They're a bit loud for my taste."

She looked at him quizzically. "You think? I rather like them."

"So why did you ask?" He wondered if she had contemplated the possibility that he might live there too at some point when selecting them.

She shrugged. "I'm excited, that's all. And I like them, so that's what I've decided."

His heart sunk. She hadn't considered him at all. In fact, it appeared she was quite content moving along without his input.

CHAPTER
TWENTY-SIX

By the day of the engagement party, Arthur's silent exasperation led him to down two whiskeys before anyone even arrived. George had come early, as usual, and they sat together speaking of business in the den while Sophia readied herself.

She arrived downstairs in a knee length red skirt, cream sweater with a loose-fitting jacket tossed over it, and low heels. Arthur wondered if she borrowed the jacket from her father's old clothing with how baggy it fit her. On her head, she wore her red felt cloche hat with the flower. Arthur supposed she wanted to hide her hair while she got used to its new shorter length. Her eyes were dark with make-up and lips bright red.

Elizabeth was overjoyed with the informality of the party, insisting that she wanted everyone to feel as though their engagement was something to be celebrated warmly. Arthur remained skeptical, but even Benjamin appeared more light-hearted than any time he'd seen him before. Still, Arthur watched the faces of the guests as they arrived and thought he detected a look of surprised judgment. He cringed with self-consciousness for Sophia.

Henry approached and bumped into Arthur's arm. "What say you? This is all odd, isn't it?"

Arthur was relieved that someone else finally acknowledged it. He hadn't seen the other three since before the visit with Dr. Narudo.

"Yes," he said with relief, "I am confused."

But then Henry shrugged. "She seems happy."

Arthur looked at her from across the room chatting to Trixie and one of Benjamin's business associates. Trixie flirted with him and made no attempt to be coy about it. Sophia gestured with her hands, telling a story Arthur imagined he'd never heard because he'd never seen her move that way. She reached up to her head and grabbed her hat, pulled it off and then used it to fan herself. She laughed. Then she placed her hat down on the table next to her, her hair a mess underneath.

"Excuse me," Arthur said to Henry and the others who had joined them. He walked to the table and grabbed her hat and then followed behind her, catching up to her.

"You forgot this." He offered her hat back to her.

She looked down at it. "Oh I was warm so I took it off." But she didn't take it from him.

"Don't you want to put it back on? Your hair is a mess," he said, attempting a laugh.

Sophia frowned. "Would you like me to put it back on?"

He wanted to say no, that he didn't care, but he looked at her with the top of her hair matted from the pressure of the hat and the rest disheveled. "I just thought that you might want to look a little more... presentable."

She took the hat from him. "I see. Well thank you." She pulled the hat back over her hair to his ashamed relief. Had it been only their small group of seven, he would've thought nothing of it. But in a room full of high society, her lowbrow party was bad enough.

Emily "Millie" Stanton, a family friend of Elizabeth's, approached him and Sophia. "Sophia, look at you." She held out Sophia's hands to get the full effect of her outfit. "You young women can get away with such interesting clothes. And, I must say what a fun idea for this party."

Arthur feared he heard a hint of disapproval in Millie's voice.

"Thank you, Millie. Have you met Arthur Malcolm?" Sophia asked.

Millie turned toward him and reached out her hand. "I have not, but I have heard a lot about you."

"Oh?" Arthur asked. He was dressed in a navy suit and tie, which upon comparing himself to the others who complied with the casual theme, felt out of place.

"Yes, and I know Betty, your secretary. Her mother used to clean my house in fact," Millie said. Arthur felt a lump of shame form in his throat. "I hear that she is engaged to your business partner, William Henly, is that right?"

Arthur nodded, confirming. He wanted to shrink away from Millie but she continued.

"How wonderful for the two of them... And what about the two of you, are you next?" Millie smiled expectantly.

Arthur froze, they hadn't ever talked about marriage. He knew what he wanted and he'd thought about it many times, but he'd been trying to let things settle some before he broached the topic with her.

"You know me, Millie, never doing what people expect of me," Sophia joked.

Millie softly laughed and then excused herself, not used to a woman being so dismissive of the idea of marriage.

Arthur looked down to find Sophia holding a glass of champagne. She put it to her mouth and took a sip. He frowned. "What was that supposed to mean?"

She shrugged. "You know how people can be with me. What was I supposed to say?"

"Nothing." He shook his head, appearing angry, though inside he felt more hurt than anything else.

"It didn't mean anything, Arthur."

"Ok." He kissed her on the cheek. "I need to excuse myself for a moment."

He walked to the den, trying to shake off the feeling. He found Henry and George already there, both seated on the couch facing the door.

"You too?" he asked as he entered.

"It's a lot," Henry agreed, "to go from all that worry to see her the best she's ever been, it's a bit to wrap your mind around."

Arthur nodded, appreciative of Henry.

"I just wanted the good whiskey." George smiled, holding up his glass. He was oddly evasive, especially given his usual defenses of Sophia.

"Did Dr. Narudo do anything else, prescribe her something?" Arthur asked.

George shook his head. "No. He sent her a book by post. That was odd. But if he would've given her medicine, you were there. You would have seen it."

"A book?"

George nodded. "Some new book from France. *La Garçonne.* He knew how much she liked to read and she'd never heard of it, I suppose."

"I cannot fathom why she'd accept anything from that madman," Arthur said. Then momentarily distracted, he asked, "Sophia speaks French?"

George nodded, thinking Arthur sounded as disjointed as he was accusing Sophia of being.

"But anyway, I was thinking more along the lines of opium because she just seems..."

"Happy?" suggested George.

"Maybe, but it's different than just that."

George dismissed him. "Perhaps that's not such a bad thing."

Henry nodded. "Arthur, you must admit that she seems happier. As though the Sophia we see has been finally unlocked to the rest of the world. Perhaps a little more... colorful."

"A little more? She is practically unrecognizable. I cannot believe that you are not trying harder to do something about it." He motioned to George.

"What would you have me do, Arthur?"

"Save her from herself. Talk to her. She listens to you."

"You want me to tell her to stop behaving happily?" George challenged.

Arthur motioned to Henry. "When you were worried about George, you did something about it then! Why not Sophia?"

George looked perplexed. "You were worried about me? Why?"

Henry sent Arthur an annoyed glance, then addressed George, "I promise I will tell you later. Let's keep focused for now?"

It took George a moment to be convinced but then he nodded.

Arthur sighed. "You both know what I am trying to say. I do not understand why you do not intervene, shift her in the right direction."

George took a sip and then answered. "I do not pretend to know what the right direction is for anyone, even Sophia. I would not dare to make Sophia into anything or anyone she does not want to be. Sophia's life is her own, Arthur."

"Then I can only just hope this is a phase."

"A phase?" George asked.

"Yes, you have heard her talking about renovations, seen her clothing, speaking of Africa. It is like she cannot be wrangled. It feels like the behavior of a madwoman. I can only hope that she comes back to Earth and remembers who she is."

Henry's eyes darted to the entrance of the room in an attempt to signal Arthur. Arthur spun around to find Sophia standing behind him, holding onto a half empty glass of champagne.

"And who exactly did I forget I was?" She took another step toward him.

Henry and George both stood and Henry said, "I think perhaps we should go." But Sophia stopped them.

"No, please, stay. I would like to hear this conversation."

They both sat again, looking like children who'd just been scolded.

Arthur stood to face her. "Sophia, please, you have to admit this is unusual."

She crossed her arms over her chest, still holding onto her glass. "What if I am happy, Arthur?"

"I am delighted if that is the case!" But his tone was not of joy, rather disbelief. "I just think that this is all a little much, don't you?"

"Too much?" She frowned.

"Yes!" he shouted, as if his volume would convince her to agree. "Don't you know who you are? You cannot behave in such a way!"

"Again I ask, who am I?"

"I don't know how to have this conversation with you, you are being so obstinate." He turned to Henry and George for help, but they diverted their gazes, wishing they could sink into the couch.

"Arthur, do not force me to ask again. Who is it that you are so adamant I be?"

He shook his head. "Sophia Kingsley. Who you are. Socialite, heiress, of proper society."

She frowned. "I am still all of those things, Arthur."

He laughed. "I would hardly recognize you as such now."

"Whatever is that supposed to mean?"

"Sophia, I care about you. I just think that you should know what people are thinking of you so that you can stop this embarrassment."

George coughed reflexively with the insult and Henry grabbed his arm to keep him from lunging at Arthur.

"Embarrassment?"

"You are not behaving in a sophisticated manner. What is this party? What is this way in which you're dressing and speaking to your guests? The Sophia I first met would've been appalled at your behavior."

"The Sophia you first met? The one who was refined and polite and quiet and always said the right thing, dressed the right way, behaved the right way?"

"Yes!" He threw his hands in the air in sure victory that she could understand him at last.

"And that is who I really am?"

He frowned. "Well of course. This is just madness, a reaction to what has happened to you. You can get back to your old self, Sophia. I promise."

"And what if this is who I am? If this is how it is going to stay?"

He scoffed. "That's utter nonsense. You know, and we all know, that you are not... this." He waved his hand up and down over her.

She looked at him calmly, uncrossed her arms, and then made the same motion over him. "And this, this suit and tie, formal Arthur, the one that the public sees—that is who you are?"

He shook his head confused. "What?"

"The Arthur I first met dressed in ill-fitting suits and stood to eat his fifteen cent soup. But this Arthur wouldn't be caught dead doing those things now."

"Of course not! Because I know what it takes to be the one with Sophia Kingsley!" He dropped his arms and stepped toward her. "Please, Sophia, I am just trying to help. I love you. I am worried about you."

"And helping me is this? Insulting me?"

"I don't mean to insult you, just to remind you." He grabbed for her hand but she pulled away.

"I don't need to be reminded of anything, Arthur."

"Sophia, think of how it looks, of what harm you're doing to your reputation. Of what you're doing to me."

Her stomach twisted in knots at his words. "What I'm doing to you?" she asked in disbelief.

"You don't think this has any effect on me? Of course it does. You're changing the way you dress, the way you talk, the parties you throw, the décor in your house. Having Sophia Kingsley by my side means something to me, but it's as if I don't even exist. What you do doesn't just impact you. It impacts me, my life. Am I not important? Now you dismiss me and don't even care enough that I'm standing right next to you when you do it."

She shook her head. "With Millie? Arthur, that's not what I meant...."

"Then what did you mean? Now that there are no prying eyes around."

She swallowed and stared back at him, frozen.

He waited and when she didn't reply, he nodded slowly. "I see. Well I suppose that it's all for the best anyway if this is what it's going to be like."

"What do you mean?" she asked, angrily.

"I've worked really hard to get where I am, Sophia. I thought you would fit in well with the life I want, but you don't—not like this."

She took a deep breath. "Then perhaps you should not be associated with me."

Her words caused him to realize what he'd said and how it sounded. "That's not what I meant. Sophia."

She shook her head. "That's what I meant, Arthur. You should leave."

His heart pounded and he swallowed hard. He spun toward

Henry and George whose faces were twisted in the same pained expression. When he turned back, Sophia was walking away from him and out of the room.

He started after her, calling her name, but George jumped up and caught his arm.

"Arthur, I think you better do what the lady asked."

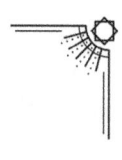

CHAPTER
TWENTY-SEVEN

"She doesn't want to hear from you," George was saying on the phone. "Arthur, you need to stop calling here."

Two weeks passed after he said those dreadful things to Sophia and while at first he imagined she would call when she was ready to talk, she hadn't. He spent every night thereafter tossing the interaction around in his mind, berating himself for agreeing to leave. He'd tried calling every day since.

"George, please, I just need to speak to her," he begged.

"She doesn't want to speak to you," George replied and then hung up the phone.

Arthur groaned and slammed his receiver down. It was eight o'clock and he was still at his office unable to leave because he knew he'd be met with his empty and hollow house.

Just then, the door chime rang and Arthur looked up in some vain hope it was her.

"Arthur, I have been trying to contact you," Henry said as he walked to Arthur's desk.

Arthur hung his head like a child being punished. "Yes. I know."

"Well then you should return my calls. I have been worried." Henry smiled but his tone was not light. He took the chair in front of Arthur's desk.

"I need to talk to her," Arthur demanded.

"You know I have no power over that, Arthur. Perhaps you should give her some time to heal."

Arthur sneered. "Time to forget me."

"You assume you mean so little to her. To us all," Henry countered.

"Don't I?"

"Of course not," Henry replied, offended.

"Why are you here?"

"As I said, I wanted to see how you were."

"How is she?"

Henry sighed. "Come Arthur, let's not talk about her."

"You've come here to tell me we cannot speak of her?' Arthur's eyes locked his.

Henry broke first. "Of course not. But I have no information to share. You know I care for you both. This is not my place."

"I suppose George gave you permission to come, but revoked your right to provide me any information?"

Henry looked down at his hands and attempted to hold his anger. "I am here of my own doing and speaking for myself."

Arthur laughed. "Please do not treat me like a sap, Henry. You may say that you are all friends but Sophia and George dictate each and every one of you. You told me not to be so afraid of him but all you act in is fear."

Henry nodded and then stood to leave. "I am glad to see that you are alive. Please ring me and we shall meet for drinks, or dinner. Whatever you like. I will be around."

***

By the following week, Arthur still had not heard from Sophia and George stopped answering the phone. Henry's visit remained in his mind but he tossed it away, remembering how he refused to speak of Sophia. His habit of chewing the ends of pencils returned until he had shredded the erasers of all of them with his teeth. His desk looked like a pencil graveyard with little pink fragments littered about.

"Have you heard from her?" William stood over Arthur's desk, looking down at him. He didn't mention the pencil massacre.

Arthur pulled the pencil from his mouth and looked up, noticing eraser pieces stuck to his gums. He stuck his tongue down and attempted to clear them out, then wiped his tongue with his handkerchief. William averted his gaze, pretending that he didn't notice Arthur's behavior.

"No," was all Arthur replied, but then tried to sound more confident. "I'm sure that she needs some space."

He kept lying to himself in an attempt at self-comfort, but when he heard it out loud, it became all the more obvious that he didn't believe it. He swallowed and looked down at his desk.

William scrunched up his eyes and twisted his mouth in an expression of comfort and concern. He hadn't witnessed Arthur in such a state for some time.

William tapped on his desk before he walked away. "I'm sure you're correct."

In all the time William had known Arthur, he'd never seen him as elated as when he was with Sophia. He also had never seen him so devastated as when he perceived her rejection. The first time they met, Sophia invited William and Betty to dinner at her estate before they left for Europe as a celebration of their engagement. William liked her just fine, but he sensed that something was askew, though he'd never been able to say what.

The uneasiness he felt about her had little to do with the way she interacted with Arthur and more to do with Sophia herself. It was clear that she adored him, but she seemed uneasy in herself, like she was trying hard to stay put together. William tried to convince himself that she was nervous around new people, that she wanted to make a good impression. And he said as much when Arthur later asked him what he thought.

They stood outside overlooking the estate grounds, smoking cigars and sipping on whiskey. Arthur looked pleased when William shared that Sophia was just as sophisticated as Arthur described, and even more so when William suggested that Arthur might make her nervous. He saw then how much Arthur savored the words and felt a twinge of guilt hit him in the gut for not being fully honest. If he had been, he would've told Arthur that Sophia seemed to be forcing something.

William broke his attention from the past with Arthur's voice. "Or perhaps she has realized that what she really wanted all along was George. Strong, rich, accommodating, George."

William sat silent trying to craft a response. He had to admit that he believed it long before Arthur spoke it. Perhaps not that Sophia wanted George, but that Sophia could not help her destiny in ending up with him.

"I don't believe she loves him, Arthur." It was the most honest response he could give that might still provide comfort.

"Perhaps not, but she may learn to. She never loved me anyway."

"How can you say such a thing?"

Arthur shook his head. "I told her several times of my feelings, and I did not realize until later that she never said the same in return."

"Do you ever consider that she was protecting you?"

"Protecting me?" Arthur asked, confused.

"You have always been convinced of George and Sophia, though never enough to keep yourself from her. You told me once that they appeared more as brother and sister than lovers. But there was still something cautioning you, despite this assertion."

Arthur nodded. "Yes."

"If she was always a little removed from you but at the same time appeared not so attached to George, perhaps it wasn't that she loved George over you, but rather that she knew she had to eventually choose him over you."

Arthur nodded. William had suggested it before. "Because she was already promised to him."

"Perhaps," William suggested.

"I am not sure that makes me feel any less wounded."

"No, certainly not," William agreed.

"She should have sooner left me rejected the first night we met than catch me only to release me."

"I cannot disagree with you, Arthur. Sophia's behavior was self-ish and cruel. Using you and disregarding your intentions and feelings for her."

William's suggestion had no errors of judgment. Still so, nothing quelled Arthur's desperation to somehow change her mind.

***

After one month passed, Arthur wrote to Sophia. His despair and worry became too intense to ignore. With no response to his letters, he drove to her estate to find the front gates closed and locked. Arthur stood in front of the gate, looked down her driveway, and wondered what might be happening inside or if she had fled to Africa as she suggested she might.

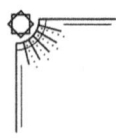

A few weeks after he stood in front of her gates in desperation and resigned himself to the fact that maybe it had all been a dream, a long shot by the poor boy turned rich businessman, his agony again grew. This time it was unbearable and he couldn't sleep. He tossed and turned in a cold sweat, thrashing his blankets around on his bed, and found himself only able to fall half-asleep, in the space where he was unsure if he was dreaming or it was reality. Sometimes he would see Sophia and attempt to speak to her, to ask her where she had gone and then he'd fully regain consciousness again only to stare at the ceiling for the rest of the night.

William never mentioned his partner's decline in productivity. Never lectured him about coming in late or not coming into work at all. If William had been angry at Arthur, he never let on that it was there. In fact, William became so caring that if he'd been able to pull himself out of his own self-pity, Arthur would've been mortified at how far he'd let himself fall. Perhaps it was Arthur's way of getting the care he so desperately longed for since his mother passed, or perhaps it was deep grief, but William proved himself to be the better friend between them.

Two weeks into sleep deprivation, Arthur's desperation took him to a place he never thought possible. He stood on the front stoop and scanned the directory beside the door. He traced his finger under the name and next to it read: *204*. Arthur searched for an intercom system like the one he'd had in his and William's apartment but there wasn't one. The door flung open and an old man in a beige suit stepped out. Arthur caught the door and let himself inside, the old man not even noticing.

The door opened to a hallway on his right and a stairway in front of him. Arthur proceeded up the narrow stairs; the sounds around him were nostalgically familiar—screams of children's laughter, deep voices of their scolding fathers, mothers singing. The smells of different spices wafted around him and reminded him of sitting in his mother's kitchen, fascinated at her talent for making a pleasant dinner out of nothing.

For a moment, he felt like a teenager again, like he might unlock the small apartment door to find his parents sitting behind it, his father engrossed in reading the newspaper and his mother flitting about the room, oblivious to the fact that her husband wasn't listening to her. She'd see Arthur come in and run to him, grab his head, and kiss him on the forehead, delighted to have him home from school. She acted as if she hadn't seen him in months every day when he walked through the door. He would never again know that pure kind of love.

Instead, Arthur found himself in front of a dingy door marked 204. He pulled the door knocker out and then tapped it into the door. He heard a rustle inside and wondered if he interrupted a family dinner but his selfish motives overtook his decency to care. Arthur straightened his tie nervously as he waited.

When the door swung open, Arthur was surprised to find the man alone behind it.

"Arthur Malcolm, you can't imagine how surprised I am to see you." James Calwell's round eyes stared back at Arthur, gleaming with hope. Arthur sighed.

"May I come in?" he asked.

James pulled the door open wider and gestured for Arthur to enter. Arthur stepped inside as James closed the door behind him. He removed his hat and for a moment, was self-conscious of how his hair might look under it, and put it back on immediately. He hadn't been taking care of himself well and up until that moment, hadn't thought to mind.

He was aware that he was standing in the living room of a journalist who was hungry for a story. He thought about excusing himself before saying anything, worried that James might write a gossip piece out of all of it, but he pushed ahead, determined to find some answers. James was always lurking around Sophia and he was the best chance Arthur had left.

"Would you like to sit?" James asked, motioning Arthur toward the small table that sat next to the living room. Behind it was a modest kitchen, much like the one Arthur had grown accustomed to when it was just him and his mother. He shook his head.

"No, that's alright. I apologize for interrupting." He paused and looked around the apartment. There didn't seem to be anyone around. As annoying as he considered James to be, he was still surprised to find him alone without a family.

James laughed. "You are doing no such thing." James' politeness took Arthur off guard; usually he was intrusive and pushy.

"I am curious what you are doing standing in my living room."

James's voice snapped Arthur back to the moment. He realized he hadn't explained his perplexing presence in the home of a man who he normally seemed to detest.

"Right. Well James, this may seem odd given," Arthur considered his phrasing, "our respective relationship to the Kingsley's, but I have a favor to ask of you."

James nodded and appeared confused.

"I was wondering if you might have any recent information on... her." Arthur heard himself ask the irksome man for the information he should've known. The information he had been privy to for months.

"Recent information?"

Arthur wasn't sure if James was sincerely asking or fishing, but he risked it anyway. "Her whereabouts. Anything, really."

James stood for a moment looking expressionless at Arthur. "I'm not entirely sure what you're asking me, Arthur."

Arthur's annoyance returned, but more so toward the lack of information than at the man who didn't seem to have it.

Arthur tried again, realizing he might need to be more direct, something he was hoping he didn't have to be. He told himself it was because he didn't want to give James too much information, but he knew it was more likely that he felt ashamed of himself.

"I haven't heard from Miss Kingsley in quite some time and I've grown worried about her. I was hoping you might know if she is alright." Referring to her so formally made the distance between them feel larger.

James nodded and wiped sweat from his forehead; even though it wasn't particularly warm in the room, the man always seemed to be sweating. Arthur took a deep breath and reminded himself that despite his advancement in class, he'd come from a place much like James and probably had more in common with him than with Sophia.

"Let me get you some tea. Please sit."

This time, Arthur obliged. He had wanted to talk about Sophia for months; her name was always on the tip of his tongue, but he was afraid that if he let it out, she might break loose and never return.

James filled the kettle and lit the stove, then placed the kettle atop the burner.

Arthur glanced around the apartment. It was quaint and bare; there were simple curtains on the windows that hadn't been cleaned any time recently, and apart from the sofa, coffee table, dining table, and two dining chairs, there was no more furniture in the place. The walls hung bare; no photographs giving clues to James's life, no painting representing his taste in art. James could likely disappear and not leave any indication of himself behind. The kitchen was also sparse and Arthur noticed some splatters on the backsplash that hardened and dried with time.

"Not much. I'm sure you're used to a little different," James apologized as he took a seat at the table.

Arthur waved him off. "You know my history."

James nodded, appreciating Arthur's civility.

Curiously, Arthur no longer felt the anxiety to have his questions answered. Sitting at the table with James had quelled something inside him for no obvious reason at all and he was content with the silence. Conceivably, the chance to say some things out loud had relieved the pressure that was building inside him.

James broke the silence. "Arthur, I'm afraid I may not have the information you want."

Arthur was reminded of the time he was turned down for the first job he applied to after his father had died. Before working in the factory, Arthur took his shot at the railroad. He thought that the long days inside might kill him and so working on the railroad was more appealing. But when he went in to speak to the foreman, the man glanced him up and down and then looked back up at Arthur. The pause between that and when the man succinctly said "no," was heavy with rejection. Back then, he had been rejected because he was too weak, but it all worked out in his favor. He met William's father, then met William, and was standing where he was because of that man's no. But now, he couldn't fathom how any bad news about Sophia would ever lead to a positive outcome.

"Any information is what I would like."

The kettle whistled and James rose to fetch them both tea. As he handed Arthur's to him, Arthur lifted the cup to his nose and let the peppermint steam fill his nostrils. He never thought he'd be grateful for James but he was sitting drinking his favorite tea with a man he'd tried to avoid, needing something from him that he never thought he'd need. Arthur's life had been like that—ending up where he'd never thought he'd be.

"I haven't seen her." James set down his cup and waved his hands, a gesture that Arthur was familiar with when James was trying to signal innocence. "And I can't say I know exactly *where* she is now, but I do know that one of my colleagues spotted her about a month ago."

Arthur set down his cup and asked, "Saw her where?"

"At her estate," James replied straightforwardly. "She was with George Carlyle."

Arthur waited for his stomach to drop but it simply gurgled a bit to accept the hot tea, and then stopped. He glanced around the ceiling and noticed the lights were covered in dust.

"And that's it? Your colleague saw her at her estate with George?"

"Well, I don't know why this would matter to you but I might as well tell you all I know. She recently sold him some property she owned upstate. Wasn't a public record, but as you know, well, I have ways to get my information."

"She sold some property to George? Why?"

James shrugged. "Who knows. Property exchanges hands all the time. She certainly doesn't need the money so my best guess is she wasn't going to do anything with it and he wanted to develop it. Like I said, I don't know why it would matter but it's the only other information I have."

Arthur nodded and took another sip of his tea. He knew it likely meant nothing, but it was the kind of nothing he'd have known about months before.

When Arthur finished his tea, after changing the subject away from Sophia and onto business and real estate, he excused himself for the evening. James walked him to the door. Arthur was again struck by his manners. He had come to think of James as something other than human—a pest—and this visit reminded him that there was a person behind everyone he encountered, like them or not.

Arthur pulled open the door then turned around and thanked James for the tea and the conversation. Just before James closed the door behind him, Arthur stopped it with his hand. Not expecting it, James jumped a bit.

"You were expecting I'd come at some point, weren't you?" Arthur asked, realizing that James knew everything that could be known about him, especially since he had been getting closer to Sophia. So it was probable that he also knew Arthur hadn't been with Sophia and maybe even saw him visit her estate looking for her. Arthur felt foolish for a fleeting moment.

James nodded. "Not expecting, but considered that it might be a possibility. Sophia has a tendency to leave an impact on people," he said, as if he'd been in Arthur's shoes at some point lifetimes before.

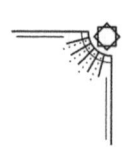

CHAPTER
TWENTY-NINE

On a morning long after the engagement party, Arthur arrived to work earlier than anyone else. The mail had been delivered after the office already closed the previous day and the postman stuffed it in the slot. Arthur found a pile of it at his feet when he pulled open the door.

Arthur set the mail on his desk, then made his way to the office kitchen to prepare tea. As the weather warmed and winter gave way to spring, Arthur made his usual switch from peppermint to green tea. He boiled the water in the kettle and poured it over his tea, the leaves swirled in the water and then floated to the top. Arthur stirred and they again sunk to the bottom and made their way back up. Again and again they played this game until Arthur was satisfied with the shade of brownish-green the water had become and removed the leaves to discard them.

He carried his warm mug to his desk and sat down. For a moment, he leaned back in his chair and looked up at the ceiling. For an inexplicable reason, he sat up abruptly and leafed through the mail as if he knew something in the stack lay waiting for him. In the middle of the pile was a thick envelope—a familiar envelope with familiar lettering. It was addressed to *The Offices of Malcolm and Henly*. Arthur sat upright in his chair and stared down at it; the formality and impersonal nature of it slammed into him.

He considered not opening it, considered throwing it into the trash can and ignoring it, like she ignored him. His curiosity won and he reached for his letter opener. This time, unlike the last, he used less care in tearing open the flap. He set the letter opener aside and pulled the yellow cardstock from the envelope.

You are invited
Please join us for the Kingsley Annual Spring Party
10th of May, 1924

Arthur fixated on the bright blue letters and wondered how Sophia had determined to invite him. How she decided that William and he were at the same level of importance to her.

He pushed the invitation aside and went through the rest of the mail. But nothing was as emotionally evocative as the invitation, so despite his wishes, his mind drifted back to it perched at the edge of his desk.

He reached for it again and stood up, carrying it to William's desk. He tucked the cardstock back into the envelope and placed it carefully on top of William's calendar. He knew that William would understand why Arthur wasn't in the office.

At the moment that Arthur shot up in his seat to dig through the mail, Sophia had taken her first sip of tea that morning. When he discovered the envelope, she sat down in her chaise on her balcony. The cool winter weather lingered in the morning but the sun warmed her skin and she wrapped a blanket around herself. As Arthur ripped open the envelope and pulled the invitation from its slumber, she saw something sticking out from the chaise under her. In the instant that Arthur read the taciturn words and felt the weight of them crush him, she reached under and fetched whatever it was. And when Arthur decided that the day of her party was the day he would die, Sophia held *Romeo and Juliet* in her hands and remembered the night she met Arthur.

She had been searching for the book for quite some time and had not yet procured another copy because she was hopeful that this one would be found. It was strange how she searched everywhere, was certain that her staff searched everywhere, and yet it was so obviously present underneath her. She frowned. *They must have missed it, but how?* She unconvincingly concluded that someone borrowed it and felt too ashamed to admit it. She turned it over in her hands; the last time she had seen the book was the day after she met Arthur.

Sophia reached her hands to her hair and recalled the Sophia she had been that night—lost, alone, bored. She tugged at the ends of her shorter hair and felt pity for that woman, the woman she was before Arthur changed everything.

Violet stepped onto the patio. "Excuse me, miss? It is time for the meeting about the Spring party."

Sophia set the book on the table next to the one Dr. Narudo sent and looked at them lying side by side. Before and after.

Sophia Kingsley was many things, but she was not an uncaring or cold person. Arthur knew that, which is why Arthur remembered her fondly as he set down the whiskey bottle in front of his mother's headstone. His pants were damp from sitting on the ground in the morning dew that hadn't yet evaporated. He knew the soil might stain them. At that moment, he didn't care so much that they might be ruined. He reasoned he didn't need pants wherever he'd end up anyway.

"I miss you every day," Arthur was speaking to his mother out loud, "it seems impossible that you have been gone for so long. I think you'd be proud of me. I hope you would be." The warmth from the liquor creeped into his cheeks flushing them red. "If you can see me, I hope you are. I hope you are too." He gestured toward his father's headstone.

Arthur stood up and grabbed the whiskey from the ground. He didn't intend to leave the half-drunk bottle in a sacred place; even a man on the edge of death should have the decency to protect what he cares most about, he presumed. Arthur brushed off his pants as best he could before turning to leave. Once more, he turned back to his parents' graves, lifted the bottle, and took a hefty swig.

William arrived at work and found the invitation waiting for him on his desk. Instead of taking off his coat and settling in for the day, letting Arthur grieve on his own, William turned and immediately left for Arthur's house. When he found it empty, he tried the cemetery. He noticed that dirt around Mr. and Mrs. Malcom's graves had been disrupted, but that was the only sign of Arthur. William stood and looked at the engravings on the headstones for a moment and remembered what it was like when Arthur lost his mother. He thought he might descend into madness and never come back. William had taken it upon himself to care for Arthur after that; without ever explicitly saying it, he knew they considered each other like brothers.

William inhaled deeply and then watched as the warm air escaped from his lungs into the early spring air. William only knew to search for him at his house and at the cemetery. He was lost at where else he could be.

***

Sophia wanted to astonish everyone when they arrived at the spring ball to find the estate adorned with all the colors of the spectrum. Purple and red streamers, silver and gold glitter, yellows, greens, blues celebrating the arrival of spring. The arrival of new life after the slumber of winter. She spun around the empty ballroom imagining the music and laughter of her guests. She looked forward to finally enjoying one of her annual parties.

Sophia stopped spinning the moment that Arthur walked out of the cemetery and dropped the whiskey bottle outside the entrance gate. William found the bottle on his way out and knew that Arthur was somewhere out there, drunk and alone, grieving the loss of something he didn't understand.

Arthur, already drunk, stumbled his way to the laundromat and through open the door, then made his way to the back and pushed open the second. Landing in the small room, he saw the broken laundry cart was still there. He knocked on the door at the back and to his gratitude, it swung open, the same large man behind it.

"Arthur Malcolm," the man bellowed, catching Arthur off guard that he remembered his name.

The man stepped aside to let Arthur through. He stumbled down the stairs, grabbing at the hand railings to keep himself from falling. When he made it to the bottom, he pushed apart the dark curtains and let himself into the bar.

There were already plenty of men there, likely in the same state as Arthur, and the music blasted just the same as it had the first time he'd been. The only difference between that time and this one, outside of Arthur's will to live, was the daylight that still shone outside.

Arthur slid into the booth where he'd sat with George and Henry. He tried to push away the memories, the time before he had known Sophia returned his feelings and sat feeling insecure and unsure of himself. He wanted there to be a before Sophia, but never an after.

Ginny was there and she glided over to him with her same drawn out voice.

"Hi Arthur," she greeted him, unfazed by his inebriation and distress, "what would you like, honey?"

He squinted toward her, trying to bring her into focus. "Ginny," he slurred and she smiled, unaffected. "Whiskey please."

"Sure thing," she replied and fluttered off to fetch his drink. The music was loud and between that and his drunkenness, he managed to drown out most of his thoughts. Ginny returned faster than he thought possible, though his sense of time was warped in his state, and set his drink down in front of him.

"Anything else?" she asked, not even bothering to feel concern that he was drinking alone on a Wednesday afternoon.

"Is Margaret here?" he asked and even in his intoxication knew it was a bad question.

But Ginny shook her head. "No, honey, she only works Thursday, Friday, and Saturday."

"Oh," he said and picked up his drink to take a sip, "thanks for the hooch."

Ginny winked. "Of course, doll." She started to walk away but Arthur stopped her.

"Ginny," he called after her sparkling silver dress, "wait."

Ginny spun around on her heels and returned. "Yes?"

"Would you like to have a drink with me?"

"We can't drink while we're working, honey," she explained, but then, upon seeing his despair motioned to another waitress to watch her tables for her and sat down. "But I can sit with you if you'd like." She smiled and he didn't care whose warmth it was next to him.

***

The bell to the office rang and William looked up, hoping to see Arthur. Instead, Henry walked in, also hoping to find Arthur sitting at his desk.

"Henry?" William rose and greeted him, concerned that he might bring bad news.

"Hi William, I'm looking for Arthur. Do you know where I might find him?"

William shook his head. "I was going to ask you the same thing." William held up Sophia's invitation and Henry nodded.

"I got mine too. I was hoping maybe Arthur's hadn't come yet. I wanted to check on him."

"That's big of you." William replied.

Brief annoyance passed over Henry's face. "I am sure Arthur spun many tales of betrayal. I would engage in telling you of evidence otherwise, but at the moment, I have bigger concerns."

"Do you have any idea where he is?"

"I might." Henry held up his keys as William began to search for his. "I can drive."

William grabbed his coat and rushed out the door, shouting to Betty on their way out. The men climbed into Henry's car and he turned around in the middle of the street, too impatient to do it properly.

"I think he went to *Seventh*," Henry said as they whizzed through the streets, cutting corners and swerving past unsuspecting drivers. William nodded; he'd heard Arthur speak of it but had never been.

They pulled up and parked right in front of the building, scrambling out of the car as fast as they could. Henry had seen how quickly and easily Arthur had been persuaded to go into the back room with Margaret and feared he might make the same mistake again.

Henry practically shoved his way through the bouncer and in seeing their haste, he stepped aside and let them by without giving William a hard time. William was overwhelmed as he pushed through the curtains and tried to keep his focus on finding Arthur. He couldn't imagine why Arthur would ever have wanted to spend his time in such a place.

Henry spotted Arthur in the booth, Mary sitting on his lap and Ginny by his side. They were all laughing and Arthur was visibly drunker than William had ever seen him before.

William shot Henry a look of concern and the men stepped toward him in tandem. Arthur didn't see them approach because he was fixated on Mary.

"Arthur," William called him to attention and he turned his face away from Mary, who was playing with his hair.

"William!" he said, muttering the words with less enunciation than he thought. "Have you met Mary and Ginny?"

William shook his head and didn't respond. Henry, in his stern voice, looked at the women.

"Get up," he ordered them. Ginny wiped the smile off her face and Mary slid off Arthur's lap, a hint of fear across her face. "Beat it," he commanded. With that, both women stood and left them.

Arthur whined, "Come on, Henry." He held out his hand in the direction the women had walked.

Henry glanced back to William. "Would you mind getting him some water?"

William made his way to the bar where Lawrence was working. Henry sat down opposite Arthur and leaned on the table.

"Henry, why are you being so...?" Arthur slurred and stopped, not realizing he hadn't finished.

Henry shook his head. "Arthur, what are you doing?"

"I was trying to get bent," he replied.

"Well you've accomplished that I think," Henry replied dryly.

"Pfft." Arthur waved him off.

"Didn't you learn your lesson with these broads last time?" Henry scolded.

"Everything's jake now!"

Henry stood and walked over to Arthur's side of the booth, then leaned toward Arthur, placing his hand on the back of the seat, bringing his face closer.

"Arthur, it's time to go."

"You disappear and then come in here and try to tell me what to do?"

Henry stood and straightened his back then rubbed his face in contemplation.

"What are you doing here, Arthur, really?"

Arthur smiled. "Well Margaret isn't working, so I thought..." He leaned to look around Henry and in the direction of Mary.

"What? You came here to fuck her and think that it's going to solve your problems?"

Arthur snapped his face back to Henry; he had never heard him use such language before and it was unsettling. The whiskey turned in his stomach and he lurched forward and threw up. The brown liquid splattered across the floor and onto Henry's shoes.

"Shit." Henry looked down and then over to William who had seen the whole thing. Ginny came rushing over and snapped her fingers, signaling for a mop.

"You fellas oughta go," she directed to Henry plainly.

Henry nodded. "Come on, Arthur, let's go." Arthur stood and Henry caught him, hoping he didn't decide to throw up again. William joined, leaving the glass of water sweating on the bar.

The two men helped Arthur up the stairs and he quickly flipped back and forth between grateful to see them and angry that they had taken him away. When they made it to the top and then out, the daylight hit Arthur in the face and he doubled over, putting his hands on his thighs.

"You alright?" William asked as he placed his hand on Arthur's back.

"No," Arthur replied, focused on the concrete underneath him. "No," he said again, this time sadder and not referring to his intoxication. "I don't," he slurred, "I don't... I'm all balled up." William attempted to bring him upright.

"Let's get in Henry's car. We're going to take you home," William instructed, trying to get Arthur's mind away from what was plaguing him.

William opened the door, Arthur climbed in willingly, and immediately passed out in the back seat.

THIRTY

Arthur awoke to a strange ceiling. White ornamental tiles floated above him and he clutched his head as it pounded in pain. He rolled over to his side and was in a strange room, in a strange bed. The sky outside the large window was dark; Arthur had no concept of time. He looked down and noticed he was still fully clothed, save for his shoes which were strewn haphazardly on the floor. For a moment, he worried he had gone home with one of the women, but then realized that the room was far too nice to ever be one of theirs.

He sat up, which briefly made his headache better, then it all came rushing back twofold. He closed his eyes and tried to remember. He recalled vomiting and looking down at a man's shoes.

Eventually, he decided to exit the room in hopes that he would find someone friendly on the other side. He pulled open the door and it led to a long hallway. The hall was plainly decorated and he ruled out George's house. He walked down the hall one direction and upon reaching a dead end, turned around and tried the other. He found a staircase and descended, nervous for what he might find.

The house was quiet and no one seemed to be awake, so he tiptoed down and then explored the floor below, which he determined was the ground floor. He passed by a bathroom and then a sitting room, the door slightly ajar. He stopped when he noticed a flicker of light.

He carefully opened the door but it creaked and the man sitting in the chair next to the fireplace popped up his head. Henry smiled at Arthur and put down his book.

"Arthur, glad to see you alive," Henry teased.

Arthur rubbed his head again trying to rid himself of the headache. "Henry," he said as he walked into the room, "is this your house?"

"It is. We brought you here so that someone could watch you."

"We?" Arthur asked, concerned.

"Me and William."

"Oh, I don't really remember."

"I'm not surprised to hear that, you were half seas over when we found you."

"At *Seventh*?" Arthur asked, half hoping the answer was yes.

Henry nodded and Arthur continued trying to get his bearings. "What time is it?"

"About ten. You've been asleep a while," Henry replied.

"I think I should go home and go back to bed."

"Stay here," Henry offered, "it's late and you have a bed to sleep in upstairs."

"Thanks," Arthur said, knowing he needed to be horizontal again as soon as possible. And then before he left the room he turned back toward Henry. "And thank you for saving me from myself."

Henry smiled.

When Arthur awoke in the morning, he was pleased to find his headache mostly gone. He attempted to ignore the shame of having William and Henry find him in self-destructive ruin, and hoped that they wouldn't share it with anyone else. Despite everything that happened, Arthur still wanted those around him to have a certain opinion of him, one that was carefully constructed by him.

Henry was just as gracious as he'd been the night before when he found him at the dining table. He insisted Arthur sit and eat before he left. Henry's maid brought him biscuits with jam and coffee, which Arthur willingly accepted, recognizing how hungry he had been without eating for over 24 hours.

"I hope I didn't make too much of a fool of myself." He shook his head between sips of coffee.

Henry set his newspaper down. "We've all been there, I'm sure. I've just been worried about you."

"I couldn't bring myself to be anywhere near her. Near you felt like near her," Arthur explained to the question Henry had not asked.

Henry smiled. "I know. I cannot say that I was not miffed, but I do understand."

"How are you? How is everyone?"

Henry let his lame attempt at selflessness pass. "Everyone is well."

"You still won't speak of her."

"Sophia is well."

Arthur hadn't heard anyone say her name in weeks; it hit him hard in the chest. At least when he was alone, or with William, or anyone disconnected from her, he could pretend she wasn't real, like she wasn't out there living a life without him. But now he was one connection away from her, hearing her name from someone who still spoke it to her.

"I'm sorry for what happened."

Arthur shook his head. "You had no part in it."

"I know, but I wish there was a way to make it alright again. We really did enjoy having you around."

"I don't know so much that everyone felt that way."

"I think you have the wrong idea about him," Henry said but was interrupted by his maid who came to refill his coffee and ask them if they wanted more breakfast. Henry shook his head and thanked her.

"I better get going; I'm sure William has been left behind the eight ball because of me," Arthur said, not wanting to hear any further defenses of George.

"We'll see you at the party?" Henry asked cautiously.

Arthur stopped mid-stand. "I think that remains to be seen."

"Well I know that we would love to have you there, just know that."

"You've been a good friend to me, Henry," Arthur replied, almost like it was a goodbye.

***

Somehow, Arthur managed to fake the following weeks quite well; he bathed, dressed, went to work, ate his lunch and took business meetings and phone calls as if he was fine. William watched his friend hollow out day by day until nothing but an empty shell of Arthur remained behind his desk.

The day that seemed to completely suck the life out of him was the day they had to meet for the Carlyle account. William suggested that Arthur stay back while he met George for lunch at the *1913 Room*, but Arthur knew that it was bad business manners to skirt a meeting. Besides, as much as he didn't want to see George, he wanted to face him so that he knew he hadn't beaten him in every way possible.

William and Arthur arrived well before George; William thought that it would be better for Arthur to get situated and stake his claim to his seat so that he felt as stable as possible. He even allowed Arthur to have one whiskey to calm his nerves. In anticipation of the tension he'd have to manage, William allowed himself to have one too.

When George arrived, he walked to the table with self-assurance and poise, and when he greeted the men, it was almost as if he'd wiped away their entire history, leaving only the remnants of business. Arthur did his best not to flinch when George shook his hand and looked him in the eye.

Most of the lunch went as any business meeting would; cold, calculated, and formal. William thought that they might get away with walking away unscathed, but as they were drinking their after lunch coffee, George unintentionally sparked a fire.

He had been talking about the final details of one particularly challenging account. Without thinking he casually remarked, "It was nice to be away from this for a while and let someone else manage it while I was in Africa." He sat back. "But the stress was back as soon as I stepped on American soil."

William swallowed and glanced toward Arthur who looked like he'd been struck. He shifted in his seat, trying to think of something to say to steer the conversation away, but the crash was already inevitable.

His voice heavy, Arthur commented in return, "Africa? I wasn't aware that the trip had been taken."

George only flinched for a moment, perhaps realizing his folly. "Yes."

"Henry didn't say anything about it," Arthur commented, trying to somehow hurt George with his continued connection to Henry.

"Henry wasn't there."

Arthur stopped, realizing that if Henry didn't go, that surely meant Trixie didn't go, which certainly meant Elizabeth and Benjamin weren't there either. His stomach twisted as he thought about the two of them alone, away from the world.

William cleared his throat. "Alright gentlemen, I think that it's time to wrap up this meeting." But neither of the other men moved.

George's expression didn't change. He grabbed the files he had laid on the table and gathered them together calmly.

Arthur didn't move but muttered loud enough for them to hear, "I thought we had become friends, I see now that was never true, that you were always against me."

In a cool voice George replied, "You've always been your own problem, Arthur."

At hearing George's arrogance, Arthur could no longer contain what little composure he had left. He leapt from his chair, almost knocking it over on his way up. William grabbed at the back of his jacket and attempted to pull him down, but when he wouldn't budge, William stood and positioned himself as close to in between the men as he could manage.

"George, I apologize. As always, it is nice to do business with you, unfortunately, we have to leave now." William knew his attempts at civility were futile and he cursed Arthur for risking their business over his own emotionality.

George nodded, still unruffled by Arthur's display. "Same to you, William. I hope to see you both at the Spring party." George placed the file back into his briefcase and walked away.

Arthur slumped back into his seat; In that moment all that he had left, call it dignity, will, or hope, drained out of him and he sat, hollowed out and ashamed.

CHAPTER
THIRTY-ONE

"Arthur, I think it's the bee's knees you decided to join us." Betty smiled as she messed with her hair in the rearview mirror. Arthur sat in the back seat wishing he could jump from the car. She continued on, staring at herself in the rearview, clearly nervous to socialize with powerful people at the Spring Ball. "I think it will be good for you. Truly I do. Show her how spiffy you look and give her the icy mitt."

They all knew it was a lie. He had lost weight, his eyes were tired and lifeless and when he'd put on his tuxedo, he thought that it was appropriate that he looked like he was going to his own funeral.

"Baby," William said with warning in his voice, "let's lay off him, huh?"

She raised her eyebrows in a protest Arthur couldn't see and William reached over to grab her hand, which made Arthur's stomach turn all the more. He had been watching the two of them frolic in engaged bliss for months but wasn't so selfish that he'd tried to dampen it. He just secretly wished everyone was miserable so that he could drown in his own self-pity without anyone trying to lift his spirits.

He opted to go to the Spring Ball for several reasons. A secondary one was to see Henry, Elizabeth, and Trixie. He hoped he might ease their minds for later, when they'd question what they could've done. He also wanted to see Sophia; he had been holding onto the hope that he would see her, once again recognize her madness, and realize he was better off without her. He knew in his heart that wasn't true and he had been wrestling his shame about his cruelty toward her.

The flowers along the drive were starting to bloom. Once Arthur walked into the party, he would round out the year, having attended every one of her annual balls. He thought that it was fitting for his end to come in such a tidy way.

William pulled up the drive and turned off the car, giving the keys to the valet, who would park it among the masses of others. Plenty of cars were left there overnight; drunk men and women were sold on taking taxis that waited at the end of the drive, knowing that the Kingsley balls were a sure place to make money.

"Are you sure you want to do this?" William asked as the valet got into his car. Arthur stood next to William on the driver's side and nodded. When the car pulled away, there was nothing left between him and his fate.

Betty tried to contain her excitement, but as a nineteen year old girl from humble beginnings, she had a right to be thrilled. Arthur recalled his excitement and nervousness the first night he walked through the front doors. How he could feel her presence from across the room and even then, wanted nothing more than to be close to her.

They made their way through the entrance and were greeted by her staff with a glass of champagne. Thomas was there directing and he nodded at Arthur as he passed. The house was decorated in bright colors; it was not the sophisticated palette Arthur was used to, instead it reflected Sophia's mood the last night he had seen her—free, wild, and energetic.

"Wow," Betty muttered as she stared up at the elaborate decorations that hung high from the ceiling. "How do you think they got those up there?" she asked in awe but William was too busy eyeing the mountain of food at one end of the ballroom.

Arthur sucked in his breath and wondered why he had chosen to join them, wondered if he selected his end correctly. William didn't let him drive because he assumed Arthur would try to flee without them in a fit of anger. He didn't know Arthur never intended on leaving.

When they entered the ballroom, Arthur felt someone tug on the back of his jacket like Sophia had done at her second party; his heart jumped but when he turned around Trixie faced him with a big smile.

"Arthur!" she said and wrapped her arms around him. She had never hugged him before and he stiffened into it. She released him and grabbed a glass of champagne from a passing tray.

"Oh I'm so glad to see you, Arthur." She tilted her head and he swallowed; he knew that the pity would come from all ends.

"You too, Trixie. I've missed all of you."

"We've missed you so much, really. You have no idea how high-hat this crowd can get without you."

He frowned, unsure of what she meant. Elizabeth saw Trixie talking to Arthur and joined, expressing the same sentiments. Arthur responded politely, trying to be friendly but feeling like an outsider from their world again.

"Have you spoken to her?" Trixie asked. Elizabeth nudged her in the side. "Ow, I know." She shot a look at Elizabeth. "But it's not like he doesn't know she's here. This is her house."

Elizabeth conceded and stopped trying to intervene.

"I haven't," Arthur said, trying to sound casual, "how is she?"

"Oh, you know." Trixie sighed, but Elizabeth stared at her and she backed off. "She's alright."

Arthur nodded, realizing that even Elizabeth was going to be tight lipped, but something about the way Trixie answered led him to believe there was more going on than they'd let on.

"Ladies, if you don't mind, I am going to say hello to someone." He brushed Trixie's elbow to get around her and acted as if he was headed somewhere important.

He ran into James and briefly spoke to him, too occupied with the idea of getting drunk so that he could numb his misery. He said good-bye and spun around in the direction of the bar, but as he did, he ran into someone, almost knocking her glass of champagne out of her hand.

He caught himself and her arm, then looked up to see Sophia's dark eyes inches from his.

He snapped up and stepped back, bumping into someone behind him. She took a graceful step back and smiled.

"Arthur, hello," she said hesitantly, "I didn't know if you would come." She sounded nervous and it satisfied a sadistic part of him.

"Of course, I wouldn't have missed it."

She swallowed and the color almost drained from her face, but being Sophia Kingsley, she somehow managed to keep her cheeks rosy. Her red lips stopped smiling and she slightly hung her head, reminding him of the Sophia he'd known around the New Year. His stomach dropped at the thought of that night and Margaret's vile behavior.

Sophia wore a loose red dress that fell just below her knees, sheer black stockings, and heels. A thick, black sequined headband had been wrapped around her short hair, and the necklace Arthur bought her hung around her neck. Her eyes were painted with dark make-up, making them all the more captivating. His plan to see her and feel nothing quickly went awry. He glanced at the necklace again, wondering if she meant to torture him.

"Arthur, I have to greet some guests." She gently touched his arm. "It was nice of you to come," she said politely, letting him know he had been cast into one of the many meaningless faces among her guests.

He let her walk away without replying. His stomach turned and he caught sight of Henry who was watching him with concern. Henry pushed his way toward Arthur upon seeing Arthur's inability to move.

"Arthur," Henry said gently, tapping him on the arm. "Arthur," he said again, getting his attention, "will you come outside with me?"

Arthur followed Henry through the back doors and onto the terrace. The air still held onto a chill from the winter, and unlike a fall breeze that blows in warm, it caused Arthur to shiver.

"Arthur, I don't think it's such a good idea for you to be here. I know I said that I hoped you would come, but I didn't know then that..."

Arthur was facing the house while Henry faced the gardens. Arthur caught himself staring at the people inside and caught sight of George, who was laughing and smiling along to a brunette's story. He watched him silently turn his attention to his right and reach out his hand. Sophia appeared through the crowd. George wrapped his arm around her shoulder and she smiled.

"You didn't know what?" Arthur had been listening as he watched the silent movie unfold in front of him.

Henry paused and Sophia glanced up, feeling Arthur's gaze. But she didn't look away, instead she stared back at him like she was waiting.

"Henry?" Arthur said irritably, "what? You want me to leave?"

Henry shook his head and Arthur turned his attention away from Sophia and looked back at Henry.

"I think I should tell you this before, well I asked if I could because I thought it was the right thing to do." Henry was shaking his head afraid to make eye contact.

"Henry, just tell me. I don't know what all this drama is about." Arthur was growing more impatient by the minute. Sophia's eyes and Henry's tentativeness both grating at him.

"They're going to announce their engagement."

"Why would I care if Elizabeth and Benjamin announce their engagement?" He looked up to see Sophia still looking out the door at him. George had his arm around her waist.

Arthur snapped his attention toward Henry whose eyes were filled with pain. If he'd had enough in him, he would've puked on Henry's shoes again. He couldn't breathe, his chest seized, and he clutched at his stomach.

"I thought I should tell you before it happened, I didn't want you to be caught off guard. I'm sorry, I..." Henry stopped when he realized Arthur couldn't hear him.

Arthur stepped back and then glanced back to Sophia, but she had disappeared. "When?"

Henry shook his head. "I don't know. I only discovered myself this morning. They told no one."

Henry appeared to feel betrayed, but it was no match for the level Arthur felt.

"Arthur, I am very sorry. I will have you know that I do not agree with the match. I do understand it but I don't..." Henry turned his head to the side as his voice caught in his throat. He was struggling to tell Arthur such news, struggling to be the one to crush him even more than he had been.

"I think I need to be alone," Arthur said aloud, but not particularly to anyone.

"Of course. I'll be inside."

Henry left him and Arthur turned to go down the stairs. He walked across the lawn and through the garden then took a left, aimless. He finally stopped in front of the stables, unsure of how he'd covered so much distance.

Two of the stable boys were smoking cigarettes outside the east entrance and they nodded to him.

"Hi, Arthur," one called and offered him a smoke.

He shook his head. "I thought I might go inside and say hi to Daisy."

They nodded; they had no qualms about Arthur, in fact, they often enjoyed his company when he'd been around. Reading his mood, they both threw their cigarettes on the ground, stomped them out, and made their way back to their sleeping quarters.

Arthur pulled open the door, the smell of hay and horses filled his nose and the darkness inside the stable forced him to squint to see his path. An eerie quiet filled the place, the noises from the party disappeared. He almost tripped over a gas can but kicked it away easily, the empty tin falling out of his way.

He made his way to Daisy and she whinnied upon seeing him.

"Hey, Daisy," he said as he rubbed her snout. "How've you been, girl? I've missed you."

"She's missed you too," a voice called softly from the other end. He froze and swallowed.

She stepped closer to him and his eyes adjusted enough that he could see her figure clearly moving toward him.

"Sophia." He stepped back and let go of Daisy's face. "What are you doing here?"

"Henry told you?"

He didn't answer, angry that she had interrupted the one goodbye he wanted to leave untainted.

"I'm sorry, Arthur," she said softly as she hung her head.

She stopped a few feet in front of him and lifted her eyes. The pity in them, the pity for what she had done pierced through him, ripping apart his heart and leaving behind an anger so palpable, he gritted his teeth and clenched his fists at his side. His irritation grew inside of him, then it became too large to contain and it forced its way up his throat and out of his mouth.

"You're sorry? That's what you came here to say to me?" he yelled at her, startling them both with its resonance.

She shook her head. "I know that you're angry and I understand, but I..."

"You what? You didn't do anything I didn't know you would. You always knew how this would end!" He flung his arms out then let them fall limp to his sides. "You used me, made a mockery of me, you broke my heart and now you get to marry the man you're supposed to marry."

He remembered what Henry said, remembered how they all told him to be careful. He hadn't realized they were referring to Sophia because he couldn't see past his feelings for her.

He took a step toward her and got closer to her face, lifting his finger in front of her. "But let me tell you something; he is the safe choice and you know he is. You'll be bored in no time."

Sophia looked straight into his eyes, hers hardening. They stood there in a face off, both teeming with rage and pain and the leftover lust that never quite quelled between them. He could smell her and feel her warmth. Finally, it became too much and he softened and stepped back.

"I don't know what to do, Sophia. I never meant to hurt you. I never meant to say those things I said at the engagement party; I never thought of you that way. I don't know why I got so caught up and..." he trailed off, his head spinning.

"Arthur," she said softly and reached out her hand, lightly grabbing his, "where did you go?"

He flinched at her touch, feeling her soft skin against his fingers. He swallowed and looked into her eyes, searching for an answer. All he wanted was to pull her close, to feel her body against his. He longed for the slant of her neck, to bury his head in her and breathe her in deeply.

"I never left. I never left," he choked out, "you made me leave."

She shook her head and pulled his hand to her chest grasping at it with both of hers. "No Arthur. Where did *you* go? The man I met on the balcony. The man who sat with me on the bench, who sucked on cheap peppermints and slurped soup while standing in a deli. Who wore his father's suit to my Halloween party and didn't care what anyone thought of him."

Tears welled in his eyes and he pulled his hand away. "You mean the man who could never stand by your side, the man who never felt like he belonged in your world? The man who day after day stumbled through life and love for you so desperately unsure?"

"No, Arthur. The man who seemed to not care about what I was. The man who wasn't fazed by my status or money or my name."

"That man never existed. You are wrong if you think that a day passed that I didn't think about it, worry about you, about money, about security."

She clenched her jaw and studied his face. The wetness from his tears made his green eyes brighter. She looked down, needing to avert her eyes. "I never needed you to be who you thought I did. I wouldn't have cared if you were one of those street vendors in England. But you think you want something... something I am not."

Arthur frowned and dropped her hand, shaking his head at her continued ignorance. "You still think that life is something to romanticize? You're wrong. You have no idea what you're talking about."

"All I'm trying to say is... think of when it was just you and your mother-"

"You know nothing of my mother!" he yelled. "So don't you dare say anything about her!"

She stepped back. "You're right. You never told me much about her. You didn't want me to know that part of you."

"Don't you dare try to blame this on me."

She shook her head. "I'm not trying to blame you."

"Of course not, because you knew that you were going to do this all along. But you coming out here to tell me how less is more whilst you announce your engagement to the wealthiest man in the city is laughable." Arthur's anger again swelled inside of him. He wanted to walk away, to leave her hurt and angry, but stronger was the part that wanted to grab her and push her against the stalls, kiss her, and let his fury drain out of him in passion.

"That's not what I intended to do, Arthur."

"Then what?" He crossed his arms over his chest.

"I didn't intend any of this! You, what happened to me, any of it!"

He had never heard her raise her voice before and it stunned him. He swallowed. "You know I thought for a moment that you wanted me for the rest of your life. You could've at least been honest with me from the beginning so that I didn't get comfortable thinking I had any kind of security."

She took a step back and searched his eyes, then wiped a tear as it fell down her cheek. Seeing the pain in his eyes became too much and she stepped forward to wrap her arms around his tense body. He stiffened into it, his heart pounded into her and he couldn't breathe. Against his will, his anger began to soften into her.

She pulled back enough to look into his eyes again. "I wish that things would've turned out differently. I do. But I don't know how to make you understand."

He swallowed and studied her face, first her eyes and then her lips. They stood there, holding each other, their anger morphing into unbearable longing. Unable to stop himself, he leaned forward and kissed her. Any will she had to keep herself from him drained out of her, and she kissed him back passionately, her hunger overtaking everything else.

He ran his hands up her side and into her hair, then pushed her back against the stable wall. She wrapped her arms around him as he kissed down her neck, burying himself in her scent. She grabbed his hair and pulled him back to her lips as he moved his hand up her leg, pulling the fabric of her dress with it.

The sensation snapped her to reality and she pushed him away. "Arthur, I can't."

His heart pounded, the happiness of once again having her ripped from him. They stood there, staring at each other until he finally said, "I don't understand. You're really going to marry George?"

She averted her eyes. "I want to marry him, Arthur."

He searched her face. "You're lying."

"I shouldn't have come here. I shouldn't have let that happen. I'm sorry."

Arthur's hands shook as desperation consumed his entire body. Then his heart began to harden as he tried to pull on some armor to defend against the impending crash. "Sophia, I know that's not what you want. Don't do this." He reached forward and grabbed her arms.

"I have to go, Arthur. I'm sorry. Please let go of me."

He dropped his hands and let her walk away, too defeated and exhausted.

"You're lying to yourself!" he called after her.

She paused and turned back. "I do hope you find... what you're looking for."

And then like that, Arthur was alone again.

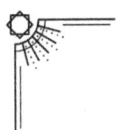

CHAPTER
THIRTY-TWO

Arthur stood in the stable for another moment, his already shattered heart breaking into even tinier pieces. His anger toward her, toward himself for letting himself believe she might change her mind, filled the space in his chest. Then, in an act of misdirected petulance, he lifted the latch to Daisy's gate. He walked to the west entrance, lifting the rest of the latches too before pushing open the door so there was a space large enough for the horses to escape if they wanted.

Before he slipped out, he turned back to them. "You can have your freedom if you want it."

Arthur wasn't certain why he'd felt it was an appropriate reaction, but he felt compelled to do it anyway. He wanted Sophia to feel the loss of something she loved.

He slowly made his way back to Sophia's house, but instead of entering through the doors off the terrace, he walked to the side where he knew the staff entrance would likely be unlocked. He pulled at the door and it opened with ease. He had gotten to know her house well enough from the time he spent there that he could navigate even the lesser known parts.

He walked down the long narrow hallway past the staff quarters and then found a back staircase. He took it up three flights of stairs and stopped at the top, fatigued. He gathered his breath, wandered down the hallway, then turned the corner to Sophia's bedroom.

Sophia's room had transformed. The expensive fabrics of navy and gold were nowhere to be seen, in their place materials of all colors and patterns. None of it made any sense, it was a mixture of clashing styles, messy and confused. Arthur ran his hands over the sheer curtains that framed the balcony door then twisted the handle and pushed it open. The cool air hit the sweat that formed during his exertion and he shivered. He pulled his jacket tighter around his middle and stepped toward the stone railing. The moon and stars shone brightly overhead.

He turned and saw Sophia's chaise, still there and the same as before. Nothing about the balcony was different. It was as if the Sophia of old had been preserved there. On the chaise was a book, face down.

Arthur walked over to it and picked it up, then turned it over in his hands; the same copy of *Romeo and Juliet* he found the night they met. He swallowed and opened it to a page she earmarked. On it, she had underlined a passage:

> *The roses in thy lips and cheeks shall fade*
> *To paly ashes, thy eyes' windows fall*
> *Like death when he shuts up the day of life.*
> *Each part, deprived of supple government,*
> *Shall, stiff and stark and cold, appear like death.*
> *And in this borrowed likeness of shrunk death*

He sat on her chaise and perused it further, wondering why Sophia was fascinated by the devastating story. Though he understood Romeo's agony at finding his Juliet dead, it was indisputable to Arthur that rejection was worse. As long as Sophia was alive, he would live with the knowledge that she was somewhere without him, somewhere sharing her time and body and laugh with someone else. He scanned the underlined iambic pentameter; there seemed to be no pattern to her choices.

He glanced to the side table and another book, small and yellow, laid closed. *La Garçonne*, The book she received from Dr. Narudo. He set down *Romeo and Juliet* and opened the new one to where she earmarked a page and ran his fingers under an underlined passage.

> *Mais, dans son instinct d'absolu, elle se voulait détachée,*
> *instantanément et pour jamais, de ce qui, tout à l'heure*
> *encore, était sa raison d'existence. Partie d'elle-même*
> *amputée. Illusion pourrie,—chair morte.*

The words meant nothing to him, locked and foreign, much like Sophia now. He turned his head to the sky, wondering what she might do when she discovered his death. Arthur was lost in that which was still yet to be when he heard a roar come from below.

Cheers, screams, applause. Arthur swallowed and closed his eyes, imagining George and Sophia clinking their glasses, hugging their friends, George blissful in his victory, Sophia trying to drink away the taste of Arthur's lips. Then the noise subsided and left him again in quiet. *Shrunk death. Smashed death. That's how they'd find him.*

He walked toward the railing, placing his hands on the stone. Something in the distance to his left caught his eye, but just as it did, a voice broke out behind him.

He spun around to find William standing behind him, a frown on his face.

William whispered, "Arthur, what are you doing? Are you mad?"

Arthur simply acknowledged him by name but added no more.

"Arthur, I heard the announcement. I've been searching for you."

Arthur swallowed again and wondered about the smile on Sophia's face as she gushed over her happy news.

"How did you know I'd be here?"

"Henry," he answered, then asked again impatiently, "What are you doing? You shouldn't be in here. She could have you arrested for this kind of behavior."

William saw that Arthur was not concerned. And then he replied strangely, "Well, they'll take me out of here one way or another."

"What?" William asked; Arthur's mood was unnerving.

Arthur shook his head. "William, you have been so kind to me, truly the best friend a man could hope for."

William took a step toward Arthur, whose back was to the stone railing. He reached out his hand. "Arthur, what are you doing? We must leave."

William saw the look in his eyes, an eerie calm juxtaposed against his inner turmoil. William then realized what he hadn't before, that Arthur intended to jump.

Arthur lifted his foot to take a backward step as William took a cautious one forward.

"I'm sorry," Arthur said. "You should go, William, please."

"No, Arthur. No."

Arthur shook his head, pleading. "Please, William. There is nothing you can do. Please let me find peace."

"Not like this, Arthur. No. You're not leaving me with this."

Arthur paused and for a moment and considered how cruel it would be to William, then his misery again usurped him. "You have Betty, your parents, soon you'll have your own children. You'll move on."

William nodded and took another step cautiously forward. "So will you. You'll see. Someday, this will all be a distant memory. Please, come with me. We'll find Betty and get the car and never come back here."

"It's not just her. I have nothing to live for. I have no one. No family."

"You know that's not true. I'm your family, Arthur." William's voice cracked as he took yet another small step toward Arthur, slowly gaining ground.

Arthur squeezed his eyes closed. William had ruined everything. When he opened them again, William's eyes stared at him, crazy with worry. Tears welled at the bottom and almost spilled over his cheeks.

For some reason, seeing William's face express so much emotion pulled Arthur back. He stared into William, needing someone to ground him in something other than his misery.

"I have no idea how to recover from this."

"Sure you do. You've been through worse. We all have to go through heartbreak at some point in our lives, right? It's part of the deal." William closed the distance between them and grabbed Arthur's shoulder. Relief filled his body as he felt his hand secure Arthur to his spot on the balcony. "Come on, let's leave."

Arthur nodded, but as he turned his head to fight away his tears, his gaze caught on something and he gasped.

William still jumpy, grabbed him tighter, but then twisted his head in the direction of Arthur's.

The stable, the one that housed Sophia's horses and the one Arthur had come from less than an hour before, was ablaze—brilliant reds and oranges raged against the black sky. People were gathered below and then Arthur heard their screams. Mere seconds after Arthur and William first saw the fire, the entire thing was engulfed.

Arthur panicked and scanned the countryside fearing Sophia's horses had been trapped inside. He hoped maybe his childish behavior saved them. More people flooded from the mansion and ran toward the stable. Men threw out their arms, women screamed, chaos unfolded below as William and Arthur watched from above. The fire was too far away to hear its roar, but the stables were constructed of wood and home to straw, and the fire burned furiously as it devoured its prey.

Arthur turned to William, his eyes wide, and muttered, "Sophia. I have to find her." Then he dashed off the balcony and out of the room.

William followed close behind, sprinting through the hallway and then tripping down the stairs to get to the ground level. By the time they joined the masses below, they were heaving with labored breath.

Arthur pushed through the awestruck guests and made his way to the lawn. William followed but stopped when he found Betty and wrapped his arms around her, happy to find her safe. Arthur continued and spun around amongst the few people who dared to move close. He frantically searched those standing near him; they stood motionless, their eyes stuck on the massacre before them.

George found Arthur as Arthur ran back toward the house. "Arthur!" he shouted over the noise, "have you seen Sophia?" Arthur shook his head and then suddenly, Henry was there too, out of breath.

Concerned, George grabbed Henry's shoulders. "Have you seen Sophia?"

Henry shook his head too. "No," he replied breathlessly, "I'll go back inside, try to find her. Maybe she went to the front and has no idea what's happening."

"Ok," George agreed. "Arthur, go search the crowd, I'll find Thomas." He turned away and then stopped. "Arthur!"

Arthur stopped and spun back his direction. "Meet on the terrace when we find her!"

Arthur nodded in agreement and then the men split, both calling out her name. Arthur stopped and asked a few people but they just shook their heads and then returned to gawk at the fire. He soon found Trixie, but she shook her head too as she held a crying Elizabeth.

He nodded at Trixie. "Ok you stay here with her, we'll keep looking. Please tell her to find us if she comes to you."

Trixie nodded. "Of course."

Arthur ran the distance to the house, pushing his way through swarms of guests. When he arrived, he found it nearly empty. George faced away from him, talking to Thomas, and then Thomas turned the other direction.

"George!" Arthur called.

Hearing his name, George turned and ran toward him, shouting, "The stable hands have already gathered all the buckets they can find and are throwing water on it as fast as they can. The rest of the staff are searching for Sophia. There are enough here we should be able to find her quickly. Let's go back outside; she has to be there by now."

Arthur, too shocked, upset, and exhausted from the day's turns, obediently followed George's orders.

As they exited, Henry ran up the steps toward them. "We searched the entrance and couldn't find her there, so I rounded the house. She's not there either." He frowned, confused. "You haven't found her?"

George shook his head, thinking. His concern grew with each second that passed. He looked to Arthur, then scanned the country-side, his mind reeling.

A light of recognition went off inside of him. "Her horses! She has to be near the stable, trying to make sure they're all ok!" He nodded emphat-ically to the other two, hoping their agreement would ensure its truth.

Without answering, they exchanged a look and then took off in its direction.

George shouted at some of the partygoers to move back from the fire; its heat was suffocating even from a distance. Even so, the men approached as quickly as they could, shielding their faces from the heat as they got closer.

"You go left, we'll go right!" George called and Arthur peeled off to his left, sprinting as fast as he could.

Arthur stopped and tried to catch his breath when he spotted one of the stable boys, one he'd seen smoking earlier. The boy held a half full bucket in his hands and was barely managing to carry it. Water splashed over the sides, soaking his boots.

"Have you seen Sophia?" Arthur asked, his breath heavy.

The boy stammered out a response, "I, I, no, I haven't seen her. We've been back at our quarters since we saw you last. Been trying to put out this fire since. We got at least twenty buckets but not enough men or height to do much."

Arthur placed his hand on the boy's shoulder. "You're doing a good job. If you find her, tell her to find me."

The boy nodded his head in shock.

Soon, Arthur spotted Henry and George running his way, their figures emerging through the smoke. Arthur coughed and covered his mouth. George spit soot to the ground and Henry wiped at his eyes.

"Nothing?" George asked desperately.

Arthur shook his head. The heat was pouring off where the stable once stood and he wiped the sweat from his brow. He bent over to try and help himself catch his breath, but the air was suffocating. Adrenaline pulsed through him and his heart thumped furiously in his chest.

When it was clear that there was nothing they could do to put an end to the fire, the stable hands gave up their efforts. Empty buckets were strewn across the lawn as they backed away from the fire and joined the masses in watching helplessly.

Henry looked around and saw the futility of their actions. "We need to get back from it," he said, wincing at the heat.

George shook his head. "Where is she?!"

Henry grabbed his arm. "We need to step back!"

But George shook him off and turned to Arthur. "Arthur, where is she?!" His voice broke. His eyes were red and tears began to spill over his cheeks.

Arthur shook his head, his eyes too starting to burn from the smoke and the heat. He coughed and wiped at his mouth.

The two men stared at each other, searching, desperately wanting to make the other have an answer. Then, everything stopped. They could no longer hear the roar of the fire or Henry as he called their names, attempting to pull them away from the inferno. Arthur breathed in the smoke and ash, and attempted to blink the heat away from his eyes. And then slowly, they both turned their faces to the fire, both coming to the same horrible conclusion at once.

George opened his mouth and Sophia's name escaped in a guttural scream. He lunged toward the stable. Arthur caught his arm, pulling him back, but George struggled forward, screeching in desperation.

Henry grabbed at George's other arm, attempting to restrain him. George pulled, using all of his weight to drag himself forward, attempting to shake them free. "No! No! Let me go! I need to get to her!"

Henry and Arthur pulled harder and Henry screamed, "George, it's no use! It's no use! There's nothing you can do!"

Finally, George's muscles gave way, he stopped fighting and collapsed to the ground, clutching his head in his hands. He gasped for air as he tried to convince himself it was a horrible nightmare.

Henry squatted beside him and wrapped his arm around George's shoulders. He looked up at Arthur who kept his gaze fixed on the stable, which barely resembled the structure it had been.

Arthur looked beyond to the pasture behind the stable, and saw Rosie and Lily, running without aim, obviously scared but free and safe. He scanned for the others, and desperately tried to find Daisy, but the smoke clouded his view.

Unable to keep himself upright, Arthur sat down in the grass next to Henry, the heat turning his cheeks red as sweat poured down his face. Henry reached out his other hand and rested it on Arthur's shoulder.

"How?" Henry asked quietly. "She isn't really... is she?"

Arthur shook his head. "Where else could she be?"

George lifted his head and closed his eyes, then choked out a cough.

"I can't be here," George said as he lifted himself to his feet. Henry followed him and looked down to Arthur, but Arthur shook his head, refusing to budge.

As George stood, Arthur's anger returned. George had taken on the job of being her future husband, and therefore keeping her safe. "Why weren't you with her?!" Arthur shouted.

George turned around and looked at him, his eyes tired and empty.

"You were supposed to be with her! Why weren't you with her?!" Arthur screamed again, his voice breaking.

George didn't reply; he turned away and Henry opened his mouth but Arthur stopped him.

"Leave me be."

Henry obeyed and escorted George away, neither speaking as they returned to tell Trixie and Elizabeth the news, hoping in vain Sophia would be there waiting for them, but both knowing the chances were small.

Eventually William found Arthur, who had moved away but still sat on the lawn, and placed his hand on his back.

"The firefighters are on their way. We should go inside."

Arthur looked up at him. "Have they found her?"

William shook his head.

Arthur turned his face back to the fire. William sat with him as Arthur's dream disintegrated to ash, until finally, there was nothing left to burn.

CHAPTER
THIRTY-THREE

The next morning, Arthur awoke to sunlight shining in his face. Sophia's staff allowed him to spend the night in one of her guest bedrooms. The staff ushered most of the guests away around two a.m. Arthur left Henry, George, Elizabeth, Trixie, and Benjamin sitting in Sophia's den around four a.m. William offered to stay, but Arthur insisted he take Betty home and get some sleep himself. Arthur rubbed his eyes and blinked them open. He saw the tile ceiling above him, the tile that was in each of the bedrooms, even Sophia's.

The unimaginable reality of the night disappeared while Arthur was sleeping. It all vanished and transformed into a dreamless sleep where time and reality fell into the void of unconsciousness. When he woke, the realization washed through Arthur's body, twisting his organs and seizing his breath. He struggled to cast out the thought of Sophia's terror as her flesh burned.

By the time the firemen had arrived, the stable was unsalvageable. All they could do was contain it so that it didn't spread anywhere else on the property. It burned through the night and by morning barely anything remained, aside from a few smoldering pieces of ash. Metal objects were the only thing left somewhat intact, but even they were charred, pallid versions of their former selves.

***

The color of the flowers around the estate stood in stark contrast to the debris that surrounded Arthur as he stood at the edge of it all. He knew that Sophia was no longer there, but he wanted to find some trace that she never had been, that she somehow left for the evening and forgot to return.

The fire foreman approached him. "Excuse me, Mr. Malcolm?"

Arthur nodded at the man, dressed in his uniform with his helmet perched crookedly on his head. His demeanor was calm but Arthur thought he saw his mustache twitch as he addressed him.

"I am going to have to ask you to step away from the scene, sir."

The scene. The scene of Sophia's death.

Arthur walked with the foreman until they were about thirty feet from where the stable once stood. Arthur looked at his shoes covered in soot, his shiny black tuxedo shoes he planned to die in, now covered with ashes. Sophia's ashes. He gagged.

The foreman was talking, "Mr. Malcom, we are working with Mr. Carlyle; we've assured him that we are going to do everything we can to understand what happened here last night."

Arthur took a deep breath and then regretted breathing in the air so close to the ashes. He thanked the foreman. He was tormented by the idea that no one witnessed the last moments of Sophia's life, that no one had been there with her.

Arthur stood aside and watched as the foreman interacted with the estate staff, as he handed out instructions to the other firemen. He watched as a few of them scoured the area. Occasionally, they would squat down and run their gloves through the debris, searching for something that wasn't completely ash.

One of the men, a shorter one without facial hair, who Arthur thought appeared too young to be working such a dangerous and important job, squatted and didn't stand up for some time. He appeared to be examining something intently. Then, he called out to his foreman who pulled his attention away from Thomas and walked his direction. The young man stood up, holding something in his hand. The foreman approached and the young man handed it to him, then turned whatever it was around in his glove for a while. They both looked at Arthur, then back to each other. The foreman thanked the young firefighter and turned back around. Arthur didn't want to know what the young man picked up.

Arthur made his way back to the mansion and sat in the sitting room. It wasn't until Violet, also exhausted and grieving, broke his attention that he looked away from the window that faced where the stable had been. She offered him tea and breakfast. Although he didn't feel like eating, he politely accepted the offer.

She escorted him to the breakfast room and then brought him tea and a few biscuits. Arthur stared down at the biscuits. Finally, he forced himself to pick one up, then he picked at it, attempting to feign eating.

When he finished, or rather when he broke up the biscuits and crumbled them into pieces all over his plate, Violet cleared his dishes for him.

Thomas approached him and softly said, "Mr. Malcolm, I apologize for interrupting, but George is speaking to the foreman and suggested you might want to have a word with him before he leaves."

Arthur rose from his chair and let Thomas escort him to the entry, where the foreman was standing. Arthur was grateful that George had been aware enough to leave them alone.

He wore a pained expression, but his voice still came out cold and collected. "Mr. Malcom, we recognize that this is a difficult time for you." Arthur looked around for the "we" but it was just the foreman standing with him. "But we needed to be able to say with some certainty that Miss Kingsley was in the stable to confirm her death."

"I don't know. I didn't see..."

"Yes, I know no one witnessed her entering the stable, but we searched through the debris and were able to recover..." He stopped and then shook his head, realizing he shouldn't finish his sentence. No one except the people involved in the investigation needed to hear any upsetting information. "Anyway, one of my men also found this."—he lifted his glove and there was something small and black in it—"Mr. Carlyle already confirmed that she was wearing it last night, but he asked me to give it to you. We don't need it for the investigation."

Arthur glanced up at the forearm and then back to the charred item in his glove. He reached into his hand and gingerly lifted it; It was a chain, blackened but intact. He rubbed some of the ash away and uncovered a red stone, then rubbed another and found a sapphire. He didn't want to let Sophia go, but he couldn't stand holding onto something that remained when she had burned inside of it. It took all of his will not to call out in pain and drop it on the ground.

***

In his shock and grief, Arthur's perception of time altered so violently that it no longer fit into any recognizable pattern. Seconds became months, hours became minutes; everything twisted in such a way that it either passed by so quickly there was nothing he could grasp or so slowly that every moment was painstakingly stretched.

If someone asked how much time passed between the moment he last saw Sophia and the one with the charred necklace in his hand, Arthur would've bet it had been no longer than five minutes. But he would've also been sure that the time he spent searching for her among the crowd while the fire blazed was at least four hours. He desperately wished for those last moments in the stable again even though his heart had broken hundreds of times in the matter of minutes. He longed to see her gentle eyes, to feel her lips against his.

The truth was, no amount of time more with her would've been enough. If given another hour, Arthur would've wanted another day. If given another day, he would've asked for another week. But to lose her having only known her such a short time was reality's cruelty at its worst.

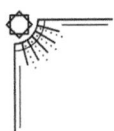

THIRTY-FOUR

George pulled open Arthur's office door to find him sitting at his desk, bent over nothing and instead staring intently at the wooden desktop. He cleared his throat to get Arthur's attention. Arthur looked up at the man standing above him, but instead of feeling intimidated or jealous, he simply ached. The grief had taken over his entire body and replaced every single part of him with hollowed-out pain.

George held an envelope in his hand and seemed uncharacteristically hesitant, afraid of Arthur's fragility.

"Good morning, Arthur... I..." he stopped himself, knowing there was nothing else to say.

Arthur looked at him but didn't reciprocate. He expected to be angry, but instead he wanted to be left alone. Arthur hadn't come to work for three days, and then decided he couldn't tolerate the echoes in his house any longer. After the foreman gave him the necklace, he placed it in his jacket pocket and left without saying goodbye to anyone. The jacket still hung in his entry, untouched.

Henry and Trixie had called but he refused them; he only allowed William to come into his house twice. When he showed up to the office, both Betty and William appeared to be holding their breaths. The air was thick and heavy with sorrow. They spoke in whispers as if they might break him with any louder volume.

George walked closer and sat in the chair in front of his desk, then he turned to William who had been eyeing him.

"William, do you mind giving us a moment alone?" William nodded skeptically but brought Betty with him outside.

The door chimed shut behind them and Arthur hadn't spoken a word. His emptiness had returned with a force greater than he knew possible.

"I know that you probably don't want to see me, but I thought that you should have this." He motioned toward Arthur with a letter and when Arthur didn't reach to take it, he set it down on his desk. Sophia's handwriting spelled out his name on the front.

Arthur glanced down at it and then back to George. His jaw was covered in stubble and his eyes looked weary. Arthur wondered if he tossed and turned at night like him, playing over the last moments of the night, desperately trying to change the ending somehow.

When Arthur didn't speak, George stood up. "Anyway, she wanted you to have this. I'm sorry she wasn't the one to give it to you." His voice cracked on the last sentence and then he cleared his throat. He turned and pulled open the door, the bell breaking the tension with its clash.

"See you around, Arthur."

Sophia's last words for him laid inside and he wasn't sure he could bear to read them. Then there would be nothing left, nothing new, nothing of her in his future. Arthur stared at the letter in front of him for hours, or perhaps it was seconds.

Finally, he lifted the letter from his desk then turned it over and saw that it was sealed. Her words saved only for him. He picked up his letter opener and ran it under the flap, then removed the papers from inside. Instantly, he could smell her and his heart lurched.

The papers were folded into thirds and he unfolded them slowly.

My Dearest Arthur,

How can I ever put into words all that needs to be said? How can I let you into my mind without revealing too much of what you are not ready to see? I know that you want explanations and I wish that I could write them in a way that might lead you to the answers you seek. I so badly want you to see clearly. But I know that I cannot be the one to make you see clearly. It is something you have to do on your own. Do you understand, Arthur?

First, I must admit how selfish I have been. When we met, I was lost and empty. I had never before felt the depths of love and joy you offered and I wanted to hold onto it as tightly as I could... but what I thought rescued me eventually brought me into such deep and dark despair I could no longer see the light. I see now that I had to find that light within me, Arthur. Brightness outside eventually dims, the stars fade, and the sun sets, but internal flames burn forever.

Next, I must remind you of our trip to England. Remember when we

strolled down the street and I spotted the necklace in the window—
the one that reminded me so much of my mother's? I'm wearing
the one you got me now, thinking of how angry you were with me
when I wished for a life like the docks men. I dreamt of simplicity,
of freedom. Sometimes we must make choices that appear mad to
everyone else in order to find our dream. Do you understand, Arthur?

*Finally, I must explain the three days after our visit with Dr.
Narudo. I slept for a day and a half after, but when I awoke,
I felt different. I climbed out of my bed and sat in front of my
dressing table mirror. I feared the worst when looking into it, that
what I'd find staring back at me would cause me such shame and
embarrassment that I'd have to climb back into bed for several
weeks. Instead, Arthur I cannot explain this to you, but I saw that
I was looking back at me. My hair was chopped and messy around
my head, my eyes were tired, and my skin was dull, but the woman
in the mirror was Sophia. It was the first time I had recognized
myself as I am.*

*For the very first time in my life, I see that the person I thought I had
to be isn't me at all, that the life I was leading wasn't mine. I thought
I was sacrificing parts of me to make the world a better place, but
that is absurd. When you finally see yourself for who you really are,
only then can you truly shine your light into the world. Do you
understand me, Arthur?*

*After I stared at myself for some time, I walked out to my balcony
and sat in my chaise. I stared out at the hills and gardens below—do
you remember that view, Arthur? Oh, how it reminded me of you, of
that first night we met. Of your wittiness, your smile, how different
you were from anyone I'd ever before met. I saw you in the flowers
and grass, in the clouds and bright blue sky. It was marvelous, as
if I was seeing it for the very first time. I do hope you somehow see
that view again.*

*Perhaps this all reads like madness, but if there is one thing I know
for sure, it's this—If we are mad, it is the madness that will save us.*

I beg you to remember your madness, Arthur. I saw it that first night and so many after. I saw your boldness. And have been thinking that perhaps it does us good to sometimes be a little lost.

Love,
S

The Malady of Elegance trilogy will continue with *The Onset of Madness.*

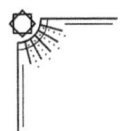

ABOUT THE AUTHOR

Jennifer Simmons is a clinical psychologist and writer who has always been fascinated by the mind. This passion has fueled her quest for understanding what it means to be human. Through her writing, she hopes to explore how we are all inextricably connected through the experiences, emotions, and dilemmas inherent in life.

When she isn't working with her clients or writing, you can find Jennifer traveling, teaching yoga as a certified instructor, and working as an adjunct professor with psychology graduate students.

www.ingramcontent.com/pod-product-compliance
Lightning Source LLC
Chambersburg PA
CBHW072349020726
47506CB00004B/1070